P9-CJN-229

BAD BLOOD, GOOD NEWS

"I knew Vivian Sinnott."

The bombshell exploded with enough force to silence the room. Suddenly I was on center stage. Taking a deep breath, I gave them the straight facts any competent reporter could've tracked down.

"Number one... Andrew Sinnott is a member of the D.A.'s office. Number two... yes, I was hired to prove that he was a cheat. Number three... yes, he was, and his wife had proof. Number four... yes, it was rock-solid proof—she had a video of her husband performing in a sex club. And," I added for my own protection, "you will report that I just happened to be here when the news came in..."

"The truth angle, eh?" answered Green. "I like it."

Then I added, "And don't worry, I won't do anything to tarnish the reputation of the *New York Post.*"

"Is that possible?"

SOMETHING FOR NOTHING

SOMETHING FOR NOTHING

C. J. HENDERSON

JOVE BOOKS, NEW YORK

This is a work of fiction. Any
resemblance to any persons living or
dead is purely coincidental.

SOMETHING FOR NOTHING

A Jove Book / published by arrangement with
the author

PRINTING HISTORY
Jove edition / November 1993

ISBN: 0-515-11235-6

A JOVE BOOK®
Jove Books are published by The Berkley Publishing Group,
200 Madison Avenue, New York, New York 10016.
JOVE and the "J" design are trademarks
belonging to Jove Publications, Inc.

PRINTED IN THE UNITED STATES OF AMERICA

10 9 8 7 6 5 4 3 2 1

This book is about a lot of things, but the essential core of it deals with *friendship*—the trust, the loyalty, the comradery, the sense of fraternity that comes when you know someone so well, so keenly, that they become more than an acquaintance, more than a pal or a chum or your bro' or any of the thousand and one other terms we use in place of "friend."

Many people use the word loosely, never meaning to actually include within the sacred inner circle of their lives most of the people they do when they call them friend. I'm talking about those few people who come to be the brothers and sisters we never had, or wished we had . . . the people we really love. My grandmother told my mother, who passed the words on to me . . . "If you have one true friend in your lifetime, then you've been blessed."

If that's the case then I've been blessed several times over. Honored to be one of a special group whose membership is made up of men and women who share the aforementioned bonds, I find I have no choice other than to dedicate this book to:

THE GENTLEMAN'S CLUB

Its ranks are made up of absolutely the finest assembly I've ever broken bread with, helped move, sung, danced and gotten plastered with, laughed and fought and cried and just plain lived life with, the people who are—when all is said and done—the best damn friends a man ever had. I could have done worse.

"Solitude makes us tougher toward ourselves and tenderer toward others: in both ways it improves our characters."

—FRIEDRICH NIETZSCHE

"To dare to live alone is the rarest courage; since there are many who had rather meet their bitterest enemy in the field, than their own hearts in the closet."

—CHARLES CALEB COLTON

"Loneliness is and always has been the central and inevitable experience of every man."

—THOMAS WOLFE

CHAPTER 1

THE OUTLINER HAD struck again. New York City's police were still baffled over their newest serial murderer, one who so far seemed to actually be killing at random. His—they were certain of his sex, at least— claim to notoriety came from drawing chalk outlines around the bodies of his victims. Why he did it was apparently as big a mystery to everyone on the force as it was to Chet Green, the *New York Post* reporter who'd set out to make the city's latest freak his own personal story.

So far, the red-ink rag informed us, the Outliner's score was holding at eight. The first had been an unceremoniously white-chalk-surrounded knifing on 116th up in Harlem. The next two had gone down in Brooklyn, one in Flatbush, the other in the Heights. With the fourth he switched from white to blue chalk, and came off the back streets to leave his prey in the dairy aisle of a Queens Key Food Mart. Pulling that one off during business hours stunned a lot of people. The fifth he left on the observation deck of the Staten Island ferry, sketched around in pink chalk, budding out at all the appendages in crude but recognizable roses. The sixth became his first female victim. No rape, just the familiar slash across the throat and a five-color rainbow made up of four lines of chalk and one of blood.

The latest was his masterpiece, though. In a World Trade Center men's room, he left two known homosexuals locked in anal intercourse nailed to the wall with railroad spikes. Again, no one had a clue as to how he'd pulled it off. Police estimates insisted he would've needed a minimum of forty-five minutes, even with the dearly departeds' cooperation.

The suspicions of cooperation came from: A, the fact the purple chalk surrounding the couple was underneath the blood that had flowed from their individual stigmata; B, the suggestion of the jockey's penetrating genitalia, a detail impossible for the Outliner to have arranged if his subjects had already been dead; and C, the tales told by the victims' family and friends that they were both AIDs sufferers and both suicidal.

The *Post* had run the photos available to it, the chalk outline, the scablike pool of crusting blood, the smear-covered body bags being wheeled out of the room, et cetera . . . all part of the people's sacred right to information.

Weary of the people and their sacred rights, I folded my newspaper, shoved it behind the counter I was leaning against, took a full drag on my Camel, and turned to look out the window. Reading newspapers and smoking cigarettes was how I'd wasted the better part of the previous seven days, and it was wearing a little thin. I'd spent the time in a small-aisled, packed-to-the-rafters grocery store on Mott Street, one of the busiest in Chinatown. It was a guard-duty job, and I was not what you might call enjoying myself. Not by a long shot. I'd been foxed neatly by an old dog who must've seen me coming six miles off. He was a Chinese— roughly five-seven, his black hair cut old-man style, muscled shoulders, working businessman's gut—who called himself Lo Chun. When he'd padded into my office I'd figured some easy coin was ahead. Of course, in my time I've figured the government is my friend and that my wife would love me forever, too. Sometimes it's depressing to see how little my intuitive boundaries have stretched over the years.

It was February outside the window—the worst part of the year in New York City. By that time of winter, everything is cold; everything hurts. Every inch of stone in the buildings and sidewalks and streets is frozen through, solidly bitter to the touch, or even to be near. Manhattan snowscapes may look pretty in the movie theater or on TV, but walking just a few blocks in the reality of its biting canyon winds takes the romance out of the scene quick—as can just looking out the window.

New York in winter is ugly—monstrously so. What snow that falls reduces to slush on contact, immediately shot through with the gray and black of the city's soot and grime. Grease from the town's million and one restaurant cooking vents combines with the salty, cold blasts of wind that screech in off the ocean to turn the dark ichor into a freezing, slippery mess that does nothing for the soul save hinder and depress. The vision of it grows especially bleak once the fine folk who live here finish decorating the heaping piles of cinder-rough slop with chicken bones, foam cups, used tissues, diapers and condoms, pizza crusts, urine, bottles, cans, and every other scrap and tatter they don't feel like bothering with any longer.

Looking out the window got me through another five minutes, but it wasn't enough. I was bored. Straight through. Bored down to my ass and still upset with myself for being jerk enough to take such a boring job in the first place. Laughing at me, my memory replayed the meeting Lo and I had the day he came to see me about guarding his store.

"Mr. Jack Hagee, sir . . . ?"

He asked everything as politely as he had my name. A fellow detective, Peter Wei, had given the old guy my address. To make a long story short, the street gangs were getting out of hand in Chinatown. The mayor's office had released the story that they were all trying to raise cash to finance the making of Black Dreamer, a new synthetic opium flooding the city, supposedly being

funneled through the major oriental neighborhoods. To
gather capital, they were planning to hit each other's
territories on the Chinese New Year, demanding as much
revenue from each other's pigeons as possible. As Lo
told it,

"I no care about pay gang. You keep shop, you pay
Tong. Always been. Always be. No one get rid of Wah
Ching. Not for thousand year. That okay. But now, big
trouble. Now, all gang fight. All kids go crazy. Want
each other dead, take each other space. Now, gangs no
can keep store safe. Store all my family have. I not lose
it. No care about pay gang who rule when New Year
come. Fine okay. No problem. But won't pay loser and
make winner mad."

I ventured the mayor's explanation about the drugs,
but Lo wasn't hearing it. He insisted the whole thing
came down to territory and that it would all be over
after New Year's.

"Pay you thousand dollar. You stay all New Years.
Keep bastard kids away from store. I pay good, you
protect store. Make deal?"

I tried to tell him he was offering too much money, a
lot more than double my daily fee, but he wasn't hearing
it. Peter Wei had said I was the best, and that was what
he wanted. We argued back and forth for a while, and
then I figured "what the hell," if the old man wanted to
be beat out of his cash so bad, I could put the grab on
something for nothing as easy as the next guy. Taking
his check, I told him,

"Okay, pal, I'm yours for New Year's."

"All New Years. Whole time. You no leave store. I
pay good. You protect store all New Years."

"Yeah, you got it. The whole thing. I won't budge.
When you want me there?"

"Tomorrow. New Year's start tomorrow. Finish next
Tuesday."

I looked at him for a second as if I'd missed a beat,
and then I remembered. A floating holiday, determined

by the movements of the moon like Easter, the Chinese New Year is a ten-day long celebration. Peter had told me that before. And, I was willing to bet the old man knew I knew.

Damn, I thought, cursing both him and myself. I'd been thinking he wanted to grossly overpay me for one day's work—because I was willing to be condesending and greedy. Suddenly, however, I was forced awake, finally aware that my indifference had not worked in my best interests. For the first time since Lo had walked into my office, I looked him over carefully. That was when I realized he was older than I'd thought, when I stared into his happy dark eyes and saw them waiting for me to catch on, saw them smile when I did.

"So," he asked, "now you want to say something about deal?"

I bit at my lower lip, running things past in my mind. I had no jobs on the docket, but a thousand bucks for ten days of risking my life against who knew how many bands of highly efficient young murderers was not the best deal I'd ever made. There was plenty of dough in my bank account, but on the other hand, a lot of money there had come from Chinatown and Chinatown referrals. Not that I'd miss them much. I'd reached the comfort zone where dirt jobs weren't nearly as attractive as they'd been when I hadn't had the faintest idea where my next burger might be coming from.

The worst part, though, was that I'd known the difference between European and Chinese New Years before Lo had come through my door. A guy with scruples would've refused point-blank to take so much money for one day's work. The old man had maneuvered me into the position where it was up to me to call myself a cheat or a coward.

I asked him for his address instead.

And that was what had brought me to closing time on day eight, looking out the window, wishing I had something better to do than read the paper I was reaching for for the fiftieth time that day. So far I'd had no trouble, but the news was getting so boring I was beginning to wish for some.

I'd read the story of the court battle over "Tan Fran" twice. A Caucasian girl with a great tan, she'd gotten a job in a law office because everyone there had assumed she was Puerto Rican, and they needed someone good-looking and Puerto Rican or black or something to prove what correct left-wing liberals they were. At her first promotion, however, they found out she was white, and thus useless since they already had a few women around to prove they weren't sexist. The result: she was fired. So she sued them. And on it's dragged for two months.

I'd read my friend Rich Violano's column—a tale of a guy who spotted his ex-wife in a department store—six times. I always read Rich's stuff—and not just because he's a pal. I like it. I liked that one a lot.

Apparently, seeing his ex just drove the poor bug-fuck nuts; he killed her by breaking her head open with a bottle of ammonia, which he then emptied into the crack he'd made. Then he just sat back and smiled, watching her scream as her brains boiled up out of her skull. He didn't run away or resist arrest. He just smiled and watched, even after she was long dead, even after the cops cuffed him and took him away. Once they got him in the squad car, though, he suddenly came to life and slammed his head through one of the passenger windows, purposely tearing his throat open on the jagged edge left. Nice family entertainment, the *Post*.

Skipping back to the leisure section again, I let my eyes retravel over the notice announcing that Cassandra Brown was going to be at The Cat Club in a few days. That made me smile. Then again, the fact that Cassie was going to be back in town was probably lighting more than a few smiles across the city. If they'd had the class to run a picture of her, I'd have had something to do for the rest of the day. As it was, I spent a few minutes remembering her in my mind, rewarding myself with the knowledge that I could see her in the flesh soon . . . all I had to do was live out the week.

I turned the page then, realizing that daydreaming about Cassie Brown might not be the most comfortable way to pass the rest of the day. The next page offered the latest pronouncement of our newly elected mayor. He had called for "A Day of Healing" in response to the screams of the public over the drug wars that had been tearing the city apart lately. The article had a sidebar on Judith Siegel, the new head honcho of the district attorney's office. Her choice words about the mayor and his "approach" to the city's problems were always good for a laugh, making her sound like she was actually more fed up with his honor's shenanigans than we in the streets were.

They did run a picture of her—one that showed her off quite flatteringly. As attractive a package as she appeared, however, the photographer had managed to capture her best feature with exacting clarity . . . her eyes. They were hard-nailing riveters, the kind that tear up lies the way rottweilers do steaks.

It was the first clear picture of her I had ever seen— one that gave me a fast insight into her unusually high conviction rate. Staring at her picture, I wasn't sure what kind of lies I could maintain on the stand if I had to look into those eyes, either.

I was about to turn to the back of the paper where the article on the mayor was continued when suddenly I found myself rolling the newspaper back up, tight and solid. Looking around the store, I saw what my subconscious radar had spotted. Two youths, heavily bundled against the cold, had entered the store, looking at items their body language said they had no interest in whatsoever. Finally they walked over to Lo and began a high-powered sales pitch in Chinese. I walked over, too. One of them greeted me.

"Back off, qua'lo."

"Why, boys? What's the problem?"

"No problem, white shit whore-licking maggot suck-er. Go buy a vegetable. Get a big eggplant and take it home to sit on while you dream of my dick."

The second youth gave the first a nudge and a whisper, probably a hint that most likely I wasn't some daffy Good Samaritan.

"What're you? Cop? You got some reason to fuck with us, shit bastard?"

"Yeah." I slapped the talker across the face with the rolled-up newspaper. "I do." Another slap in the opposite direction. Hard. Cracking. "I work here." Two more, one on each ear, sharp and stinging. "I'm the trash man, you see." A reverse sent the blunt end into his left eye. "I gather up all the useless crap and put it out in the street."

A stiff, slamming poke in the guts sent the talker fly-ing, bouncing him off the counter behind him. A dozen or so cans of something heavy fell on him, slowing his responses and adding to the confusion. Grabbing him by the hair, I jerked him to his feet, ignoring his screams and the blood running from his face.

The other hadn't moved yet, He was clearly the bag man, the negotiator. Without his strong arm, he was terrified. I tossed the first out the door, making sure his back would hit badly and hard against the Ford parked at the curb. It crunched. So did he. Good, I thought. I don't like Fords much better than I do punks. Turning to his partner, I asked,

"And what do you want?"

"Nothing. No, no . . . nothing."

He was scared. No one had thought collection was going to be much of a problem. If someone refused, the gang would just come back later and take care of things. But fighting back—defying their goof shit little band of thugs—his eyes told me that such a thing had never crossed any of their minds. Not even for amusement. I said,

"What do you mean—nothing? You came into a store

for nothing? I think you must be with that real tough guy out in the street."

"No! No I'm not. I'm not!"

"Then what are you here for?"

The sweat was beginning to break out on his forehead. He was carrying the money they'd already collected. He was a runner, not a fighter, but I was between him and the door. If he lost the money he had, he'd be in for even more trouble than the talker outside.

"I mean no trouble. I, I—I came in for"—his eyes darted in every direction, finally hitting on an idea— "for some candy. Yes! Candy!"

"Well, then . . . buy some candy."

As the runner dug into his pocket, I told Lo,

"Sell him a crate of candy." As the punk's eyes came back to me, I said, "A big crate. Something expensive."

Lo disappeared into one of the back aisles and then returned with a large cardboard box on a hand truck. Total cost: four hundred fifty-four dollars. I asked,

"This is what you came in for, right? Candy?"

The runner kept his eyes on the newspaper still in my hands and nodded vigorously. I opened the door for him after he paid for the box, watching him struggle his purchase out behind him. Just as he began to pass through the doorway, I slid the paper under his chin to catch his attention.

"Now; you collect up your future cellmate out there and you go tell the rest of your crew that this store is off-limits until after the New Year. You tell them this . . . Mr. Lo will happily pay his respectful fees when you kiddies have sorted out your boundary problems, but not before. Go shake down someone else. Anyone else. But not this store—not until after the New Year."

He nodded vigorously, keeping his eyes away from mine. I pulled the newspaper away from his throat and let him pass. As soon as the door shut, he abandoned his crate, running over to the tough guy still pulling himself up off the sidewalk. They stared at the store for a long time. I lit a cigarette and waved. Finally they walked off down the street, leaving the candy behind.

The box sat in the snow, abandoned like the Japanese gun emplacements along the beaches of Okinawa the day after the Marines landed. It sat in view as a marker, commemorating the winning of a battle before the war had actually started. With a shrug, I went out and fetched it back inside. Then I helped Lo pull the steel shutters down over the window and door.

Satisfied we'd secured the bunker as well as we could, we went upstairs to the second floor where the old man and his family lived. I took my by-then familiar place at the table and started in with everyone else on Mrs. Lo's spread. As usual, it was terrific. The food sat in colorful bowls on a large lazy Susan; celery and crabmeat, bamboo shoots with red and green peppers, freshly roasted cashews, pork ribs and chicken wings crusty with barbecue sauce, two different kinds of steamed fish, bean sprouts and hamburger heavily doused with black pepper, and a bowl of large, batter-dipped shrimp flash-fried so evenly you could eat them shell and all without even noticing the crunch.

The food wasn't the best part of dinner, though—it was eating with Lo's family. It had been a long time since I'd eaten a meal with other people at the table. My own childhood hadn't had a family that met at the same time every day to eat together. My own childhood hadn't bothered with a family much, period.

Lo and his wife had five children, as well as a few brothers and a sister who gathered every night to eat and discuss their businesses and jobs and school. The first few nights I made the mistake of filling up on whatever I saw in front of me, forgetting the dessert to come. I remembered that night, though, and left some room for the peaches, apple cakes, coconut rolls, and oranges that followed.

Keeping the pounds off wasn't easy under Mrs. Lo's watchful eye. She'd figured out what kind of eater I was the first night and made sure plenty of what I liked was on the table at every dinner after that. She didn't speak more than a handful of English, but so far we'd had no trouble communicating. I'd been made to feel like an adopted son, and what loving mother can't communicate with her little boy?

Lo told the assembly what'd happened in the store earlier, the end of the story meeting with everyone's approval—everyone, that is, except his oldest son, Kong. The kid didn't like his dad's and my approach to things. As far as he was concerned, we were just begging for trouble, and looking to take the whole family down with us.

Mr. Lo just shook his head. It wasn't that we didn't think the kid had a point. Neither of us really disagreed with him—hell, nobody did. The general consensus of the entire family was that more of them would be back the next day. What Kong didn't seem to understand was that I'd known that when I'd started in on the tough guy—his dad had known it before he'd come to hire me.

That there was going to be trouble had always been inevitable—that was why I'd been hired in the first place. And now we were in it with no turning back. Figuring I might need some extra beauty sleep, I excused myself from the table and headed downstairs to my cot.

I thought about the family as I lay in the cold aroma of sawdust and dried fish, trying to figure them out. They were proper people, loving and happy—the kind I don't spend much time with usually. They all had their own chair around the table and their own place in the living room for watching TV. They even changed clothes for bed, wearing pajamas or nightgowns, one of the smaller girls even sporting a little tasseled cap. As I scratched at my underwear, the same I'd worn all day, I had to admit a lot of their life-style was very appealing.

In their home, which was in effect their own little world, they had so far managed to keep the rotting decay of progress out of their lives. True, they dressed in mostly Western clothing, owned stereo systems, televisions, a computer, and a garbage compactor. The girls wore makeup and the boys had Walkmans. The travel pictures we went through one night showed me they'd seen a lot of America—a lot more than most of the people born here.

And yet somehow they'd managed to work and live here for years, in the heart of one of the country's dirtiest, nastiest, most corrupt, and violent cities and not be overly affected by it. They had a set pattern to their lives, and the backbone to hold them erect against any kind of outside interference. Every day as we worked and ate and lived together, the time seemed to go faster. Actually, deep down, I had to admit the eight days we'd spent together had practically flown by.

Closing my eyes, I scrambled toward the back of my mind, searching for sleep. Day eight was going to be day nine before I knew it.

CHAPTER 2

THE MORNING *POST* was its usual treasure trove of laughs. BACKYARD BODIES SURFACE THROUGH AIDS CONFESSION was the field day they picked to go after to catch the commuter crowd, reporting on the activities of a pair of lesbian dominatrixes and their male slave. One of the women had posed for a number of bondage magazines. Chet Green, the dutiful reporter on the story, only had room to list *Punished!, Hot n' Helpless,* and *Whipmaster*. The other had made a splash for a while in a variety of HOM, Inc., videos.

The slave would go out to bars, pick up some man or woman, bring them home, and then turn them over to his mistresses. They would then "punish" him for "seeing" someone else, getting around to the "someone else" he'd brought home a little later. His punishment would be to get his plugs and rings lovingly replaced, along with a short whipping and perhaps a few maternal kicks and punches, just to let him know what a good puppy he really was. His date would be beaten, slashed, burned, urinated on, and in other ways abused for as long as he or she could be kept alive and enjoyable. Then the slave would bury the new victim in the wooded hillside behind the house and go shopping for his ladies fair once again.

The whole thing broke up when the neighborhood dogs nosed up one of the shallower graves for a late-night snack. That brought some human bits and pieces to the back porches of a few of the neighbors. It also brought the slave forward to confess, something he'd wanted to do ever since he'd discovered that he had gone HIV positive somewhere along the line. "God's punishment for their evil ways," as he'd put it. The story then let the public know how many graves'd been uncovered so far, and what'd been found in them.

The paper had a string of other fun tidbits as well: the man who cut off three of his toes in the lawn mower, more on the ex–Miss America who'd been embezzling from her company, updates on the attack-dog situation, as well as the search for the hit-and-run driver who'd tagged out a cop and his baby daughter, the continuing crackdown on Black Dreamer, and the never-ending indicting of city officials. That last was especially fun to follow.

When the new mayor had come in in the previous January his administration had begun rooting out the former's thieving hangers-on. Political hacks who had felt secure for over a decade were suddenly in a runaway competition to turn state's evidence on each other, especially as our deadly-eyed new D.A. kept tying one after another of them to the city's drug traffic. The *Post* hadn't had this much fun material in years.

Of course, there still wasn't much on the national or international front, but what the heck? It was the kind of quality reporting one expected from the newspaper established by Alexander Hamilton in 1801.

Quality reporting or not, though, the paper hadn't managed to capture my complete attention. I'd been keeping my eyes open, watching the door, who came through it and when they left, as well as the front window, who went by it and how often. Which is why I was ready when the friendly foursome came into the store.

They arrived quietly, without any rude fanfare, but everyone in the place knew what was coming down. The majority of Lo's customers vanished in less than a minute. Some remained long enough to check out, hurrying away with their plastic-bagged purchases. Most of the others simply abandoned their baskets in the aisles and fled.

Two of the quartet were big, each bigger than the previous day's tough guy. One was scarred—right cheek and forehead. The other was unblemished but with a badly broken nose. They were followed by a medium-sized one with a joke of a mustache and a look in his eye that dared me to find the punch line. The last one—black hair, long, greasy—was a runt, but one with shooter written all over him. It seemed obvious that at least one of the others would be armed as well. I sized up Mustache as their leader and moved on him; positioning myself between them and the back of the store, I kept two stacks of heavily crated canned fish nearby in case I needed the cover, then pulled my .38 and said,

"Far enough, boys. Give out with your message and slap pavement."

"What's the gun for? Need something to suck on, faggot?"

"History lesson, kids. Bernie Goetz only got six months for gunning down punks with an unregistered weapon. My gun's licensed. So am I. I'm on the job. I'm protecting my employer's property and life. They'll slap my wrist.

"You children are only someone else's voice. So, just give me your message and get back to kindergarten."

"You know, you talk real big for a dead man—but you've got guts." Mustache regarded me with all the care his perhaps four-month career as a professional tough guy had ingrained in him. "Not much gray fuel in the upstairs—no; brains are your short suit all right—but guts . . . yeah, that you've got."

"Fuck the anatomy lesson. Get to the point."

Mustache pulled a joint from his pocket and lit it. It burned slowly, leaving thick, purple-gray billows of smoke, indicating it was laced with coke, or crack, or hash, or Black Dreamer, or something else even newer than Dreamer that I'd never heard of. Stabbing it at me, he said,

"The point, Caucasian, is that the Time Lords have secured this territory. The war is over. The old man isn't your concern anymore. His store is ours. You should have been on the last train back to white pig happy land."

"Do tell." Mustache and one of the giants took a step forward. I warned them off. "Step it easy and backward. If you're in charge now, the word'll be streeted soon enough. So, go back and tell the king of the Time Lords you did your duty and let's all get out of this the easy way."

The midget and Mustache looked at each other, judging the percentages open to them. For a moment I thought they were going to rush me, but their mood broke off in the direction of reason. Mustache pointed the others toward the door with his reeking baton, laughing as he told me,

"Okay, ghost, why not? We got nothing to prove here. Too cold to bother with you now, anyway. But tomorrow, collections go back to normal. We'll be back—all of us. And you—we will not want to see. So, put away your little gun, Caucasian, and book passage back uptown to the mainland. You'll be a lot happier that way."

As the four left I slid my .38 back into my shoulder holster. The wind howled coldly as they passed through the door, its bark cut off sharply as wood and glass slid back into place. Lo looked at me with a question on his face. I tried to pull enough confidence into mine to answer him. Finally, he asked,

"You think it all over?"

"Don't know—could be. It'd be nice to get out of this without getting my clothes dirty."

Tossing me a crystal pear, the kind that are all water and sugar, but with no substance to them at all, he said,

"I don't think things so easy. Gang boys all too young to be so reasoning. Too easy you believe their words and forget their pride. They be back tomorrow, all right.

"Tomorrow be big trouble."

I shrugged and kept on chewing, not really having an answer. Feeling a little up-against-it-all, I went to the back of the store to where Lo's tiny office was to use the phone. I called my main information broker, Hubert, so I could get my mind onto something else. He answered in his usual manner.

"Hey, hey, Dick Tracy. W-where'd you park the squad car?"

"Can it, mutant."

"Oh, in one of yer surly moods, eh? Oh, w-well, w-what's on yer mind?"

"I'm still stuck at that Chinatown gig and I'm getting a little bored. Thought I'd give you a ring and see what was doin'."

"Not much. I have that videotape we need for Th-Thursday. Outside of that, t-though, I was thinkin' of skippin' town 'til then. Why? I mean, I mean, what's up?"

"Ahhh, nothin'. Not really."

Hu went quiet for a second and then asked,

"You okay, Jack? You need a little backup or somethin'?"

"Nah," I told him. "I'm just bored. This job's a piece of cake. If I can't handle this one, I'd better get out of the business."

"Okay," he answered slowly, "okay. Guess I'd better get movin', then. Maurice should have the car downstairs w-waitin' for me. I've got t-to hustle out to the airport. Little job to oversee down southwise. Yes, sir—it's B-Bermuda fer me fer the next couple days."

"Don't get sunburned, ya little weasel."

"Yeah," he laughed. "I'll try real hard not to. Don't you freeze yer balls off up here in the Ice Age."

We laughed at each other for another minute. Hu made

sure to remind me not to take any wooden nickels, and then it was quiet again. I hung up the phone and went back to finishing my pear. For pieces of fruit with no weight to them whatsoever, those pears can sure lay heavy in your stomach. At least that one did.

CHAPTER 3

THE WHOLE WEEK had been a continuing racket of fire-works, bottle rockets, and pinwheels. Nothing, though, in the first nine days of that Chinatown New Year's could have prepared anyone for the tenth. Tiny, brightly colored bombs went off constantly in every alley. Rattling strings of explosions peppered the din—two, three hundred at a shot. The air hung dark with burning gunpowder, new plumes rising from every corner to further choke those in the frozen streets. Explosives dropped out of windows and off of roofs; missiles flew upward, lit the sky, and then crashed back to earth.

All in all, the perfect time if ever I saw one for a mob of punks to stalk the neighborhood and empty machine guns at each other and the rest of society.

Lo and I opened the store at the regular time, leaving ourselves somewhat open, not wanting to encourage the gang to perhaps torch the whole building just to get at us. Most every other place around was closed for the holiday, which sent Lo's business through the roof. While we worked, the old man told me the story behind the ten-day tradition.

Over the centuries, as the farmers in China celebrated the coming of a new year, since they couldn't really do any work in January or February anyway, they just got in the habit of partying longer and longer. The traditional length is actually fifteen days, which was easy to pull off three thousand years ago; just shut the country down for two weeks and let everyone get shit-faced—not possible in our enlightened age, of course. Thank heaven and all its angels for the legion of bloodless, leeching old ladies who run this nation. Without them to protect us from ourselves, God only knows what kind of fun we might have. Before you know it, someone might drive at fifty-six miles an hour after having a beer—or maybe light a cigarette in a restaurant.

Anyway, normally the biggest night of the festival is New Year's Eve, just as it is for us. This year, though, the new mayor's Minority Focus Group planned events throughout the city to show how in touch he was with everyone but heterosexual, Anglo-Saxon males. Unfortunately, the boob's people got everything backward, not realizing the ten days of the Chinese New Year worked like the twelve days of Christmas, with the biggest day of the holiday coming first. And, of course, they got all of their media coverage lined up before anyone could straighten them out. So, doing the only thing the fearless leader of a City Hall can do, he had the police street the news that people who celebrated on the tenth day instead of the first could expect no tickets for illegal fireworks, illegal congregation, et cetera, but that those trying to celebrate before then could expect major hassles. He even arranged for the side streets to be blocked off— no traffic to interfere with the festivities.

Which explained why on what should have been a business-as-usual day the streets were raining explosives, and most of the stores were closed, their owners trapped between their fear of the gangs and the mayor's indifferent stupidity. Welcome to New York.

Lo's business, of course, was the best it'd been in ten years. That brought half the family in to help. At lunchtime, Mrs. Lo and the youngest granddaughter brought down two trays of large bowls filled with noodles and pork, as well as some side plates of fish balls, fried rice, and shrimp toast, plus tea with cakes, cookies, some mixed pastries, and a large platter of orange slices—just to keep us all from starving before dinner, you see. While everyone else was eating, Lo's youngest came over to me.

"Mr. Hagee, sir?"

"Yeah, Git'jing, what's up?"

"Will things be bad today?"

I looked into her ovaled face, past her short, unmoving lashes, into the inking darkness of her solemn eyes.

"They could be," I admitted. Telling the truth to their offspring seemed to be a routine matter with the Los. Besides, this was one of those kids to whom you just couldn't lie. "What makes you ask?"

"So far you have been very lucky. But we can't ask you to use up all your luck for us. So I have brought you this."

She handed me a chain with what looked like an ivory dragon on the end of it. Closer inspection showed it was actually one large dragon with eight smaller ones crawling all about it, some of them pushing balls, or possibly eggs, with their front paws or holding them in their mouths. I wasn't sure if they were supposed to be playing or fighting.

"Thank you," I told her. "Is this supposed to bring good luck?"

"Nine dragons in the home always means good fortune. Every home needs nine dragons in it somewhere to bring good luck. They don't need to be the same, or in the same place, or anything like that. You just have to have nine of them in your home somewhere for the luck."

"But I'm not in my home," I joked with her.

Quite seriously, she told me, "You do not have a home."

"Sure I do," I replied. "I live in Brooklyn, in Bensonhurst."

"No. You may eat and sleep there," she let me know, "but it is not your home. Your home is still within you— you have not yet begun to bring it out. That is why you can carry your dragons with you—because you have only a place to stay, not a real home."

That said, she smiled politely and then ran back to her grandmother when the old woman started to collect up the dishes. I wanted to argue with her, but didn't see the point. She was right. I lived in a barren apartment that I kept clean by keeping it empty. Half the time I slept on the couch in my office instead of going home. If it wasn't for Elba, the girl from downstairs who takes care of my dog, the poor mutt would've probably starved to death by now.

The thing that made me wonder was how Git'jing could tell all that just by looking at me. After all, everyone hates being obvious. Figuring it wasn't worth the questioning, however, I slid the chain over my neck and hung my dragons inside my shirt. I feel luckier already, I told myself. Besides, the way things looked I was willing to take any advantage I could get my hands on.

The morning paper had given an update on the situation in Chinatown, one so wrong I wondered how it could've been printed, even in the *Post*. Not that the other New York rags were ever any more accurate; the *Post* might be the most flamboyant of the main quartet of papers keeping the city "informed," but it has no monopoly on inaccurate reporting—not by a long shot.

Luckily, for all the news that mattered to me that day, I had other resources. In Chinatown, as in all real neighborhoods, not fancified motel parks for the rich like Sutton Place or Park Avenue, the vocal grapevine is as strong today as it was in the first grove of trees that ever knew human congregation. Sadly, that day it was not carrying good news.

Despite the message the Time Lords had delivered the day before, the word on the street was that they were bluffing. They were still in dispute with the Angry Ghosts and Mother's Blood Flowing over three prime real estate areas, one of which was Lo's block of Mott Street. They had given the same message to a number of stores looking to see what the popular reaction was.

Most everyone else locked their doors to see who got picked to be made an example of; you can guess who got picked.

I thought about calling in help, but decided against it. When the gang showed, another gang waiting for them wasn't going to slow them down. They'd picked Lo and me to teach a lesson to, so we were the ones who were going to get it. Face demanded it, which meant there was little hope of stopping it merely with force.

Actually, I couldn't imagine how much muscle it would take to back down the Time Lords. I'd been able to send the first two packing because they hadn't expected me. The next bunch had only been sent to deliver a message. But this time . . . this time was for all the marbles and they would move forward no matter what.

As we waited, Lo told me,

"No worry. I know this first day talk to you. What else to do? Take chance they no burn store, kill me, wife, children? Hope not to be a dead man? Crawl on floor, beg for mercy from animals who kill just for chance to laugh? No thank you bullshit very much not. Standing better way to die than kneeling.

"What you think?"

"I think you've got a point," I told him.

"Good," he answered, slapping me on the back. "Damn good. You get ready. Trouble come soon; be sure. I go sell rice."

Lo was wrong, he got to sell rice for another five hours before our troubles finally came home to roost.

CHAPTER 4

THERE WAS NO mistaking what was happening when they came. You could feel the attention focusing on the store before our playmates were even in sight. Lo could feel it; so could his wife. She came downstairs to chase all the kids back to safety while I was still putting on my coat. I hit the sidewalk just as the evening's entertainment came into view.

There were at least two dozen of them; hard-muscled, impressed with themselves, young—the oldest not more than twenty. Some were carrying ball bats, some had bricks. God only knew what was hidden from sight. I could see all my old pals from the previous two days intermingled with the fresh troops. Their leader was a new face, however.

At best he was seventeen. The way he walked, the power in his step, the way he ignored the blasting chill killing its way through the streets, showed he held his position by being the toughest animal in the pack. His eyes, plainly etched with privilege, were what betrayed him.

He was a child, one used to snapping his fingers for whatever he wanted—money, women, drugs, police protection, transportation, invisibility—whatever. It had all come too easily to him until now. He was more than sure he was in charge, more than aware that his word was law—he was certain. If he believed in any gods at all, it was only so he could rest assured they'd appointed him master of all he surveyed.

Looking into the master's eyes, even from a distance, I knew he was the reason for all of Chinatown's current troubles. It was *his* needs, *his* desire and greed that were tearing the neighborhood apart, setting the gangs at each other's throats, killing a total of twelve so far in the last three months.

Expectedly, there wasn't a cop in sight. No one knows the grapevine like they do. I could count on them not showing up until things were long over, one way or another, using City Hall's stupidity as their excuse. Hard to blame them, really. Pulling out a pad and scribbling with a Bic is a hell of a lot easier than taking on a drug-confident, wildball, gorilla-rough teenaged killer. Or two. Or who knew how many.

A hand signal, fingers over the left shoulder, stopped the gang's advance. The leader took three more steps toward me and then planted himself between me and his boys, playing the scene for all the drama he could remember from the last WWF match he'd seen. I leaned against the stone of the next building, lighting a cigarette, waiting for him to start it. Things were beginning to fall into place for me. All of Chinatown had known trouble was coming for New Year's. The residents and the police had all prepared to the best of their abilities to stay out of the gangs' ways, hoping a lot of winnowing might befall the ranks. Lo had decided on protection instead of prayer.

The gangs had knocked the crap out of each other, the police had let them, and now the top three were ready to divide up the remaining plums. For whatever reason, the Time Lords were the ones making the first move. Maybe they were the strongest gang after all— they'd been the ones making all the moves I'd seen. Word had it they weren't, though, and I was betting the word was right. Their strategy was wrong; it lacked finesse. It was blunt, broken-bottle, dull-eyed slugger stuff. The kind of planning that always springs into the minds of children.

I've never liked that aspect of childhood. It is necessary, I suppose, but there's something about the way
people think until they finally go mad and reach adult-
hood that is almost tragic. The smug condescension of
youthful righteousness is almost unbearable to watch.
Whether it is unbearably funny or painful depends on
both the child putting on the exhibition as well as the
audience gauging it. But no matter how much sympathy
one has for them, the end result is that they make an ass
out of themselves and there's no way to warn them off
from it. Adults know this because they can remember the
things they once believed from which no one could warn
them away.

All it boils down to, though, is that no matter what
one might think to the contrary, there are certain things
that make the world run, and that make human beings
tick. Those who play by these rules are called grown-ups.
And those who think the rules can, even for a millisecond,
ever be broken are called children.

Children.

"So," snickered the leader, "qua'lo so stupid he just
can't find his way home? That your problem, old man?"

Christ, how I hate children.

Letting a lungful out, I responded through the smoke,
"I'm tired of playin' jacks with you and your boys,
Sonny. Go on—take 'em on out of here. Get smart,
juvenile. This store ain't worth it."

"Then why don't you leave?"

The chuckle of his gang broke through the distractions
around us—through the cold and the noise. Pulling in a
long lungful of smoke and ice, I drew out the moment
until it was mine again, and then I told him.

"I have a contract that binds me here until dawn.
I don't have any other place to be. You—you're the
Time Lords. You can go anywhere you want to. Show
the wisdom in mercy, boys. Let this place stand."

Sonny cracked his innocent prankster's look just
slightly, his eyes narrowing as he forced himself to

consciously take my measure. Rechecking his footing on the ice, I caught another secret hand sign directing two of his troops forward on either side of him. One of the giants I'd seen the day before. The other, bigger one was new to me.

"You were told to go home, Kojak."

"European powers were told to stay out of this hemisphere. Nobody listens."

Conversation stopped with a snap of the fingers—the shorter giant's cue to attack. He was a rusher, sweeping forward at me like a runaway train. I planted my cigarette firmly, taking another drag, waiting for the right moment. When his foot touched the walk I sidestepped out of his way—quick—letting him ram his fingers into the bricks I'd been leaning against.

The second giant was already moving. Him I took more seriously. He came in calmer, with a sharper idea of what he was doing. Waiting for him to swing, I stepped inside his arc, throwing him off balance just by being so close. He stumbled for a second. I bounced the back of my fist off his nose and then pivoted, catching his ear with my elbow. He staggered off, but by then his partner was up.

He was more cautious this time, but I couldn't afford to congratulate him. Before he could overcome his hesitation over doing his fingers any further damage, I reached out to the point of being off balance, something he never expected. Grabbing his left hand, I jerked him to me— crushing his fingers together while I dragged him across the ice. He howled. I let him. He swung at me blindly, swatting to stop the pain. I dodged him with a chuckle and spun him around, letting him fly into his partner, bouncing his skull off the other giant's back. They sat on the ground together, shaking their heads, wondering what had happened.

Crossing to the street, I stepped on the first giant's hand, drawing screams so loud you could hear them blocks away despite the fireworks. Good as I figured my moves had made me look, however, I could feel the years catching up to me. Had it really been ten years earlier . . . the training and the fighting and the killing? Back in my oh-so-enlightening Military Intelligence days—taking guys like Sonny's bruisers apart like clocks—a little tussle like the giant brothers wouldn't have mussed my hair—then. Now, even despite the cold, I could feel trace lines of sweat along both ears—my tongue pressed against my back uppers.

I curled and uncurled my fingers, making two casual fists, stopping in the middle of the street ankle-deep in the growing slush. Ignoring the freezing moisture soaking into my boots, I took my Camel out of my mouth as casually as I could, blowing smoke and asking,

"Got any more acts you want to audition before you go home?"

Sonny's waving hand brought forward a quartet, two with baseball bats, two with knives. The first to try his luck was a knifer. He stabbed, danced back, stabbed again. I stayed out of reach. This bunch was better—not in each other's way. The blade came at me again, but only as a feint. He was setting me up for the batters. Noting that in time saved me from getting my head splattered. They'd moved forward together, not swinging but stabbing, limiting their range but keeping their distance. Almost worked.

I ducked the first blade again and then grabbed out, catching the punk's wrist. Twisting, I got him to lose the knife; then I got him jumping. As long as he was hopping around in pain, no one else could close in on me. He tried to swat me away, but was in too much agony to connect.

I had his wrist caught firm between thumb and forefinger—nerve-jamming him. The pain, I'm sure, was tearing through his brain in screaming electric flashes. Pouring tears, strings of snot, and screech-propelled spit arced away from his shaking head. Finally, I grabbed the back of his head and bounced his face off the closest

car—cracking glass—more to put him out of his misery
than anything else Then, reaching down, I came up
under him, getting a good enough hold to hoist him
over my head. The others backed off as I knew they
would, thinking I was going to throw him into them.
Very dramatic, but hardly ever workable. I flipped him
backward over the car I'd just bounced him off of. He
thudded against the roof, then fell over the other side,
landing in front of the sidelined giants. The others got
the idea. I'd forced them to flinch needlessly—bad loss
of face. Then I showed them I was going to take them
out one by one and stack them like firewood.

The batters came forward again, rising to my challenge. This time they were swinging. I tried to time
my catch but I was off. One caught me in the side.
Hard. I slid on the snow and rammed into a parked
car. The second batter stepped up, the cheers of his
fellows making him reckless. Swinging down, he went
for my skull—took out the Toyota's windshield instead.
I kicked sideways, burying my foot to the cuff in his
side. Bones cracked. His. Good, I thought.

The first batter came back again, stabbing. I sidestepped twice, then faked a slip. He struck again, too
quickly. With better timing I grabbed out and took his
bat from him, sliding it out of his gloved hands with
a twist. He turned to run, but I put everything I had
into a spinning return hit and broke his ankle, sending him rolling through the street, screaming for mercy.

The second blade carrier debated facing me on his
own for a second, then stepped away, melting back into
the ranks with his head hung. Smarter than he looked.
The gang stood their ground, silver breath mixing with
the burning gunpowder and smoke wreathing through the
air. The frozen night continued to hammer noisily around
us, the constant explosions becoming our silence. I'd lost
my cigarette in the slush. Lighting another one, ignoring
the pounding in my ears—my chest—working at keeping

my bare hands from shaking too badly, I asked the boy in charge,

"Had enough, Sonny?"

His eyes bore through me, heating buildings on the other side of the street. Spitting into the slop at our feet, he growled,

"Full of tricks, aren't you, ghost man?"

"Oh, cut the crap." I exhaled smoke at the gang, sucking breath, knowing opportunity's knuckles were inches from the door. If he was an adult, I was dead. He'd have someone gun me down and that would be it. I was gambling I'd figured him right, though. If I acted like I wanted everything to end then, I was sure he'd misinterpret and go for me himself. Which was, of course, the only way out I'd seen since the gang had first arrived.

"I'm tired, and you're scared," I told him. "You can't afford to lose any more face, and you don't know what to do about it. My advice is 'give up.' Take this band of rejects to whatever flop you throw yourselves into at night and get out of this the easy way. No one's been hurt too bad yet—especially me."

Without hesitation he began to shrug off his coat. "So you haven't been hurt too bad yet, eh, ghost? Well, let's see if we can't change that."

Knock, knock, motherfucker.

He'd taken the bait, Now, if I could just live through another fight with the toughest beast in the pack, I might be able to get through the night. Winded and trying not to show it, I shrugged off his attitude, grabbing down as much nicotine as I could before I had to start moving again. Sonny stared at the baseball bat in my hand and then picked the fallen one out of the frozen mess it lay in, wiping it off on his sleeve. He pointed at a large construction industrial trash bin and walked away toward it. I followed. So did the gang. He said,

"Emperor of the mountain. Winner decides what happens."

"Yeah," I answered, "doesn't he always?" The boy looked at me, smiling. I pulled in a last lungful and then flipped the butt away, saying, "Okay, Sonny. Let's get to it."

The bin was filled with the guttings of an apartment building in the icy throes of winter gentrification. Ten feet wide, thirty-five feet long, six feet deep, it was filled with old wiring, rotting pipes, broken plasterboard and bricks, and nail-studded splinters of wood. One corner was a stacking of old-fashioned windows. The top layer was one of garbage, some in bags, most tossed in loose or torn free from its wrappings by hungry cats and desperate humans. A wonderful little arena.

Sonny was already coming across the field by the time I got to the top. Bracing myself, I swung my bat up to take the first hit, barely able to shift its position to take the second. He slammed at me unmercifully, swinging at me from the left to the right to the left, on and on, waiting for me to fall into a rhythm so he could break the pattern and paste me. I matched him, blocking hit after hit, feeling the numbness starting to climb my arms.

Knowing I couldn't keep taking such punishment, I waited for a weaker strike and then pushed, putting our bats off to the side and our faces up against each other's. Letting my weapon go, I caught his bat arm with both hands and threw him off balance, unfortunately only into some soft garbage bags. He started to get up but I threw myself on him, forcing him back down into the trash. He thrashed about, trying to stand, but I kept the pressure up, pushing him down as deep as I could into the bulging plastic sacks. His raking fingers tore several open. Our bouncing around freed more.

Snow started to mix with the frozen grease and decaying pus from the bags, making it impossible for us to hang on to each other. Sonny slipped away from me, clawing his way across the arena, gasping for air. I tried to grab his ankle but sank to my knee in the trash, suddenly finding my leg trapped in the bricks and debris below.

"Now," came Sonny's rasping voice, "I'm going to kill you."

I jerked at my leg, tearing pants, skin, and muscle, but freeing it. Sonny came forward, swinging one of the bats at me so violently he almost threw himself from the bin when he missed. I dragged myself out of his path just barely in time, grabbing up a couple of broken bricks as I stood. He came at me again. I lobbed the first at him— missed—only denting a parked car's door. Weighing the second in my hand for a moment, I let it fly; he hit it away with the bat. It fell to the street, almost clobbering one of his followers.

"No more jokes, ghost man? No more tough talk?"

My breath was scorching my throat. Blood was sluic- ing from my leg, the pain filling my eyes with tears. My side still hurt from the first batter's swing in the second inning.

"Naw," I admitted. "No more jokes."

"Well then—if you can't amuse me anymore, fag- got, you know what that means, don't you? It's dying time!"

He stepped across the trash gingerly, watching his footing, coming with a smile to dash my brains out. Too tired to dodge or resist his attack, too close to the end of my resources, I pulled out my .38 and gut-shot him, sending him thudding into the street below.

Instantly, shots rang out. Five of the Time Lords started to clamber up the sides of the bin. Two in the background began pulling out guns. Conserving ammo, I grabbed up one of the stacked windows and flung it at the first three heads coming over the side. One ducked; one got a broken chin; the other lost an eye. I pitched two more windows into the crowd, catching one of the marksmen, sending another backpedaling for cover. A knifer came over the wall, tearing through my coat and nicking my side before I could get hold of him. I slammed him across the jaw with all I had left, sending him falling into another behind him. That one's screams told me he'd fallen onto something sharp and nasty. Too damn bad.

As more guns came loose I readied my .38 again. My head was empty of thoughts except for how many of the enemy I could take with me and which ones I wanted the most. I'd hoped to bring things down to just their leader and myself—to take him out and then bluff the others into leaving. Hadn't worked. A hail of automatic weapons' fire gouged at the metal of the bin sending thick sparks and ricochets off into the surrounding fireworks. A couple of slugs went by me. I took aim at the main shooter and was just about to fire when I suddenly spotted dozens of figures moving through the gloom at both ends of the street. A bullhorn sounded, orders barking at us in Cantonese. The Time Lords lost interest in me immediately, looking to the left and right instead, sizing up what was happening.

A Chinese youth in a good suit—five-ten, medium build, round face framed by a sharp-edged haircut—came up to the bin. Offering me his hand, he called,

"Come on down, Mr. Hagee. Join the party."

The newcomers were armed to the teeth, not looking for anything except cooperation. After a second it dawned on me what was going on. Shoving my .38 back into its holster, I answered,

"Ah, I'm going to have a little trouble getting down from here, and—um, well . . . as gracious as it is for someone of your importance to offer his hand, I wouldn't want to ruin your suit. Sir."

The newcomer smiled an expansive, dangerous smile and turned to Sonny. Roughly nudging the still-howling gang leader with his foot, the smiler told him,

"You see—respect. This warrior knows how, and when, and to whom to show respect. Too bad you never learned that, William."

Turning back to me, he answered, "Don't let it trouble you. What are clothes? An artificial shell. A dozen suits are not worth what you have done. Take my hand."

I did more than just take his hand; I slid out of the bin like a mouthful of spit going down a bathroom wall. Smiler caught me and held me up on my feet. Whispering, he asked,

"You're not going to die on me, are you?" When I assured him I wasn't, he said, "Good. You hang tough for two minutes—let me gather up the face to be gained here and you'll come out happy."

I nodded. He turned to the crowd. His speech was simple. I knew he was the head of either the Angry Ghosts or Mother's Blood Flowing. Both gangs had known the Time Lords would move first. Now I could see that they had waited for the best moment to stage their takeover and then moved in in unison. Probably planned for days.

His offer was straightforward—the Time Lords were too wild, too undisciplined, too much of a troublemaking organization. They caused more discord than harmony, and thus had to be disbanded. When someone countered that you can't disband a gang that had a leader, Smiler answered,

"Why, you are right. Debbie, my sweet queen. If you could oblige us."

A dazzling oriental girl in an expensive-looking gray fur coat came forward and pressed a sawed-off shotgun over the hole in Sonny's stomach where my bullet had entered. She smiled and pulled both triggers, splattering the asphalt with meat and bone. Sliding home two more shells, she retriggered and splattered the street some more.

While she worked at her repavement operation, Smiler told me, "This way no one will bother to look for any stray slugs from some unnamed private detective's gun, eh?"

I nodded again, with as much strength as I could. My job had been to protect the store. I'd done that. In the end, since it matched their own interests, the Time

Lords' rivals had come in and finished what I started. After Sonny, a.k.a. William, was put out of his misery, none of his followers had anything more to say. The rules had been followed; honor had been satisfied. The Time Lords split ranks and joined one or the other of the two gangs surrounding us like the last kids to be picked for a stickball game.

Smiler walked me over to the Los' store. I'd played down to him because he was the king of the moment. There was no honor to be had in provoking him into getting rid of me like he had Sonny, and little sense. He'd come in at the last minute and pulled my bacon out of the fire because he wanted to show he was the friend of the toughest man on the street. He could have just as easily waited until I was dead to make his move. I've made worse friends in my time. Check out my ex-wife if you think I'm lying.

"Okay, pal," he suggested, "why don't you go inside and get put back together before you croak or something?"

While he helped me over the curb, he quietly shoved a wad of bills into my pocket. When I looked at him, he whispered again,

"Look, gangbuster, don't get all proud on me. I've been waiting for a long time for someone to do what you just did. Now, I know who really shot Billy Wong, and you know who had him finished off. I could kill you, and one of Billy's relatives might go to the cops with that to get me, and on and on it could go. Who needs it? Revenge is as ugly as greed. I like you, Big Hagee. You understand the basics. Billy . . . he was crazy. Kept trying to throw all the balance out the window.

"He had to go."

The Los managed to break through the mass of gang members surrounding us then. As I fell into their arms, Smiler said, loudly enough for plenty of people to hear,

"Everybody—know this. The Lo family, and their property, is under my protection. This noble warrior, Chinese or not, has shown us what must be done with those who upset the old ways. *He* is under my protection as well, for he is a great and honorable figure, and too much a man to be my friend for things as small as money or his life. For this, *I* owe him favor—for this"—his hand swept over the corpse of William Wong and the shattered remains of the Time Lords—"everyone in Chinatown owes him favor."

Taking in a harsh breath, Smiler's face suddenly grew dark as he added,

"So all who hear me and know how far my words travel, remember only of this night that the fireworks were wonderful, and that you all watched the skies from your windows and saw nothing of the streets."

The few onlookers took their cue and disappeared. Most of the gang members followed them. A cleanup crew restuffed the bin, finding room for Sonny somewhere in the middle. By the time the Los helped me hobble back up to their apartment, the streets were empty save for the black snow and the never-ending explosions. My leg and side were messy, but not nearly as seriously hurt as they appeared. The girls burned my clothes in a barrel on the roof while the boys scrubbed me down and treated my wounds.

Smiler had paid me five thousand dollars for eliminating the Time Lords. Less than I would have charged if he'd asked, but more than anyone else was offering once it had already happened. I wasn't quite sure at the time I'd ever get the chance to call in the marker he claimed I was holding on him, but I figured it didn't hurt to keep it in mind. Myself, I've never been one to pass by money in the street just because some people think it's undignified to stoop in public.

Mr. Lo made a big show out of paying me while I held court from his easy chair, answering the continual barrage of questions about the fight. I laughed most of it off, only playing up the dangerous parts for the youngest children.

I also added a corny bit about grabbing the dragons around my neck and praying to the gods for help. I didn't really care who else bought it; Git'jing's face lit up at the mention, and that was all that mattered.

After that, Mrs. Lo chased us all to the dinner table where the food was so deep you'd have thought the rest of the neighborhood'd been invited to join us. The family chattered about the fight, and the whole of my New Year's visit, and the excitement of it all. For a while, at least. Before dessert, however, the conversation was back to that of shop and school and business and dating and homework and babies and all the other talk that fills a happy home. Something that, come the morning, I'd be leaving behind.

Grabbing for the last piece of lobster, I pretended rage at the baby who snatched it out from under me, just to see that innocent laughter one final time. I figured if I only had one more night, I'd might as well make the best of it. If I'd had any idea at all what was coming next, I might never have left.

CHAPTER 5

I WAS HAVING lunch at Louie's, a seafood place in the Village, feeling lucky to have managed a table underneath Charlie. Charlie is the name of the stuffed sailfish hanging from the ceiling in Louie's main dining room. For a while, the management had barred Hubert and I from that part of the restaurant. We'd staged an impromptu contest one night, trying to throw onion rings over Charlie's nose. Louie hadn't been amused. Neither'd been the people we hit with the onion rings.

That was in the past, however, forgiven if not forgotten. I sat in Charlie's shadow, nursing a gin and tonic, waiting for a friend who'd called me the day before. I'd just gotten home from Chinatown when the phone rang. It was Rich Violano, one of the toughest crime reporters in the city. He'd heard about my guard-dog assignment and wanted to ask me some questions, throwing in lunch at Louie's as an inducement.

I told him "sure," letting him know that anytime he wanted to grill me, Louie's was the place to do it. We both laughed at that one, agreeing on one o'clock. Rich came in at just a couple of minutes after, knowing where to find me.

He slung his dripping coat over the back of one of the extra chairs at the table, brushing snow out of his brown hair with his free hand. Slapping his cheeks to bring some feeling back to them, he asked,

"You never get tired of sitting under that thing, do you?"

"Hey," I told him, pointing up, "how often can you hang out under that big a prick in this town and be confident you're not going to get shit on?"

"Well," he laughed, "that makes sense."

Before we could continue, though, our waiter circled back to take our orders. Rich got the salmon steak, sided with cottage fries and stuffed mushrooms. I got the Batter Boy Special—shrimp, clams, oysters, scallops, and a jumbo filet, all golden-coated with fat-soaked breading and grease. Rich asked for a continuous stream of seltzer while I switched to coffee for the duration of the meal. I wasn't drinking because I like to taste my food when I eat. Rich wasn't drinking because he never does.

Rich Violano ranks as one of New York's most interesting characters. He doesn't drink, smoke, curse, do drugs, visit prostitutes, gamble, or anything else that passes for real fun. For the majority of the guys trying to manhandle the city crime beat, such personal habits would've been a liability. Most criminals feel more comfortable around people who have at least a veneer of unrespectability. Rich manages to counter the fears of those whose trust he needs by always telling the truth.

No matter what his enemies have to say about him, the one thing they're forced to admit is that Rich Violano is an honest man. If it appears in his column, he means it. If he's ever told a lie to anyone, about anything, no one I know has ever heard about it. His word is as solid as steel, his dedication and compassion boundless, and his tenacity a street legend. Stories just don't get away from him. Which, of course, in a corrupt dump like New York has earned him a lot of very bad will. It never seems to bother him, though. Sometimes I've wondered if he's even totally aware of just how many people hate and fear him. Frankly, I don't think he ever gives it much thought. A clear conscience must be a wonderful thing to own. I wouldn't know.

As our waiter headed for the back, Rich pulled out his minirecorder and set it on the table between us. His finger ready to thumb the record button, he asked,

"All right. Anything happen to you in Chinatown worth the *Post*'s time? You've got to give me something. After all, I can't justify putting us both on the expense account without at least asking."

"I don't know. I don't think there's anything I can tell you that will net you that Pulitzer they're counting on you winning for them, but I do think something's going on downtown."

"You talking the drug connection?"

He was keeping the conversation loose, but I knew Rich was referring to Dreamer. The mayor's office's new "terror drug flooding the city via Chinatown" would be good for front-page copy for at least two more weeks. I told Rich,

"Maybe."

"You wouldn't want to elaborate, would you?"

"Yeah, I'd love to. I'm just not steady on any of the facts. It's all just feelings, really." I told Rich about my guard-duty chores and what the situation was like downtown. With a recorder going, I did some judicious editing of the truth, but pretty much gave him the whole story. By the time I was done, our waiter had already circled around again with our bread basket and drinks. Rich lavishly buttered a thick sesame seed roll and began to tear into it. Coming up for air, he asked,

"You think that maybe the recent elevation of street violence—hard to believe it could actually be worse than last year, isn't it—could it really have gained any of its altitude because of Dreamer?"

"It's possible. The Chinatown gangs have been pretty stable for a few years now. They've all had their own territories, and everyone's been pretty happy with the arrangement. But . . . something got them stirred up. Trust me, Rich, those little monkeys haven't been gunning each other down over nothing."

"Yeah," he agreed. "There's been a lot of trouble the past few months, and the timing's been pretty close."

"How close?"

"The first whispers I got on the stuff, ah, I mean Dreamer, came the same week of the first murder, back in December."

I fished a breadstick out of the basket and took a bite, giving myself a second to let the new information sink in. Like a lot of people, I'd followed the news about all the murders in Chinatown, as well as the increasing scare bulletins over Dreamer. Also, like a lot of people, since it hadn't concerned me much, I hadn't stopped to put two and two together. Maybe the gangs were fighting for more than people thought.

Since I hadn't been looking for evidence one way or the other while I'd been downtown, I really didn't have anything concrete to tell Rich. Reflections made days after the fact about something you didn't think much about in the first place weren't the best guidelines on which someone could base anything. Luckily, Rich was a good enough reporter to know that. We continued to talk and munch bread until lunch came. Setting aside illegal drugs and city corruption for the moment, we both fork-and-knifed our way into our meals, savoring the usual excellence of Louie's.

Rich's salmon was nearly three quarters of an inch thick, pink and firm, dripping all the right juices, just a little bit smaller than a catcher's mitt. His fries were a work of art, mostly golden-sunshine brown, but shot through with those delicious hard, crunchy spots everyone loves so much. They were piled so high they looked like a mountain at sunset, with the salmon as a pink lake in the foreground. The platter they were served on was so full his mushrooms had to be brought on a plate of their own.

The Batter Boy was its usual pig's delight, twenty-nine or thirty pounds of sizzling shellfish and fillets. Louie's dips their seafood in a light, mostly bread-crumb batter that has always been my favorite. No matter how hungry I am, however, I can never finish an entire Special. Try as I might, I always end up asking for a doggie bag. My dog should be so lucky.

Digging into our feasts, we happily ignored each other for a while, only coming up for air long enough to spout "Christ, this is good" occasionally and wipe away some of the layers of grease on our mouths, cheeks, and fingers. Finally, though, once we had sated our initial greedy hunger, Rich sat back slightly and asked,

"Jack, do you have anything on the upcoming docket that's going to take a lot of your time?"

"No. Not really. Hu and I have a meeting with a client of mine tomorrow, but that's about it. I could wish for something, but nothing concrete's on the calendar. Why?"

Rich waved a piece of salmon around in a circle on the end of his fork, twirling it as if trying to reel in his thoughts. Eventually, though, he lay his silverware down, pushing himself a few more inches away from the table with the same motion. He asked slowly,

"Jack . . . where do you think the drugs that get into the city come from?"

"Ahuh, Colombia," I answered. "Mexico, Hawaii. . ."

"No," he interrupted, "I mean, who do you think brings them into the city?"

I squinted at Rich sharply, wondering what he was up to, then answered, "Well, it's a long list. The mob does a lot of business. But there's all kinds of gangs cutting in on them these days. Colombians, Salvadorians, Jamaicans . . . I know both the Chinese and the Koreans have been giving them some big trouble over the last couple of years—interrupting the heroin flow . . ."

"Okay, but who lets them get away with it?"

I continued to stare at Rich, not really sure at what he was getting, finally asking, "Okay. Where's all this leading?"

"Don't know yet, Jack. Really don't. There's some stuff coming down in the city lately . . . I don't know. It's"—he paused, his tongue running over the back of his teeth, his eyes looking nowhere—"it's getting bad. Bad government running wild, killers and dope dealers everywhere, little guys getting rammed out and crushed right and left. Something's wrong."

"Nothing new in all that," I told him.

"I know," he answered. "But this is different. I'm not talking about random incidents. There's a pattern emerging. I haven't been able to put my finger on it yet, but I think I'm starting to get close to something. Something that might cause the paper to want to hire you for a while. What do you think?"

I was a little surprised.

Newspapers don't hire detectives. They have all the snoops they need on staff. The only time a paper shells out money to bring in someone like me is when things have gotten too dangerous for someone like Rich. And that means things have to be pretty dangerous. No one really likes giving reporters a hard time. Killing a member of the Fourth Estate is almost worse than killing a cop. It focuses far too much scrutiny on one's activities. So, what Rich's little statement said to me was that the paper wanted to uncover something it felt was so dangerous, whoever was on the targeted end might be willing to eliminate people and take their chances. That did not make me feel secure. I told Rich so.

"Yeah," he answered, "I can see your point. You want me to forget I asked?"

"No. If it was anyone else I'd already be headed for the front door, but I owe you one—*one* at the very least . . ."

Rich waved his hand in a dismissing manner.

"Forget that, will you?" he said. "I was just doing my job."

"Maybe so, but you were the only reporter in town who wasn't out to crucify me then. A lot of people

tried to make me look pretty bad until the facts came
out. Then they just shut up and forgot all the nasty
things they said about me. But you stuck by me the
whole time . . ."

"And we sold a lot of newspapers doing so."

"Is that why you told my side of the story the way
you did—just to sell extra editions?"

"No," he admitted. "We thought you were telling the
truth."

I snorted at Rich's use of the word "we." His editor
had wanted to hang me out to dry like the rest of the
city. I'd been accused of trying to run off with a fortune
in diamonds. It'd taken me a long time to prove I hadn't
stolen them, and to track down who had. The especially
hard part came because I really had taken the diamonds,
but only to flush out the killer. It'd been one of those
clever gimmicks that always works on television but'd
blown up in my face like a back-country ginmaker.

Before I knew it, I was running around town trying to
hide a Boy Scout knapsack filled with uncut diamonds
and malted milk balls, being chased by the police, insurance investigators, the TV and print media, and the guys
who'd really tried to take the stones in the first place.
The only thing that kept me on the streets long enough
to prove I wasn't the guy interested in taking the stones
was Rich's editorials. I reminded him of that, adding,

"Granted, what you're hinting around at here sounds
like more than enough to allow me to call us square
on the favor—and I probably will once we're finished.
Then you'll be all happy, right? So, let me do it my
way, 'cause my way you win no matter what I do?
Okay?"

Hoisting his glass, he saluted me with it, agreeing,
"Okay."

I returned his salute with my coffee cup before
knocking back what I had left to generate a bread-
crumb-coated burp that'd sorely needed releasing. The
career women at the table next to ours lowered

their voices and their eyes in an appropriate fashion to show their extreme displeasure. I leave it to your imagination as to how much embarrassment that caused me.

CHAPTER 6

THE REMAINDER OF the afternoon brought me nothing except a chance to read another hundred pages of the *Iliad*. I'd been trying to finish it for almost a year, but somehow I was still floundering around in the middle. So, leaving the women on the beach to moan and wail and pull their disheveled hair over the death of Achilles, I reshelved them with all of the other half and three-quarter finished novels on my wall, deciding to head for home early before the rush hour built up.

Driving through a New York City February is no picnic. The poorly maintained streets develop the most treacherous pockets for sheltering ice one can imagine. Even cars as heavy as my Skylark can get caught off guard by them. Light buckets of plastic like the crap turned out by Detroit and Tokyo these days get sent into killer tailspins by the dozens every winter day. Since driving in the middle of, literally, a couple of million of them is not my idea of a pleasant evening, I generally leave Manhattan either early or late. One of the few advantages of being your own boss.

I arrived in my neighborhood at about a quarter of five, just in time to watch the sun set and to grab one of the last parking places on the street. My mailbox was empty except for a few form pleas for my moneymoneymoney, which I filed at the incinerator on my way to the elevator.

I reached my floor a few minutes later and arrived at my apartment at the same time as Elba Santorio, my combination maid and surrogate niece and grandmother. She'd just come up the stairs with my dog, Balto. From the look of them, he must have dragged her over half of Brooklyn. I smiled in their direction mostly because I hadn't seen Elba for a while. She'd been busy doing work; I just hadn't been home. Trying to keep Balto from jumping on me with one hand, I opened the door with the other and we all went in.

As Elba unleashed the mutt and dragged off her overcoat, she asked,

"Jack, can I talk to you for a minute?"

"Well, sure, sweetheart—what's the problem?"

I turned to her immediately, hearing that sound in her voice that cued me to the fact there was trouble somewhere. I'd known Elba for over a year already, ever since her family'd moved into my building. Back then, it hadn't taken me long to realize someone was teaching what should've been a smiling, happy ten-year-old her life lessons with a length of leather. I looked into things. Turned out her mother had died, and her father didn't have any better way to handle things than to take off his belt. Especially once he'd started drinking, a hobby he didn't save for the weekends.

"It's my brother, Rickie."

"Rickie? What kind of trouble can he be in? He's only—what—eight?"

"Seven."

One night I heard the screams for myself. They came up out of the courtyard, echoing through my apartment until I couldn't pretend they weren't there anymore. Her father was still beating her when I kicked their lock apart, his hand still gripping the belt, his arm still going up and down. I just walked in and dragged him to another room and kept hitting him past when he said he'd never do it again, and past when he begged, and past when he threw up on both of us and the rug and the walls. If Elba hadn't opened the door, all welts and wide brown eyes, I might've just kept beating him until he was past breathing. I almost did anyway.

"Sweetheart, what's he doing that's so bad?"

"It's not his fault, Jack. He's so young. He doesn't understand what he's doing, Not really."

"Okay. Fine, but—what's he doing?"

I let her father scramble away from me then. He left the apartment and I stayed—for that night, anyway—to make sure he didn't come back and take things out on the kids. He didn't. A few days later, when the swelling had gone down, Elba came to my apartment offering to do the cleaning. No mention of the weekend was made. The feeling was right to trust her, so I went with it, giving her my spare key without a word or a rule. After that, I headed into the city, not too worried that handing my home over to a ten-year-old might be a mistake.

I came back to find my world changed. All the dishes'd come out of the cupboards to be cleaned. Then the cupboards themselves'd been scrubbed, and the walls, and the floor. When I'd left in the morning I'd had some old blankets and towels hung over the windows—I came home to curtains. My furniture sparkled from being polished. Hell, even the damn dog was clean.

"He's . . . you won't hurt him, will you?"

"Sweetheart, he's only seven." I put a clamp on my imagination. Telling myself that the truth was going to be bad enough, I asked,

"For God's sake—what's going on?"

"He's selling the *Euforia Satanica*."

Euforia Satanica, a.k.a. Black Dreamer. For a moment, I was stunned. I sat staring forward, caught up again in just how disgustingly bad everything is in New York. All the slicks and the trades and the papers had run articles on how the pushers were hiring younger and younger help—it wasn't Rickie's age that'd shocked me; it was the fact that a kid I'd taken to Saturday afternoon cartoon matinees was now a drug salesman. Much as I listen to the argument that everything is just the same everywhere, I have trouble believing that parents in Wyoming or Idaho or a hundred thousand other places have trouble keeping their seven-year-olds from selling drugs. I asked Elba,

"Okay. Where's Rickie now?"

"I don't know. He never comes home until ten, eleven, twelve . . . sometimes not at all. I don't know when he'll be home again. Really."

"That's all right. Do you know where he works?"

She shook her head. Catching her breath, she answered,

"They take them to different places. The people looking for the drugs know what corners or doors or whatever to go to. They switch the kids around to make it harder for the police to know who is selling what or where— or who they're selling it to . . . you know."

"Yeah. It's okay. If there's nothing we can do for the moment, there's nothing we can do."

Then, after thinking for another second, I asked,

"Is Rickie keeping drugs at the house?"

"Sometimes." The word was hard for her. Pulling her lips tight together after she said it, she continued, "Most of the time, no; if he can't sell everything they give him for the day they take it back at night. But, sometimes . . . the *tiradors* use our apartment for . . . storage."

"What?"

"They will bring big cans, like you see at the gas stations, and leave them in the apartment for a day or two. They pay a good bonus for it."

I sat back again, not knowing where to go in my head after that revelation. Drug pushers were using my own building as a base. Other people had to be aware of the situation, and yet no one was doing anything. Either paid off or too scared—which reminded me:

"Elba . . . what's your father doing about all this?"

She was quiet. She lifted her head, trying to look me in the eye, but couldn't. I caught on without any trouble.

"Rickie's not pulling anything over on him, is he? Your old man is in on it. He's taking his cut and thinking himself one lucky guy to have such an enterprising son. Or did he street Rickie in the first place?"

I was getting steamed and Elba knew it. She threw herself on her knees in front of me, holding me down in my chair. With tears starting, she begged me,

"Please, Jack—do not hurt him. He did not start it. Some of Rickie's friends at school were first. They recommended Rickie for a job. He was good, and soon he was making such big money Papa could not help but notice. Sometimes he makes two thousand in a week. He almost always brings home over one thousand. Please . . . understand . . . he only did it to make Papa happy. He does it to make Papa smile. It has been so long since he was happy without having to drink—so long since Mama died."

Like anyone else, I thought to myself, Why me? I'd already had one ugly run-in with Victor Santorio; I didn't want to have another. I knew his story. He'd loved Elba's mother with a passion out of the drippiest novels you can imagine. When she'd died it took the heart out of him and beat it against the sidewalk. He'd become a lost man with five kids to raise and no will to live. Not to disparage Elba and her siblings, but working a shit job all day with nothing to look forward to but coming home to nearly half a dozen children after losing your childhood sweetheart to cancer is not most guys' idea of a great time.

I did feel sorry for him, but I was a lot more concerned about Elba and her brothers and sisters than I was for their father. I was also concerned that men with machine guns and a tendency to use them on innocent people were bringing fifty-five-gallon drums of one of the world's most debilitating drugs, or perhaps just the flammable, explosive chemicals used to make it, into my own home. It was not what I'd hoped to hear about after another freezing day at the office. I told Elba,

"All right, sweetheart—here's what we'll do. Don't worry, I'm not going to call the cops . . . not yet, anyway. I'll wait until I can talk to Rickie, and your old man, and we'll see if we can't straighten this out without any trouble."

She half smiled at me, nervous that maybe I wouldn't be able to keep myself from tearing into her father again. Urging her up off her knees with a little tug, I sat her in my lap, stroking her hair, waiting for the tears I had a feeling were behind the corners of her resolve. She broke then, spilling out bundles of disjointed words, digging her face into my shoulder, crying loud and long. I patted her back and let her cry without bothering to say anything further. Twelve years old and running a family, going to school, and working for me—I marveled that she hadn't had a nervous breakdown a long time earlier.

The cold of the outside gnawed at the minimal heat our building provides, prompting me to reach for something with which to cover the sobbing girl. Hooking my coat from the chair I'd thrown it over, I draped the dry side down her back and then just settled into my chair and the quiet. Balto came into the room and lay at our feet, sensing something was wrong, knowing there was nothing more he could do about it than be present. Sighing to myself, I continued to hold Elba, waiting for her to pull herself together, hoping that when the time came I'd be able to do more for her than the dog. Sometimes you wonder.

CHAPTER 7

THE NIGHT PASSED without incident. Elba calmed down after a while and made dinner for me, mainly for the excuse to not have to return to her family's apartment. Before Elba left we agreed she would try to get Rickie to come with her to see me as soon as possible. She promised to leave me either a phone message or a refrigerator note so I wouldn't be unprepared.

Pushing all that aside, however, I went into my office at a quarter past ten the next day, trying to get a handle on the March rents to come. True, I'd scored a nice bundle in Chinatown, but I'd already earmarked that money for a number of other things, including the college fund I'd started for Elba a while back.

Being both frivolous and lazy by nature, I've found it best over the years to hide money I get my hands on out of sight as quickly as I can manage it. Sometimes it's the only way I have of tricking myself into working another day. Sometimes even that doesn't work.

I opened my office door to find my front room more than a little cool. The heat'd gone down during the night to the point where a light face of frost had formed on the glass in my doors. I put my hand to the radiators, finding all of them just beginning to sputter into life. Ignoring them with a sigh, I went into my inner office and started my daily ritual. Hat and coat on their hooks on the tree, flip on the message machine in the hopes of good news or wealth, start up a fresh pot of coffee, light a cigarette.

Normally the morning paper would've been next, but I had other chores for once. The client I had coming in at eleven was expecting to watch a videotape, which meant dragging the office TV out of the closet and getting it set up. Hubert, who was bringing the tape, would also be bringing a portable VCR with him. The case it would be wrapping up was one of those usual sorry state of affairs.

My client was a wife who more than suspected her husband was cheating on her. The main reason she was quite sure was he had admitted it. He had also made it fairly clear to her he was not about to change his ways or grant her a divorce. He was a minor official in the D.A.'s office, one who didn't want the aggravation and trouble of a scandal. He was also a slap-'em-up artist who'd first knocked his wife around a bit, then bullied her with threats of legal maneuvers that would keep her poor and away from their children, which he'd smugly felt would keep her sufficiently in line. Luckily for my ability to meet the rents of March, he didn't know his wife as well as he should have.

She had come to me to get her proof that would carry her through any court battle. She wanted more than a few black-and-whites snapped through a hotel window. She didn't want a show that could be decried as a setup—she wanted something raw, and ugly, and final. From what Hubert'd told me on the phone, she'd be getting her money's worth.

I was just sitting down to my first office cup of coffee for the day when Hu arrived with the raw, ugly finality in question. Peeling out of his dripping duster, he cackled,

"Hey, hey, Hagee . . . what's doin', Dick Tracy? Got a great one for ya. What's the difference between a refrigerator and a faggot?"

Admitting I didn't know got me the answer.

"A refrigerator don't fart when ya pull the meat out. Hahahahahahahahaahaaa—haha, oh, God, I love it—ya get it, right? Ya get it, don't ya? Hahahaaaahhaaaa . . ."

"Yeah, honest. It didn't go over my head. Want some bean?"

"N-not that sludge you make. I plan to make retirement age with a f-functioning set of kidneys, thank you very much."

"Everybody's a critic."

Taking another long draw out of spite, I kept myself from grimacing at the taste while making a mental note to clean my coffeepot the next chance I got. Abandoning my cup for the moment, though, I asked Hu,

"So, where'd you finally catch up to him?"

"Where else? At the Buck."

I wasn't surprised. Mrs. Sinnott'd listed it as one of the places her husband used for business. When I'd seen that I'd asked her how long she was willing to wait, knowing that if he frequented the Buck we just might be able to snag him up easily. She was more than willing to give him enough line with which to hang himself.

The Buck is interesting. In most respects it's a normal, wooden-barred, brass-railed, big-mirrored drinking place. What gives it its name. though, is its linoleum. The floor is covered in money. The pattern is one of American coins and bills: dimes, fifties, quarters, singles, nickels, silver dollars, twenties, and all the rest. You can find most of the styles of each denomination as well; Indian Head and Lincoln pennies, Liberty and FDR dimes, et cetera.

Years ago, the original owner started the con of putting real money down on the floor amid the fake. The tradition was that the bar put the money on the floor and the customers, if they found it, put it on their table as a tip for those hardworking Buck girls. The rumor always ran that those who generously put something large on the table would get taken to the back room for some fun by the grateful table-hopper who benefited from their generosity.

The truth is that for years the Buck was actually a clever little sex club. The barmaids, mostly doubled-out hookers working side hours, used the Buck to meet johns they wanted to keep private. They really did wait tables; rubes were let in all the time to keep the respectable image up, but just as large a percentage of the profits came from the back rooms as they did from the front. Sometimes it made me wonder if all the interesting little places in New York have truths just as ugly hidden underneath their colorful myths.

Today, however, with everyone looking for safe sex, the Buck had become an exhibition club—a place with a lot more show-and-tease than the old days. From what I'd heard, the back rooms were gone, but not the sex. That was out in the open now, the patrons as entertainment, everyone wink-and-nodding each other into the happy carnival spirit of things, creating a new myth so they could more easily accept the vulgarity of their needs.

Since it might easily have taken months for things to fall into place, I'd arranged a sliding fee scale for Mrs. Sinnott that would charge her only for the actual time involved rather than my daily fee. After that, I'd put one of Hubert's people I use a lot, Carmine Cecolini, a tail man good for long jobs, on her husband. Carmine worked with Mrs. Sinnott, watching her husband's schedule, following him on those nights it was possible he might be headed for a rendezvous with some cutie. After eighteen days, he struck pay dirt.

"So," asked Hubert while he hooked up the VCR, "when you goin' to break down and make a real agency out of this dump?"

"What? With lots of people on salary and elevator music playing in the waiting room and charts to show clients statistics on crime?"

"You could do worse."

"I could piss blood, too."

"You may need to s-sell it if you k-keep goin' on this way. J-Jesus, Jack—the detectives in paperbacks have better operations than you do."

"Yeah. They've also got big-titted babes waiting for them behind every door and sixteen-inch skulls. They get shot and run off to play tennis, and they don't ever have to worry about digging up dirt on guys like Andrew Sinnott to make ends meet."

"Com'on, Jack. Steppin' into the nineties w-wouldn't be nearly as painful as you make it sound."

"The hell it wouldn't." Draining my coffee, I banged my cup down a little too hard, saying, "When the hell are you going to get it through your head that I like being responsible for just myself. I had enough of sending people out to do dirty work in the service.

"I like things the way they are."

"Things the way they are are g-goin' to get yer ass blown off one of these days."

"Promises, promises."

The arrival of Mrs. Sinnott at that moment kept us from discovering how morbid we were capable of getting. She came in wearing the face I've seen a thousand times—knowing and expecting the truth, determined to see everything through to its inevitable conclusion, and yet still hoping against all reason to be proved wrong. Praying for it. Her hope faded fast. Simply looking into my eyes told her she didn't have a husband worth keeping. Pushing aside the useless, she said,

"Well . . . it certainly didn't take you very long."

"No, ma'am. We were pretty lucky right out of the gate."

"Yes. Weren't you just so fortunate."

"Mrs. Sinnott," I interrupted, knowing where she was headed, "you knew what you were after when you came to me. I can appreciate how you feel, but I don't think it will help us any if you decide to take your anger for your husband out on me."

"Oh, you can appreciate how I feel, can you? And what gives you all the insight? Have you just grown so used to the parade of pathetic women who can't keep their men that the sight of us just bores you now? Is that it?"

"No, ma'am," I told her. "A few years back I tried marriage myself but . . ."

I sucked in a long breath, letting it out as I talked.

"After seven months my wife figured she could do better than a police detective and moved out on me while I was laid up in the hospital. I came home to find her drawers empty and a letter blaming me for everything from her monthly cramps to the trouble in the Middle East.

"I'm not saying this to upset you, ma'am. I just thought maybe I should let you know you re really not as alone as you think."

Steeling herself, Mrs. Sinnott slipped into one of the padded chairs in front of my desk, wiping at her face with a rolled-up tissue. My guess was her eyes were a fairly nice shade of green when she wasn't crying as much as she had been recently. Also, stripping them of a little of the suspicion, anger, and hate she was feeling toward men in general wouldn't have hurt, either. She apologized,

"I'm sorry. Obviously I'm not really mad at you."

Wives apologizing to me—I think I hate that more than any other part of my job. They try to sound sincere; they really do. Somehow, though, they always sound like a real estate merchant trying to convince a black family that the agency really doesn't have any properties in the nice sections of town. I never blame them for it. Truth knows I've done the reverse and hated everything female in sight because of the actions of only a few members of the species.

Shoving it all out of my head for the moment, I concentrated on my client, waiting out her lament.

"It's just that I've tried for so long. I tried to be a good wife. I tried! After that I tried to be a good politician's wife, and then . . . later . . . then I just tried to stay out of his way."

She looked away for a long moment, no longer in the office. Abruptly she began to root around in her purse for something and then, just as suddenly, she snapped it shut again without pulling anything out. Looking back up, she said,

"I thought for a long time that maybe, maybe he'd grow up, realize what he was doing to us . . . to our son and daughter . . . I don't know . . . that maybe, somehow, he'd think about what he was throwing away."

She laughed at herself then, turning her eyes away so she could hate herself for a moment without the burden of someone else's pity taking any of the sting out of it. The moment passed quickly, though. She looked back at me, fixing her gaze on mine, her eyes pleading for understanding.

"But that didn't happen. And . . . I don't think it's ever going to happen, either. What do you think, Mr. Hagee?"

"You might be right, ma'am."

I said what I did because it was what she wanted to hear, and because there was nothing else to say. I'd collared another cheating husband once before whom I'd sized up as partially reformable. Taking a chance on my instincts, I told him what was going down, giving him the choice of either going headlong into the inevitable divorce his actions were dragging him toward or cleaning up his act. He's straightened out enough since then to not cause me to regret my decision to bend the facts I presented to his wife.

But Andrew Sinnott was not in that category. From what Hubert and Carmine had told me, he was more than just a womanizer. He was foul, miserable, dirty water—the kind of drink you wouldn't trust if you were dying in the desert. Reaching forward for the VCR, I switched it on, splashing Mrs. Sinnott full in the face with her husband's antics.

The tape started with a few establishing shots cueing the audience in to where the action was taking place. Hubert took charge of the narration.

"Okay. Here he comes now. Th-that is your husband . . . right, ma'am?"

She studied the screen carefully, finally admitting, "Yes. That's him."

"Okay," responded Hu with enthusiasm. He rubbed his hands together to show he was just getting warmed up and then dove back in. "Well, now—here you'll see the film take a break. Watch that wall clock jump. See there? First it's a little after eight, then it—it's almost nine. All he did was have a few drinks. and t-talk with a couple of guys. We have it all on tape, but we duped out this s-shorter version for today because . . . oops—t-there he goes.

"Look there."

Hubert aimed an index finger at the screen, making us aware of Sinnott's movements.

"See," yelled Hu, still pointing with one hand, directing us in closer with the other. "See? He's pulling three one-hundred-dollar bills out of his wallet, there—right there. And now he's pretending to pick them up off the floor. See? Did ya see?"

"Yes, Hu," I told him. "We can follow the story."

"Huh? Oh, yeah; s-sorry. Anyway—now watch—here he goes, calling the waitress over. Now see, he shows her the money. Puts it on the table—and now—the moment of truth."

At that point I asked Mrs. Sinnott if she wanted to view the rest of the tape in private, but she told me "no." She didn't elaborate past that point, either. She merely sat in front of the television, her legs crossed tightly at the ankles, hands gripping the arms of her chair, waiting. I half watched the screen, half watched her, waiting for her reaction. Over the years I've seen a lot of different ones—from men and women.

Nobody wants to find out they aren't enough to hold their mate—that they're no longer attractive enough, or intelligent enough, or stimulating, interesting, or whatever enough. People raised on Snow White and Cinderella often don't understand that marriage is a tight-fisted battle of two people against the world. It's a partnership where love is important, but trust is the most highly prized ingredient. Once a husband or a wife forgets their principal duties, usually, that's pretty much the end of things.

Whether or not the couple remains together—for the children, or from a lack of financial options or imagination or courage, or out of the fear of being alone rather than departing from the hateful stranger they've saddled themselves with—does not matter. Once trust is gone, in all but the rarest cases, that's the end of things. From the look on Mrs. Sinnott's face, I could see that, sadly, there was nothing very rare about her case. Nothing much at all.

Somehow Carmine had managed to move his camera to get a short, full-body shot of the waitress. She was a heavily madeup stunner—one who had decked out her tightly muscled, athletic frame in a punk leather-and-chain version of a stereotypical French maid's uniform, with black, high-heeled ankle boots and wraparound sunglasses to complete the effect she was after.

Carmine had aimed his mike as narrowly as possible, but only one word in ten from Sinnott's table came through to us. It was enough. First he indicated he'd found the hundreds on the floor, and that he was leaving them as a tip. That got him a rousing kiss of gratitude. The waitress wrapped her arms around Sinnott's neck, pulling him half up over the table while she maneuvered herself in closer. Continuing the kiss, she slid his jacket off his shoulders and started on his tie and shirt buttons. Mrs. Sinnott's eyes grew wide. I was a little surprised myself. Hubert had to clamp his teeth together to cover the dying cartoon duck noises he was making. While we watched the straight-on camera shot, the spike-haired blonde continued tearing at Sinnott's wardrobe, dropping some of the pieces she got loose to the floor, tossing others over her shoulder.

Not at all nonplussed, Sinnott responded like a man who knew what he'd paid for and expected to get all

his money's worth. In seconds he had stripped her of
everything but her boots, stockings, and sunglasses. I
wondered at why the pair had even bothered with the
pretense of the tip. Maybe it was a rule of the management to keep the owner's legal hassles to a minimum.
Watching the screen made such questions unimportant.

Sinnott was not built like a porn star, but he made
up for his lack of musculature and penis size with an
overabundance of determination and joy. Balanced on
the single-legged table, he grappled his partner from
above like a man clinging to the face of a mountain.
The pair slammed against each other repeatedly, the
slapping noise of their violent contacts loud enough to
reach Carmine's mike. Each crack made Mrs. Sinnott
flinch just a bit more than the one before it.

The edges of the screen showed the other couples
around them. All eyes were on the pair. They weren't
waiting for the table to collapse or admiring technique.
They had become an adoring audience, using the bouncing couple on the table as surrogate release. Sweating faces, all with unblinking eyes and restless mouths,
were now crammed up against one another, constantly
jockeying for better views.

By this point Sinnott had stood up on his table, the
waitress straddling him in a locked-leg position. His
thrusts were choppy, showing his concern for the strength
and balance of the table, but his face showed only that he
was in his element. He had not paid merely for sex; he'd
paid for the chance to entertain, to be admired, respected,
perhaps to generate envy.

Regardless of my personal feelings, I had to admit,
anyone who came on a night Mrs. Sinnott's Andy did
was sure to get their money's worth. He whooped with
glee, laughing and shouting, giving out with Tarzan
yells, all the time dancing and rocking his willing partner. At one point she released her leg hold and Sinnott
flipped her upside down. She locked her legs around his
head then, arms around his waist, and then caught his

still-hard member up in her mouth, sending a new look across his face.

With greater dexterity than I would've imagined him capable of, Sinnott bounced down from table to chair to the floor without shaking his partner's sucking grip loose, and then began to stride about the club, showing off his prize. He stepped out of camera range, and all the heads of other patrons still visible to us followed him. They were the main show, after all.

Due to Hubert's editing, Sinnott came back into the picture almost immediately, but I reached out and turned off the tape. I didn't see any need to explain my actions. Mrs. Sinnott knew the tape wasn't over. She also knew if she wanted to view any more of it with us present that we would oblige her. But, like myself, she saw no purpose to it.

I asked her if she would like anything, a cigarette, a drink . . . there was no answer. I searched out the rewind button and pressed it. I told Mrs. Sinnott I was reversing the tape, checking to make sure that was what she wanted done with the same apologetic whisper a funeral parlor director uses to ask the widow where she wants the latest flower arrangement placed.

She made a quiet mumble that sounded like a "yes," but then found she couldn't let it go at that. Still frozen harshly in place, her head down, legs rigid, fists tight, she said,

"Yes. Rewind the tape. Yes. Rewind it and give it to me so I can take it home and get on with this . . . this— Yes. Yes. Rewind it. Take it back to the beginning, take it all back to the beginning—take everything back to the beginning—"

She was crying now, reaching out to me in an unconscious, desperate grab from the center of the black loneliness that had surrounded her for so long, but that she had only that moment admitted actually existed. Her tears streamed, her sobs echoed. It was a death wail—the death of her mate, her partnership, her future, her life.

Mrs. Sinnott wasn't a woman who had lived for herself.
You could see it in her eyes; I could feel it in the pain of
her agony as it filled the room. From birth she'd waited
for her chance to be "Mommy." She found herself a
marriage, a husband, children—she'd done everything
she was supposed to, when she was supposed to—and
now it was all disappearing.

"What am I, I mean, what am I going to do? Oh, dear
God Almighty . . . what am I going to do?!"

I held her, patting her back, trying to project a feeling of fatherly concern, mumbling niceties, hoping the
developing scene wouldn't grow too messy. I refrained
from saying anything of substance. As I'd explained
to Mrs. Sinnott earlier, it had nothing to do with any
"parade of pathetic women." Having been in her shoes,
I knew there was no cure for what she was feeling except
time. Even if I'd understood her position perfectly, even
if I'd had all the answers she needed—which I didn't by
a long shot—I wouldn't have bothered to say anything.
After all, who ever listens to good advice when they're
howling with pain? I never do. No one does.

While I quieted Mrs. Sinnott, Hubert retrieved the
tape from the machine, replacing it in its plastic case.
After that he put it on the desk in front of us with the
full-length version and then gave me a high sign that
he was going to go out and get something to eat. I
nodded, knowing it would make things easier on all of
us if Mrs. Sinnott was allowed to pull herself together
with less of an audience. He managed to shut both doors
without any noise.

It only took another minute for her to get a hold on
herself. Pulling away from me gently, she apologized
for her behavior. And then, suddenly, she looked into
my eyes and smiled, just a little.

"You really do understand, don't you?"

"Yes, ma'am," I told her. "I went into the service
young. Probably too young. Saw things, did things . . .
I really didn't want to. When I got out, I wanted to settle

down and have a family and lead a normal life . . . be a regular guy, you know? Just put it all behind me. But . . ."

I sucked in a breath, pushing the memories back where they belonged, stopping myself from rambling. Exhaling, I finished.

"It didn't work out. I wish it had. I'll be honest— I wish I didn't have the slightest idea of what you're going through, or how you feel. But since I do, all I can tell you is to hold on, because even though the worst is probably still to come, things will get better. Believe it or not, this all does pass."

While she wiped her face down, draining away the last of her tears and ruined makeup, she said,

"You should have been a psychologist, Mr. Hagee."

"Me?" I almost laughed. "No. Not me."

"You know a lot about pain," she countered.

"Yeah, that's true," I admitted. "But I don't know very much about making it go away."

After she finished cleaning herself up, Mrs. Sinnott pulled out her checkbook so she could clear up our account. I gave her a receipt along with the number of the best divorce attorney I knew. I'd been a little worried about her when she'd first broken down. Most of the women I've had to deliver the bad news to haven't taken it quite as badly as Mrs. Sinnott. Of course, most of them didn't have the news delivered to them in quite the fashion she did, either.

But it didn't matter. By the time she left my office her face was clean and she'd lost the wobbliness. She was injured, but not crippled. She left with a handshake and a grim set to her mouth and eyes that made me more comfortable with what had just happened. As I lugged the television back to its place in the closet, I was feeling much better about her chances for survival. Hubert returned as I poured myself a cup of coffee.

"S-so," he stuttered, "Wanda Waterworks finally got her little seizure under control, eh?"

"Can it, ya mutant."

Crossing the room, his familiar limp dragging only slightly, Hubert set his own coffee on my desk as he pulled his bulky overcoat free. While he piled it in the chair next to the one he usually likes to sit in, he cackled,

"Oh, come on, man. She was flake city. What'd she f-fuckin' expect?"

"Jesus, Hu. We didn't give her an envelope of eight by tens taken through the motel window shades, you know. We delivered a Ken Russell special. That was a hell of a rough trip for someone."

"Awwww, bullshit. Christ, b-b-but you can wimp it up with the best of 'em. That miserable bitch—what else did she expect? Trust me, Dick Tracy, her husband ain't the only one at fault in that marriage."

"And what makes you say that?"

"Were you lookin' at that tape? You saw how our b-boy likes it—you saw—wild and dirty and public. You're right. That was no b-back road motel room . . . it was a fancy club in the middle of one of the world's b-biggest cities that all kinds of people go to all the time."

Hu snorted at me, waving his arms as he continued,

"You wanta bet hubby tried to get her interested? More than once, even? You wanta? In fact, I'll b-bet there was a time she was willing to indulge little Andy in his fun and games.

"But then"—Hubert paused to gulp the top layer of his coffee down—"after that fuckin' piece of paper made them legit, my money says that's when she got morals."

"And people call me a cynic."

"Fuck that. All that guy wants is some g-good, clean healthy fun, which you can b-bet your rent money dried up in his house a long time ago. So now, just because he goes out for a little partying, his whole life is going to c-cave in. Now he loses his j-job, home, p-place in the community—everything—all 'cause he went to a hooker to put a little more fun in his life, and 'cause you wanted more cash in your till."

Sitting back, sipping at my own brew, I answered Hu wearily.

"You're so full of shit, I can't believe it. First off, you and Carmine are making more of this fee than I am, so I resent the insinuation that I'm the big bad ghoul here. Second, I don't care if you're right or not. Marriage is marriage . . . period. You take a set of vows, you're supposed to respect them. You got problems, you work them out."

"Thus speaks the expert."

"Hey, okay," I told him, "I'll be the first one to admit my marriage did not happen, and that I was just as much to blame as she was. But I didn't cheat on my wife."

"Why not?" He leered. "No opportunity?"

"No, you little weasel. Because it's not right. Plain and simple." I knocked back a half a cup of coffee in one slug, and said, "I'll tell you the truth, sometimes guys amaze me. I mean, every time you turn around, some movie star or politician or preacher or athlete or your neighbor is getting caught with his pants down—stupid morons—with some whore, or some animal, or some grandmother they knocked down, or their baby daughter—and they defend themselves with all the same stupid speeches you just made. And all because they just had to go on and on, trying each new bit of nonsense that came into their heads, because they couldn't control their cocks long enough to think about anything or anyone but themselves.

"Hey, that one's got nice high heels—oh, that tingles my favorite fantasy; better call the wife with an excuse—wonder if she takes in the back door—wearing heels like that? Sure she does. Bet she likes it rough, too. Bet she'd just love it if I followed her home and slapped her around and made her blow me. I mean, look at those shoes, will you? You *know* she's dying for it.

"No wonder so many women think we're all dirt. I mean it—seriously—when the hell are guys going to start thinking with their heads and not their dicks?"

With mock innocence, Hubert stared at me sincerely, choking back a bellyful of laughter as he answered,

"Why, never, Jack."

I looked him in the eye and knew I was being had.

"You bastard."

He'd caught me. I forced a short laugh for his benefit. Hubert slapped the desk repeatedly, cackling his duck noise, pleased he'd been able to goof on me as long as he had. What his true beliefs about Sinnott were were immaterial. Even if he thought our client's husband was really Hitler back from the grave, he wouldn't have been able to pass up the opportunity to play devil's advocate/defense lawyer just to get my goat.

Narrowing my eyes to slits, I gave him the look you give a dumb but loyal dog who's pushing his luck. Sitting back in my chair, I finished my coffee with a last gulp and told him,

"No wonder you don't have any friends."

"Don't need 'em," he said, still howling. "I'd trade most of the people wh-who've ever called me their friend over the years for a good laugh."

"Yeah," I admitted. "Me, too. But that doesn't make you any less noxious to the rest of us."

Hubert dragged on his overcoat, saying,

"It's f-forty below outside—an' I got a long way to go. I d-don't need this. I can go to classy joints to get insulted."

Pulling his gloves and cap from his pockets, he shot me a short salute before putting them on. I walked him to the outer office.

"Don't worry about the Sinnotts, Jack. You'll just g-get ulcers."

Then, turning in the doorway, he cautioned me,

"I-it's all this worrying you do about the rest of the world that causes you all your grief. Do what I do, Dick

Tracy—tell the rest of the world to go fuck itself.

"You'd be a lot better off."

As he left, I went back to my desk, grabbing down the *Iliad* as I went by the shelves. Pulling my Gilbey's bottle and a glass from their resting places in the bottom drawer of my desk, I poured myself a good handful of ounces, leaving the bottle out. Mrs. Sinnott and her husband had put me off the idea of lunch.

Going to my place marker, I picked up reading where I'd left off. The women were still wailing on the beach. I finished my drink before I got off the first page.

CHAPTER 8

TRY AS I might, I didn't get to read for very long. The phone rang as I worked my way through the slaughter at Troy. Tossing the *Iliad* aside once more, I picked up the receiver to find Rich Violano eager to get his editor and me into the same room. I offered,

"Well, I know it doesn't look good for me to be able to just drop everything and run right over—any good businessman would jerk you around for a day or two, but truth to tell, Hu and I just wrapped up my last pending job. I could blast over now if you wanted."

"No need to rush," answered Rich. "In fact, the quieter we keep this, the better. Would six o'clock be too late for you?"

"No, I could bear to stay in the city until then. But," I joked, "it'll cost you extra."

He chuckled, throwing back at me, "Well, right. What doesn't?" Then, getting serious, he added, "Anyway, I'll see you here at six in Sally Brenner's office."

We clicked off, Rich going back to his vital daily task of keeping the public informed, me to my Gilbey's. The Sinnott marriage had soured my mood to the point where even the world's oldest and greatest literature wasn't making much of a difference to me. Watching Andy bounce his way across the tables at the Buck hadn't left me much in the mood for a tale of gods and their capricious handling of all our fates.

Looking at the Howard Miller clock that hangs on my wall, I could see I had a number of hours to kill. For

some reason at that moment, gin seemed the best way
to kill them. I filled my glass again slowly, one voice
in my head questioning whether or not I should stop
pouring as the level came even with each watermark,
the other voice letting me know that the very top would
be just fine. Neither won by a knockout, but it was clear
the decision would be awarded to the latter.

I cursed Andy Sinnott with each sip, wondering how
guys get into his particular mind-set. What was it that
made him feel entitled to act the way he did? Did he
just not understand what his wedding vows had been
all about? Had he ever tried at all to be faithful? Or had
he simply been a shit from the very beginning, one of
those guys to whom marriage means nothing more than
getting to screw the live-in maid?

Filling up another glass, I cursed him again, angry at
his vulgar antics and at myself for getting caught up in
them enough to care. Once again my mind divided itself
into two teams, both of them clearly voicing their opin-
ions within my head. The one reminded me that it was
guys like Mr. Andrew Sinnott who made it possible for
me to make my rent payments most months. The other,
however, countered that that was an oversimplification
of the facts.

Sinnott, it pointed out, wasn't some seven-year itcher
who had finally given in to the despair created by his
own inability to peer inside and find anything worth
looking at. Nor had he been caught on any simple weekend fling, in some business-lunch tryst, office romance,
or in any other kind of lonely night—mistaken choice—
wrong move at the wrong time whore jump. He was,
plain and simple, a rotten son of a bitch. One who, from
all I could piece together, had hurt a decent woman
repeatedly and often, both physically and mentally, as
well as his own children, without the slightest regard for
his actions.

I drained my third glass, barely feeling the rush of
the gin, thinking about another, wondering if finishing

off the bottle could take the taste of Sinnott out of my mouth. Knowing the answer, I slipped the Gilbey's back into its drawer. Even I don't drink when I can't justify it.

A glance at the wall told me I still had hours to go before my meeting at the *Post*. I knew that leaving the office was another bad business move, but I didn't care. The answering machine could field any calls that might come in—after all, wasn't that what I bought the damn thing for? The truth was, I had to get outside. Away from the gin, and my office, and any other reminders of the Sinnotts. They were out of my life—I never had to see or think about them again—but they weren't out of my system.

Grabbing my hat and coat, I locked my door and headed for the street, taking the squeaking steps two at a time. I hit the sidewalk out front at a brisk trot, instantly pierced through by the stone-cracking chill still lingering into the afternoon hours. At least the sleet had stopped.

I walked down Fourteenth Street, staring through familiar buildings off into some unknown beyond, basically wandering, trying to use the cold to calm myself down. My hands were shaking—half from the chill, half from rage. I slammed one fist into the other palm—five, six, ten times—leaving both stinging and crippled. I think some people stared—I'm not sure. I was angry and upset—wishing for someone to kick the shit out of because I needed some kind of release and I didn't feel like sobbing. It was too cold for weakness.

Maybe, I thought, after even my short time with people like the Los, maybe I'd just forgotten how miserable the rest of the world can be. I didn't have to worry, though. It was all coming back to me.

I walked through the cold for the next two hours—past people in silk and furs stepping carefully over the beggars, past gibbering madwomen digging into trash bins, hiding their finds in the folds of their clothes, saving them for later when they were safe in their warrens. I went past some complaining about the quality of Broadway, agreeing that any seat that went for under sixty-five dollars just wasn't worth sitting in, and past some others living in boxes—tired, cold people without the strength or the will even to do something as simple as complain. I walked by it all without caring one way or the other, despising all the greed and stupidity around me equally.

When I couldn't walk anymore, the cold numbing my legs, making me stumble, I ducked inside a Blarney Stone for a coffee. I downed the first one in three burning gulps—drank the second slightly slower—sipped the third. After that, finally weary, the gin and the caffeine battling to wreck my system, I went back out into the cold and pointed myself toward the garage where my car was parked so I could drive to my meeting. Trudging inside, I threw a salute to Espo, the only one of the regular day attendants I know by name. Then I flopped into my Skylark and sat for a minute, bracing myself for the trip.

Thinking for just a moment as I inserted the ignition key, I hit the realization that if I was a normal guy—some Suit with a regular job—that I'd have been headed for home then, away from the streets to some cozy hiding place, safe from the stench and the decay and the madness. Not being one, however, I continued sitting in my cold car, getting ready to brave the dangers of winter driving in New York, all so I could go to a meeting that had all the earmarks of being more trouble than any sane man could want.

As the Skylark's massive engine growled to life, I sighed and directed it toward the street. Espo flipped me a shaking good-bye as I drove past, instantly going back to rubbing his freezing hands together as soon as I acknowledged his existence again with a wave of my own.

Then, suddenly, perversity made me smile. Things could be worse, I thought . . . I could have Espo's job.

But then, as always, whenever I try to cheer myself up, the other side of my brain chirped in to remind me that in a lot of ways even Espo's job was better than mine.

CHAPTER 9

I ROUNDED THE corner of Catherine Slip and South Street, one of the four corners of the block-long *Post* building, far in advance of my meeting time, searching for a spot. It's an area of town notorious for its lack of parking, and I was taking no chances of showing up late. Rich's boss had enough reasons to give me grief without me giving her any more.

Luckily, I found one on my third go around of the area, only having to wait for a few minutes as an old woman forced her lumbering GM product up over a hump of packed snow and cinders and ice. I backed in, leaving the Skylark in the shadow of Knickerbocker Village, a sprawling apartment complex with fences made out of fifteen-foot-high curved iron rods. These barricades fit neatly inside massive doorways, giving the place a kind of nineteenth-century penal-colony look. I've seen pictures of castles in France with weaker fortifications.

Jumping out into the cold, I hustled through the depressingly small and inadequate children's park between the Knickerbocker and the *Post* building. Kicking my way through the piles of debris underfoot, I sighed as I passed under the graffiti-wrecked murals that grace the back of the place, trying to put all the myriad images of the city's failure to serve itself out of my mind before I got inside. Like I said, dealing with the meeting ahead was going to be rough enough without being in a bad mood to start.

I was ushered into Sally Brenner's office immediately upon arrival, despite the fact I was ten minutes early. That alone let me know something was up. Rich's editor hadn't been very anxious to be in my company for a long time. Somehow, I didn't see what was going to be very different that night. As her last duty of the day, the editorial secretary pointed me toward Brenner's door, fluttered a little three-fingered wave at me, and then disappeared.

Then, figuring that watching her leave was really about the only legitimate time-killer I had, I pushed my hat onto the back of my head and put on a smile, determined to not be the one who started the inevitable fight this time. Going into the office, I said,

"Hi, Rich—Sal. The secretary said to go right in."

"Then you should have come right in and not stayed out there watching her ass disappear around the corner."

"Sal," I said, figuring that if we had to do our dog-and-cat routine, that we might as well do it then and get it over with, "I'd much rather watch your ass disappear around a corner. In fact, I'd much rather watch your ass—period—no matter what it was doing. But since you're paying for my time, you might want to do something a little more businesslike than start right up with the situation-comedy bullshit."

Her cheeks colored slightly, a passing flare that disappeared after only an instant, settling into the same look it always does—that one that lets me know just what a wonderful opportunity I missed by not doing some undefinable "right thing" by her during our one social encounter. Believe me, if I'd known what it was, I would have done it.

We'd met at a party at Rich's, one where she'd known everyone and I'd known no one. Being Rich's bash, it was a friendly gathering, but because of the nature of the guest list, it was also an upscale one—the kind of party where the loner almost always has a bad time, usually because the desire to stop being alone prompts one stupid choice or another.

Sally Brenner is an attractive woman: strikingly light skin set against black, just-above-the-shoulder-length hair—blue-gray eyes, slightly large but set just the right distance from each other to make them alluring rather than childlike, capped by sharp dark brows. She has thin lips that fill out into a nice smile whenever she can be bothered to create one, made distinctive by just enough color that she can go without lipstick and still look tasty. She's a working woman, not a fashion model, the corners of her eyes and mouth already crinkling like any other real person, but that night, or any other, she was damn attractive to a guy like me.

Normally, one never sees Brenner in other than the strictest of business clothes. When I'd first met her at the party, however, she'd been dazzling in a long-sleeved, black velvet silk number, one that came from below her knees to halfway up her neck, but only in the front. Its back was practically nonexistent, leaving nothing to the imagination, but quite a lot for hope to concentrate on. Black Italian suede shoes and a matching diamond earrings and brooch set were the only accessories she'd brought, and the only ones she'd needed. The pin was shaped like a traditional valentine's heart, the earrings little arrows. They'd worked, too.

For whatever our personal reasons, we got very interested in each other—very fast. We kept each other amused with our charm and cleverness long enough to be discreet, at least in our own minds, and then left the party with a bottle of Rich's wine. We walked around the lower West Village for a long time, talking endlessly about nothing, finally ending up on a deserted pier overlooking the Hudson.

We looked at the stars—those visible in a Manhattan sky—pretending we could see more. Then we emptied Rich's wine, and when I couldn't take the suspense anymore, I kissed her. Nothing fancy, just a brush on the lips somewhere between your sister and an old school friend. Apparently, it was enough. When I went to light a Camel to cover the following silence, she stunned me for a second by asking if I'd rather have her or a cigarette. My pack hit the water a second later. She asked me if I was sure. I threw my lighter in after it. Then she shrugged off the black velvet silk and stood before me, wearing nothing but her Italian suede and diamond arrows.

I was dead and in seventh heaven—where she was, I'm forced to admit now, I have no idea. When we finished, she was dressed and walking away before I knew what was happening. At the sound of her name she started running. By the time I was half-dressed enough to chase after her, she was gone.

I never talked to Rich about what happened, and being a gentleman, he's never asked. Unfortunately, Sally and I have never discussed what happened since then as well. I tried to bring it up once and was convinced by her reaction that such was not a good idea. I've never known what I did or didn't do, either. I've got some guesses, but no facts. All I know for sure is that it does not seem likely there will be any more meetings outside of her office or mine. So, giving her my look in return, the one that says I had a good time but that she still confuses the hell out of me, I offered,

"Look. I didn't drive over here for my health. If you want me to baby-sit Rich through some sort of trouble, just outline the problem and let me get started. I'm no more comfortable sitting in your office than you are having me sit here."

"You don't bother me, Jack Hagee. You don't have the weight. I find you arrogant and one-dimensional, like most self-absorbed males, but I've been surrounded by all of you too long to let it bother me. You're here for only one reason. You're good at what you do. Richard is getting into something that is just a little too nasty . . ."

Rich cut in.

"I still don't think anyone is going to . . ."

"Richard," Sally cut back, "let's not run it over again. I say you don't cover this without protection." Her hand pointed in my direction, "If you insist that this slab of meat . . ."

"That's it." I stood up, pulling my hat down tight over my forehead. "I'm out of here. I'll take a bullet for you, Rich, but I'll be damned if I'm going to sit here and take any more of this crap."

"Sit down!" barked Rich. I sat. Sally started to protest. He shut her up, too. "Now, I don't know what in hell happened between the two of you, and unlike the rest of the staffers here at the *Post*, I don't care. But I will tell you this"—he spun his gaze at Sally—"I suspect—call it my reporter's instinct—that this never-ending antagonism is more your doing than Jack's. You"—he turned back, not wanting me to feel unwanted—"on the other hand . . . you're the big tough private eye, you ought to be able to handle this better."

Standing at that point, he concluded in softer tones. "Now, I'm not either of your fathers . . . hate each other until doomsday . . . I've got no right to interfere. But I am going to go out—not far—just to the machines in the hall to get something to drink. Then I'm coming back. By that time my hope is I'll have a couple of adults to deal with."

And with that, he did just as he said he was going to, leaving the two of us to stare at each other over the desk and whatever else was separating us. Sally's mouth drew itself into a sharp line, everything about her telling me she was just waiting for an excuse to follow Rich out the door. Since it was also fairly obvious she was not going to be the first one to speak, I decided I would give things one last try.

"Well," I offered, "you want to try and come to some sort of understanding here?"

"I think we can just wait until Rich gets back and then start our meeting."

"You don't want to clear the air between us?"

"I don't think there's any point to rehashing the past. We both know what happened."

I closed my eyes in anger, biting down on my lower lip to get myself under control, choking back the first words that wanted to come out of my mouth, substituting others instead.

"Sal . . . yes, we both know what happened between us, but I don't think we're seeing those events in the same light. If you'd like to tell me your point of view, I'd be happy to listen. If you want mine, I'd be happy to talk. But I think we ought to do . . . *something*. The way we act whenever we have to be in the same place is just . . . silly."

"So, I'm 'silly'?"

"I didn't say *you* were . . ."

"No. No. You said it—you said I was silly."

"I said the way we've *both* been acting has been silly. *Both* of us. Get it? *Both* of us."

"But you think I'm the one who's really at fault. Even Rich said that. And why not, he's your friend. Now I'm supposed to just swallow my pride and forget everything and just smile like some teenager whenever you're around. Maybe dress up a little for you—dance on the desktop . . ."

"Goddammit!" I slammed the side of her desk for emphasis, exasperated beyond my ability to control myself. "Will you shut up? I don't know what you've cooked up in that twisted bitch brain of yours, but I'm sick of it. Drop it. Goddammit to hell and back, just drop it!"

She stood up behind her desk, staring down at me. She started to lean on her desk, started to cross her arms, finally just let them fly in exploding rage.

"You think you can have things any way you want, don't you?" she screamed. "That the whole world is just laid out for you to pick and choose which pieces you want on your plate. That everything is just a game for your amusement! It doesn't work that way, Mr. Jack

Fucking Hagee. It just doesn't!"

I looked up at her then, wondering what I could have been thinking of when I'd left Rich's with her—wondering how even I could have been that lonely. Wondering how anyone as lonely as she was could continue to reject every crumb that came her way. Suddenly weary of the clash, ready to agree to anything just to put the noise and the anger all around us somewhere else, I said,

"You're right. It's all my fault."

"Oh, no. You don't get out of this that easily."

"Oh, Jesus . . . what more do you want, Sal? I'm willing to take all the blame you want to heap on me because, frankly, I just don't care anymore. I'll do *anything* you want just to end this nonsense."

"But you don't believe you were wrong."

"Of course I don't. How can I believe I was wrong to do what I did, when you won't tell me what it is I'm supposed to have done? You're making me sound like some jerk out of a sit-com. But to get this all over and finished once and for all . . . I'll sound like one. I'm willing to believe I did something, and that it was horrible of me, and that I'm the walking shitpile. I'm saying 'You're right' and 'I'm wrong.' Without even hearing the charges, I'm pleading guilty. And, sweetheart, without your help, I just don't think I can do any more than that."

And with that, something finally broke. The anger in her turned into something else, draining her of her energy. She sat back in her chair, looking away from me. My instincts told me she was ready to cry, but I had no proof. Trusting myself as usual, though, I told her softly,

"I'm going to go and find Rich. We'll be back in a few minutes."

She nodded absently as I left the office. I found Rich at a cubicle a few yards away, sipping at a diet Pepsi. He, like everyone else in sight, was trying hard to show a lack of interest. I sat down on the desk, asking,

"What now, Mr. Violano?"

"You want to talk about it?"

"There's nothing to talk about. Just pray that whatever her problem with me is . . . that we're finally past it."

"But you don't think we should go back in just yet."

"No," I told him, shaking my head, sad that it had to be that way, "I don't think so."

"Might as well get down to business, then." Putting aside his diet soda, Rich asked, "How well acquainted are you with the Chinese Consolidated Benevolent Association?"

"Rich, I worked Chinatown almost exclusively when I first got to town. I know the CCBA."

"How well?"

"Depends on what you want," I answered, slightly annoyed at Rich's vagueness. Pushing my hat back up on my head, I asked him,

"You investigating the funding of private schools for immigrants, looking into the sanitation or police protection lobbies, checking out the start-up business loan credit associations . . . ?"

"Maybe something a little more . . . unethical?"

"Oh, you looking for a game of Fan Tan or thirteen-card poker? You want to meet oriental women for a short time, or were you looking to hire an extortion gang, or maybe just a simple murder or two? Whose prices do you want . . . On Leong's? The Hip Sings'? The Ghost Shadows'?"

"I was thinking more of Mother's Blood Flowing."

And then I understood.

"You're not looking for protection," I said, telling him what he was obviously already aware of.

"You didn't call me the other day to set up this meet because you were worried—you already knew I'd had my bacon pulled out of the fire by the MBF and just wanted to muscle in on my connection."

I stared at Rich almost in disbelief, shook that even a guy as straight as Violano would try to grift me. In his defense, he said,

"Jack, I had to say something that would allow me to get you on the payroll. Are you going to tell me that if I came to you and asked for an open door to the head of the MBF that you wouldn't have done it for me?"

"That's not the point . . ."

"Or that if I went to Sally and told her I was bringing you in on my expense account that she wouldn't have pitched a bird through the window?"

"Great," I said, mellowing, but still sore, "so you let her bounce it off my head, instead."

"Yeah," he reminded me. "While taking the rap I'm too scared to walk the streets without you holding my hand. At least this way you get paid."

"Money ain't everything, pal."

"And," he said, quieter, regretfully, "I was hoping that whatever it is that's between you two might finally have cooled off to the point where you might like each other again. You did meet in my apartment, you know."

Smiling—knowing when I was beaten—I said,

"Okay, I surrender. We're all grown-ups here, of a sort, anyway. We'll take responsibility for our actions. Come on. Let's go back in there and get this thing on track."

By the time Rich and I got back inside Sally's office, she seemed fine. Looking up at me with an expression that implied maybe the war was over, she said,

"I guess we're all ready to get down to business, so let's see what's up. Rich, how much have you told Jack about what's going on?"

"I'm going to cut right to the headlines," Rich told his boss. "Someone high up in our new mayor's administration is dirty as sin."

"My surprise knows no limits."

"Yeah," he agreed, the sarcasm in his tone matching hers. "My sensibilities were stretched to the utmost as well. Anyway, I've got a trail leading back to City Hall, but every time I get anywhere near it goes dead. Someone, with either a lot of money or a lot of power . . ."

"There's a difference?" I asked.

"Calm down, Mr. Social Injustice. Anyway, someone is plugging every leak I come across. I've got a dead nail on the notion that Black Dreamer is tied directly to our Mr. or Ms. X. My problem: got no name, got no proof. That's why I want your connection to the leader of Mother's Blood Flowing. Quiet word is that the MBF controls all of the Dreamer flow running in through Chinatown. If I can talk to him, just get an idea of what direction I'm going in . . ."

"Hey, wait a minute . . ." interrupted Sally. "You just wanted to tap a root from this guy? I thought . . ."

"Yeah." I put up my hand. "Cupid here thinks he's subtle. I won't kill him if you won't."

Sally glared at Rich for a moment. Her eyes showed that she wasn't mad enough to hate him for what he'd done, but that she was wishing she could. Rich tilted his head to one side and sent his eyes rolling just a bit—his way of again telling us both to grow up.

Before we could gang up on him, however, a noisy, frantic knocking came at Sally's door. When she gave the banger the go-ahead, a highly excited, middle-aged man—Caucasian, thin, sandy hair, clean-shaven—came in, beelining straight for Sally's desk.

"Oh, boss. I love ya for bein' here."

"Chet, before I listen to whatever wonderful scoop has you so kinetic, let me point out that we do have company that isn't family."

Rich introduced me to Chet Green and vice versa. Having a bigger audience just seemed to make him happier. "Doesn't matter who's here," he told us. "We're going to be telling the whole world this one."

"Well," said Sally in her quiet voice, the one that everyone who knows her worries about, "be that as it may, tell Rich first—outside. I want to talk to our Mr. Hagee."

As the brother reporters left, Sally asked,

"You were suckered into this, too?"

"Yeah," I admitted. "Rich just confessed when I talked to him outside a minute ago."

"Did you beat it out of him?"

"I used my charm."

She drew her eyes into a flat line, saying,

"I guess I'll have to believe you. I know how effective a weapon your 'charm' is."

"Sal," I said, bolstered enough by the cracks showing in her defenses to make one last try, "don't start it up again. Please. I don't want to talk about it anymore. I just want the two of us to get along. We don't *have* to fight every time we see each other. Maybe I'm wrong, but I don't think we even have anything to fight about."

What she would have answered had to be postponed. Rich and Chet both burst back into the office, Rich shouting,

"Boss—you re going to love this."

"Ta da, ta da, ta ta ta DA," sang Chet. "And now, the kind of news that sells papers."

"This can only be one boy . . ." suggested Sally.

"Yes, yes. Everyone's flavor of the month has struck again. And he's knocked all the theories about him into a cocked hat. The psych boys are going to be pulling out their hair over this one."

When I looked at Sally and Rich for some sort of explanation, Green suddenly wheeled around, grabbing me by both shoulders. Allowing him his excitement, I sat still while he performed.

"Don't worry, my friend, the name will be revealed. Who could it be, my brother, that could inspire such lunacy in an otherwise sober member of the Fourth Estate? What name in this town is the auto-fucking-matic headline grabber these days in this and every other paper, including the fucking holier-than-holy, I spit on their masthead, *New York Times*? Who is he? Say the name, brother."

"My guess would be the Outliner."

"Yes, yes! Send this man to the head of the class, for, indeed, the Outliner has struck again. In a new, bold, picture-worthy style, one demanding seven-hundred-and-twenty-point headline type. Our boy has changed part of his M.O. this time—most likely by accident, but too late now—and done in . . . ha ha ha, here it is, time for the flash . . . a local politician's wife."

Sally's eyes grew big. Knowing that business was about to take over, I straightened my hat, ready to say my good-byes. All in all, I was feeling a lot better than when I'd walked in. Rich wasn't in danger, which made me happy. and it didn't look as if Sally were mad at me anymore, which, like any guy, made me even happier. Seeing it all as signs that my life was going to finally get a little less complicated, I was just about to interrupt the festivity over the city's vicious serial murderer's latest foray when Green announced,

"Yep. It's going to be ugly. Nobody—and I mean *nobody* thought this guy's next strike was going to be anyone like this Mrs. Andrew Sinnott."

I stopped short for a second, and then I sat back down, a little confused, a little shocked—anger growing. I gave credit where credit was due, though. Chet Green was right. Things were going to get ugly. Real ugly.

CHAPTER 10

"JACK," ASKED SALLY. "What is it?"

It was interesting, hearing concern in her voice. Part of my brain said it was only her reporter's instinct, raw cunning sensing a connection between Green's story and the look on my face. Another part, though, wanted to believe the concern was for me, regardless of the cause. Always willing to test the waters, I told the assembly,

"I knew Vivian Sinnott."

The bombshell exploded with enough force to silence the room. Suddenly I was on center stage, all three of my companions waiting for the rest of what I had to say. Knowing I would have to fight my way out if I tried to leave without telling them what I knew, I related the whole sad tale. Green asked the obvious.

"Jack, can we quote you?"

"Keep my speculations out of it. I'm not getting sued so you can sell papers. Anything else, sure."

Taking a deep breath, I gave them the straight facts any competent reporter could've tracked down.

"Number one . . . Andrew Sinnott is a member of the D.A.'s office. Number two . . . yes, I was hired to prove that he was a cheat. Number three . . . yes, he was, and his wife had proof. Number four . . . yes, it was rock-solid proof—she had a video of her husband performing in a sex club. And," I added for my own protection, "you will report that I just happened to be here when the news came in, and that you got what information you did after catching my reaction to said news."

"The truth angle, eh?" answered Green. "I like it. How 'bout the tape?"

I frowned at him, hoping he'd get the idea. He didn't.

"Peekie, peekie? Just one little look? A few seconds for the duping of . . ."

"No." I answered him with emphasis. "I will not release copies of the tape to the *Post*. Or anyone else, outside of the child welfare board. I don't care how big a bastard this guy is, this was between him and his wife."

"How about your footmen on this?" asked Rich. "Anyone we can contact?"

"No one I'd want you to find. If they come to you willing to deal, I can't stop that. But I won't let my agency be known as a place that can't keep its mouth shut."

"That's enough, boys," said Sally, calling off my interrogation. "Chet, Jack said Sinnott is in the D.A.'s office. Have you sent anyone over there to flush him out?"

"I called for a car to pick me up out front. I'm on this one myself. Just wanted to let you know what I was up to before I took off."

"Okay," she told him, "get going. And—Rich, Jack— would you two go with him? Just to . . ."

We both had the idea before she could say it.

"Wild horses and all the king's men couldn't stop us," I told her. Then I added, "And don't worry, I won't do anything to tarnish the reputation of the *New York Post*."

"What?" she asked, certainly *sounding* serious. "Is that possible?"

Rich, Chet, and I were ushered into a large room with what seemed like every other reporter from the Eastern Seaboard. We pressed body upon body against each other, everyone juggling tape recorders, notebooks, video cameras, spear mikes, hip flasks, coke bullets, predatory smiles, and bad attitudes. Every few minutes we were told by a stiff, affected City Hall flak that a statement would be released shortly. After another twenty-seven minutes of watching the heat in the room melt the electronic journalists' makeup, finally the district attorney of New York City came out and addressed the crowd.

Judith Siegel—billed by many as the most honest woman in New York City politics—stood before us at her podium, looking as if all the sound bites in the world didn't matter a hell of a lot. It was the first time I'd seen her in person, a distinct improvement over the pulp stock newspaper picture I'd seen that morning.

She seemed vaguely familiar, but in truth I had to admit that hers was a familiar look—short, black hair framing an oval face, made up in a not-attractive, not-unattractive way. Her armor consisted of a cream-white suit, one that angled, padded, and otherwise twisted her to give the appearance that she might have a reasonably attractive figure under it. She stood in low, comfortable heels, somewhat feminine, somewhat businesslike, telling nothing about her except that like everyone else in government her basic thrust was to appeal to the lowest common denominator.

In cold, riding tones she warned the press that she would not allow it to chew up a valued employee like Andrew Sinnott as if he were one of their normal, equally innocent targets. She flashed her violent eyes, letting those assembled know she would stand for no harassment of her employees, and that anyone who dared disrupt the work of her offices for a story would find themselves with worse problems to worry about than just meeting their deadlines. Then, once the room had been given its guidelines for proper procedure and snarled down into submission, Ms. Siegel finally introduced us all to the husband of the Outliner's latest fancy.

Andrew Sinnott cut a lot better figure on video. Coming out to share the podium with his boss he looked ten years older, withered and shrunken, only the starch in his shirt holding him together. I'd be a liar if I didn't admit it'd crossed my mind that he might have committed the murder himself. I could see it fitting the kind of guy I'd sized him up as—I'd certainly seen it before.

Defied by his wife? Just kill her. He was of the type that gets too used to getting their own way—too used to being right no matter what—far too easily. He could cheat on his wife, that was "okay." He was a man—he was the boss. Bosses do what they want. But for her to do something he hadn't allowed, that had to be punished. A lot of the time, his type found murder to be a perfect solution. Besides giving them vent to their bad tempers, it saved embarrassment, let them keep the kids, the bank accounts, the house, et cetera, avoided scandal . . . other reasons.

Good as my rationalizing was, however, I scratched the idea from my mental pad after seeing him. Even through the crowd, poking and jostling everyone around them, all the fine fellows of the news trying to make sure they ruined their brothers' and sisters' stories, I could see that Sinnott was shaken. It was clear in his face: he wasn't worrying about a crime he had committed. He was worrying about who had committed it.

It's a look I've seen a thousand times before. People next to violent death always wonder if they might be next. It's an almost irrational fear, one triggered by their attachment for the victim—that bond showing the survivor that death is indeed tangible.

So Andrew Sinnott didn't kill his wife. Well, I thought, let's see what he has to say about the guy who did. When he opened his mouth, nothing came out. He gasped for air, looking sickly, then finally got the words going.

"Ladies and gentlemen of . . . the press, I, I have a short statement I'd like to make. Please. I'm going to try and tell you all everything you want to know here and now, be-because I want to be left alone. I've already sent my children out of town, and no, I won't say where. I don't want flocks of you on my doorstep, or chasing them, either."

Color began to finally find its way into Sinnott's cheeks. I had to admit, I was almost impressed as he worked his number on the media assemblage. Chastising them relentlessly, he let them know just what kind of curs he thought they were for forcing him into such a position only hours after his wife's brutal murder.

Yes, he had viewed the body. Yes, it was his wife. No, he would not tell anyone anything the police had said—that was how murderers stayed at large, by reading the papers and watching their televisions and finding out what was known about them. No, his children did not know yet, but he was sure some crusading journalist would get the news to them before he could.

Like I said, I was almost impressed. Listening to him talk, watching him lash the electronic vultures all around me, I found myself wishing he were a man I could respect. It was the never-ending problem—what *do* you do when someone you have no use for is right and you aren't? There was no getting around the fact that I'd come along to see Sinnott speak because I'd wanted to believe he'd killed his wife. Now that I knew he didn't, I was just killing time, waiting for him to finish so the crowd would thin enough so I could escape.

His talk lasted less than ten minutes, at which point he threw things open to questions. Yes, of course, he hoped the Outliner would be caught. No, he did not care to comment on the killer's mental state—that was something best left to those who understood the subject. Yes, he thought the Outliner had made a mistake killing his wife. Yes, her death would focus even more public attention on him. Yes to this, no to that. Yes, no. Yes, no. On and on.

Then Chet decided to test the waters.

"Mr. Sinnott, Chet Green—*New York Post*. Sir, would you care to comment on the state of your marriage before your wife's murder?"

Sinnott stopped cold, eyeing Green hatefully, measuring his response. When he could finally speak, he said,

"No. No, I wouldn't. Mr. Green, didn't you hear what I had to say before? Weren't you listening? I'm here to brief you people about a crime. What's your angle, anyway? What possible relevance does that question have to anything we're dealing with?"

Sinnott's face clouded over, hot and red and angry. The D.A. singled out our little group, shooting us a hateful look. Eyes narrowing, she marked us for future reference, then signaled a couple of her people forward. She was too late, though. Before they could get close enough to work their damage control, his voice cracking, Sinnott began shouting,

"Even if I were beating my wife every night, or sleeping with sheep, what in hell would that have to do with why we're here? You miserable bastard . . ."

Before Sinnott could continue, though, the two aides the D.A. had motioned for reached his side. One backed Sinnott away from his podium while the other first covered the microphone with his hand, then uncovered it to announce,

"Ladies and gentlemen, that will be all. There will be no more questions at this time."

Then, turning his back on us, the aide helped his counterpart move Sinnott offstage. The D.A. had already disappeared. Taking our cue with the rest of those assembled, Rich and Chet and I headed for the doors. A few of the other reporters asked Green what he'd been fishing for, but he put them off, just reminding them that he worked for the *Post* and that, hey, wasn't it his job to look for the worst dirt everywhere?

Once we were outside, however, he had a different tune to sing.

"What do you think, boys?" he asked. "On the level, or not?"

Rich shrugged honestly, not knowing what to make of what we had seen. I felt the same way. Green prodded us, however. "Rich," he said, "you're looking for dirt in City Hall. Jack, you just had someone you knew killed in a suspicious way. I don't know what I don't like about the performance I just saw, but I know it wasn't the fact I was called a miserable bastard . . ."

"That's true," said Rich. "Sally calls him worse almost every day."

"So what's the point, Chet?"

"That's why I love this boy, Rich . . . always cuts right to the front page. The point, Jack . . . ? I'd like to run all this mess by you two, see if any of it adds up. Couple of hours of your time. Maybe your real story is hidden in here, Rich. For you, Jack, maybe we avenge Vivian Sinnott's death."

As we let what he said soak in, he added,

"We'll do it over dinner." When we both stared, he interpreted the looks correctly. "Of course on me."

"Italian?" I asked.

"Anything."

"Sounds good to me," agreed Rich.

"Great," answered Green, slapping his hands together. "Well then, let's get going."

I followed the pair along to the company car waiting for them. Even though I didn't see any connections coming fast, I figured, what the hell, a free dinner's a free dinner.

You'd think by now I would have learned.

CHAPTER 11

RICH, CHET, AND I sat at a corner table in Fabarini's, to our way of thinking, the last decent spaghetti shop in Little Italy. Fabarini's is by no means an intimate place. Usually loud and crazy, generally filled with boisterous males, some shouting, some singing, it is, however, one of the happiest places in lower Manhattan. That joy, understandably, is a thing basically inspired by their jumbo portions, reasonable prices, and the giant basket of always delicious garlic bread they drop on each table, even if you're only having a couple of beers. Of course, anyone who knows the three of us knows we weren't there to just have a couple of beers.

We'd ordered two cold seafood antipastos and a trio of shrimp cocktails to start with, along with an order each of the fried zucchini, mozzarella sticks, and stuffed mushrooms. The three of us picked while we talked, washing down both the conversation and food with the first of a number of pitchers of beer, for Chet and I, Rich sticking to his usual seltzer.

Waving a mozzarella stick at me, Chet asked,

"So come on, Jack, spill it. Is Sinnott full of shit, or what?"

"I don't know," I told him. "I'd swear he was being straight up there tonight. I really don't think he had anything to do with killing his wife."

"But . . . ?"

I stared at Rich, knowing he could tell there was something in the back of my mind, sending an exasperated sigh at him for making me think about it consciously. I prefer to let my thoughts come together in the back of my head. It's less work that way, and when the answer to something finally does crystallize for me, I always know I'm right.

I'm not good with working out puzzles for the sake of exercising my brain. When I start juggling theories instead of facts, then doubt sets in. I'm perfectly willing to follow a gut feeling I can't explain into the worst kind of trouble—that kind of move never bothers me. But acting on some kind of Sherlock Holmes level, that's not my style. I just don't have that kind of confidence in my own powers of deduction, even when I *do* know I'm right.

Rich, however, working on an entirely different set of governing principles, never seems to have the kinds of doubts I do. He also always expects everyone else to be thinking things through as fast as he is, coming up with conclusions they can solidly back with facts.

"Yes . . . 'but,' " I told him, knowing it was useless to try to avoid the question, "I was a little thrown off by the way he was acting."

That got both the newsmen focused on me, quietly waiting to see if I was on to anything. I continued, more than conscious of their stares, trying to explain.

"I mean, I'll say it again. No, I don't think he murdered his wife, or even arranged for someone else to do it. But I do think he's afraid of something, and I don't just think it's the specter of death."

"What do you mean?" asked Chet.

"That's the tough part. I got a sense from him that . . . he was, yes, definitely afraid, but"—I groped for the right words—"afraid of something or someone, I don't know, not so metaphysical, I guess."

Chet stuffed a sauce-slathered shrimp into his mouth along with two mushrooms. The words barely able to find their way out past all the food, he asked,

"You think he knows who killed her?"

Taking the last mozzarella stick for myself, I admitted,

"Like the rabbit said, 'It's a possibility.'"

Before any further conversation could continue, however, both Rich's and my eyes jumped to the front, followed by Chet's a split second later. We had all noticed the same figure coming through the door. Never one to miss an opportunity, Chet shouted,

"Captain Trenkel, join us."

Ray Trenkel is the captain of the police precinct that covers my office. He's a better guy than Mike Fisher, the captain of the precinct in which I live, but then who isn't? Fisher is an arrogant, corrupt bastard. Nobody would ever call Ray Trenkel corrupt.

"Well, well, well," he said in his artificially friendly tone, "Jack Hagee sitting to dine with those outstanding men from the *Post*, Chet Green and Richard Violano. Am I still in time to order?"

"Did you bring the file?" asked Chet.

"A file? You're asking a New York City police captain to give you—a newshound—a confidential police file for the price of a meal?"

I looked back and forth from the two of them, shaking my head. Like I said, Chet Green is not one to miss an opportunity, but I hadn't known he was that quick. A little miffed at being surprised, I asked,

"When did you get on the horn to this dickhead?"

"Watch your ass, Jackie-boy," warned Trenkel.

"Oh, excuse me. When did you get on the horn to King Richard the First, here?"

"I called him when I went to the can while you and Rich were getting the table."

It wasn't that I couldn't stand Trenkel to the point where I couldn't sit down at the same table with him— Ray Trenkel is probably the best friend I have at the NYPD, which I know isn't saying much. The problem was I'm just not one for surprises. Especially ones that bring Ray Trenkel to my dinner table.

"So," asked Rich. "What's the file?"

"Specs on the Outliner to date," answered Chet.

"Green, you've been on this case since it started," I said. "You're just getting around to copping a peek now?"

"Don't beat up your playmate here," Trenkel cut in. "The guy who lets this one out . . ."

"Meaning you in this case?"

"Heavens, not me, Jackie-boy," answered the captain as he handed the envelope under his arm over to Green. In a slow, measured, on-the-record tone—one perfect for quoting—Trenkel told us,

"I would no more give the press access to restricted documents on a sensational case than I would allow a private investigator to look into the same case without a client." He winked at me, then grabbed up my last two jumbo shrimp, finishing,

"And even then I wouldn't let him get away with shit—would I?"

"No," I answered with a bit of a snarl, "I'll vouch for that much, anyway."

"Good," he said, cramming the shrimps into his mouth. After that, he slapped his hands together, asking, "So, what's on the menu?"

"How about a few answers?"

Trenkel looked me in the eye, gauging what he thought my interests were. He took a subtle breath, trying to get his wind up, but attempting to look as if he weren't preparing to make a speech. Finally, he answered,

"Be happy to tell you, since if I don't, Green is sure to anyway. I'll be the first one to admit that like anybody else in this world I've got a twofold purpose here. First off, just like everyone else in the city, I want this motherfucker caught. Now, I don't trust Chet here any further than I can shotput a Cadillac, but I'm counting on Violano to keep him honest. No offense, Chet . . ."

"Hey, none taken."

"Thanks. Now see there, Jackie. There's a reasonable man. He knows how to deal with the police."

"Yeah, next time I want you to do something illegal I'll buy you an Italian dinner and then pretend you're not a prick when you insult me. What's your second reason?"

Trenkel's face hardened slightly, but he managed to keep his jowls loose enough to allow him to laugh me off. Spearing a set of the zucchini sticks with a fork borrowed from another table, he said,

"The second reason is that I'm just as political as everyone else in this world. If you think I don't want to be commissioner, think again. If Green can turn anything out of this mess, I'm the one that gets the boost. He can have his story. I've got a hat that needs a few more feathers before I can throw it into any arenas."

As Trenkel chewed at the zucchini dangling from the end of his fork, our waiter came up and supplied him with a menu, napkin, and the rest of the utensils he would need. He told the waiter to stick around, flipping the menu open and making his order in just a few seconds.

All the time, however, I kept watching Ray's eyes. The way he kept averting them from me let me know he knew it. Something in both his voice and his expression told me there was a little more to what was going on than what he was saying. Once the waiter was gone, he told me what it was.

"And since I guess it looks a little odd, me helping out here this late into the game," he stopped for just a second, then finished, "I might as well add one more reason to the list." His voice going even lower, he continued,

"This Sinnott mess is going to focus attention on City Hall, and as you might guess, that's something they never like. The guy who takes that brick off the pile will be remembered. And that's definitely part of it. Another part is . . . I knew his wife, met her at a fund-raising thingus. She seemed like a nice person—too nice for a slug like Sinnott."

"You knew what kind of a guy he was?" I asked.

"Oh—no," he answered, failing to sound casual. "Not personally. He's in the D.A.'s office—they're all slugs in the D.A.'s office."

Not believing him, but accepting what he had to say to avoid an argument, I let the whole thing drop. He was right about one thing, I was a private investigator thinking about sticking my nose in police business for my own reasons. Not a smart thing to do. On analysis, they weren't even very good reasons.

Yeah, I felt sorry for Vivian Sinnott before she died, and I felt sorry for her afterward as well. In all honesty, though, I feel sorry for lots of people in this world and I don't have it in me to help even a tenth of the living ones, let alone the dead. If I'd thought that Andrew Sinnott had murdered his wife, I'd have been all over him like a cheap suit. It wouldn't have been smart, but then no one's ever wasted much time accusing me of sporting an overdeveloped intellect.

The truth was, sitting there in Fabarini's, I knew I just couldn't afford to get involved. I had no client to allow me legal access to the case. In fact, I had no clients, period. If Rich didn't really need me, I wasn't going to bill the *Post* for more than the night. Which meant that after Vivian Sinnott's check cleared, and Hubert's team took their bite, there'd be no more money coming in, and precious little lying around. Considering that Elba had more cash in the bank than I did at the moment, come the morning I was going to have to find some real work.

And at that moment the waiter appeared with our orders. Actually, the four of us had jammed so many side dishes on the expense account that the waiter had needed a busboy to help get it all out. As the two of them passed out various helpings of this and that to their proper recipients, I decided I had made up my mind on what the future held. Digging into my chicken rotella, I chalked off the following points, "knowing" they would all be true.

In the morning I would no longer have the *New York Post* as a client. I would no longer be involved with the Sinnotts, Andrew or Vivian, and I certainly wouldn't be tracking down the Outliner.

What I would be doing, I told myself, would be looking for a new client or two, people with nice, safe, unglamorous cases, and not until after I had slept in late so I could digest ten or fifteen pounds of the wonderful Fabarini's cuisine sitting before me.

That in mind, I grabbed up one of the pitchers of beer from the table, one still about a quarter full, tilted it in the general direction of my dinner mates, and then said,

"Salud, gentlemen. I'm out of things now, but I wish you all good luck in cracking the toughest case in New York."

Then I tilted the pitcher back toward me and upward, draining it before I set it back on the table. And to all of that, all I can say is, I've made mental lists and I've shown off in my time. And I've made some lists where I wasn't exactly right on every point, and I've shown off where it might have been prudent not to, at least not to the extent I did. But up until that night I'd never shown off over a list I made up where every single one of the points on it was one hundred percent wrong.

There's a first time for everything, I guess.

CHAPTER 12

WE GOT BACK to the *Post* a few hours later, Chet and I slightly drunk, all of us stuffed and feeling it. Trenkel had stayed reasonably sober since he had to return to the precinct house. Chet and I had celebrated—him, his terrific story; me, my decision to avoid it. Once we were back at the paper, I could have just poured myself into my car and headed for home, but the beer had warmed me to the point where I thought I would follow the boys upstairs and see if Sally was in.

Using the excuse of wanting to both hit their head and grab a cup of their instant coffee before driving, I followed Rich and Chet inside and then rode upstairs with them in the elevator, feeling the discomfort from the gas building within me. Trying to shift my belt without allowing any embarrassing noises to escape from either end, I wondered just how many more years I'd be able to eat and drink like a hog whenever I felt like it without having to pay too large a price for the privilege.

When you're twenty, putting away a few pounds of pasta, along with hunk after hunk of greasy bread and a few helpings of various batter-fried cheeses and sea-foods, all of it washed down with twenty beers or what-have-you is a reasonably simple accomplishment. Some guys will be just fine, some will groan and roll their eyes, and some will out-and-out puke, but we all do it and then think nothing of doing it again the next time the opportunity arises.

Once you hit your thirties, however, with a brain already indoctrinated with such bad habits, most guys suddenly find their bodies can't play the game anymore, even though their brain still wants to . . . just like mine. I had to admit that my stomach had posted its opening notices in my brain, warning that the situation was going to have to change. I'd started feeling that tightness in the jeans as well.

So far I'd resisted the urge to go up more than a couple of pants sizes when shopping for new ones. But that was only because I've been able to hold the line by sticking to my workout schedule. I had a feeling, however, that that was going to have to change. If it did, though— if some kind of macrobiotic diet was in the cards on one of those "sooner or later" signposts, I know myself well enough to realize that I'll be taking my chances and waiting for later.

Once we got off on the editorial office floor, I made my trip to the head, then said my good-byes to Rich and Chet and headed for the coffee table. There was hot water and instant crystals, but all the real milk was gone. Not liking powdered creamers or black coffee, I decided to break my no sugar rule that once just to be able to choke the stuff down.

While I stirred the bitter-smelling mess, I wondered exactly what excuse I could use for going in to see Sally again. Not being able to come up with anything clever—not exactly a new situation for me—I decided to just take my coffee and go to her office and see what happened. God knows, I told myself, things couldn't end up any worse than they were before. So armed with my cardboard cup of white sugar and freeze-dried caffeine, I knocked on her door with my free hand and then spun the knob when she called out.

"Hi, Sal. How's doin'?"

"Hi, yourself. Were you of any help to my valiant crew?"

"I don't know. You'll have to ask them."

"I'll see how big a bill you send us," she answered, not yet really looking up at me. "Then I'll decide if I'm going to question it or not."

"You wouldn't want to tell me what a fair price is so we could skip the argument?"

She eyed me, looking to see if I'd been making a crack. Deciding I hadn't meant anything nasty, she said,

"Oh, sit down, will you? I don't need you towering over me and I'm too tired to stand up."

Sliding into one of the chairs on the other side of her desk, I took a slug of the coffee and then said,

"I'd be happy to sit. I'm beat, too. And besides," I took my chance, "having a seat is a lot better than getting thrown out in the hall."

"Oh, don't worry," she assured me, some of the tone I was used to from her sneaking into her voice. "That's still possible."

"Sweetheart, I'd rather leave now than start another fight." Then, leaning forward just enough to be able to put the paper cup on the edge of her desk, I added,

"But on the chance I can say this without starting one, I'll tell you, Sal, I really liked you when we first met. Hell, I like you now. I did mean it earlier when I said I was sorry for whatever it was that got us off to a bad start. I still don't know what it was, but I sure wouldn't mind it if we could get past it. And," I hastened to add, "I don't mean that I just want to jump your bones again."

She cut me off.

"No . . . ?"

"Oh, they're nice bones," I admitted. "And they're fun to jump and all, but I like you a little more than that. I'll tell you the truth, if I was only after some cheap fun, I'd go somewhere else. You're more trouble than that's worth."

"Thanks a lot."

"You *know* what I mean," I told her.

"*Do* I?"

I dropped my chin toward my chest, half closing my eyes, not wanting to shout my answer, but frustrated that I couldn't think of anything else to do. As my breath shot out in an angry exhale and I pulled in another that I hoped I'd be able to speak with, Sally jumped in first.

"No, I'm sorry. I know what you mean," she admitted. "Honest, I do. *Honest*. And, maybe, maybe I've known it for a long while, too."

We searched out and caught each other's eyes, neither of us finding the things we were afraid we were going to see. I broke out in the kind of relieved, goofy grin most guys with too much alcohol in them would when they discovered they'd gambled and won. Sally smiled, however, a wide, beaming greeting that softened her entire face—one that flushed her cheeks and filled her eyes with the look that glued me to her side the first night we'd met.

There are moments that sober a person—some are tied to hate, some to fear. This was one of those moments, but not one tied to either of those reasons. I felt as if a massive weight had been lifted from my chest, as if a sponge that had been stuffed in between my skull and my brain had suddenly been removed. Happier than I had been in a long time, suspecting that she was as well, I started to open my mouth when the door was flung open, propelled by a Rich Violano more excited than I had ever seen him before.

"Up! Up!" he ordered. "Come on. Now!"

And with that he turned and ran back down the hall in the direction of Chet Green's desk. Looking at each other with a mixture of emotions, we hesitated for only a second, then both got to our feet, sensing that whatever it was that Rich wanted, it was more important— a one-of-a-kind moment that wasn't going to wait.

When we caught up to Rich, we found he had indeed gone to Green's desk. Chet was sitting sideways, waving us forward while talking to someone on the other end of his speaker phone. As we drew closer, he said,

"They're here. They're here. Okay, now—please. Please just repeat everything you just said."

"You're not taping this, are you?"

Green mouthed the words "don't I wish" silently to us, answering the voice on the line,

"No. I swear to you. I would have if I could but all my equipment is in my locker."

"How can I trust you?" came the voice again, male, smooth, wary, somewhat arrogant and yet hoping for trust.

"Pal," offered Chet smoothly, "if I had you on tape I wouldn't have to get you to repeat anything. But I can't run your story if no one in authority hears something. My editor-in-chief is here now, though. Just please, tell it again. She's here. She's here. Please, just once more."

There was a long pause. Nothing, no answer or background noises, no click-off, not even breathing came through the speaker. It made sense, no one on our end was breathing, either. Finally, though, the line came back to life.

"You'll print what I tell you?"

"We will!" shouted Sally, knowing who was on the other end of the line just as surely as I did.

"Okay," came the voice again. "Okay—but it's just like I told you the first time . . ."

Another pause followed—shorter—then the clincher.

"It doesn't matter what they're saying. I didn't kill that Sinnott woman."

CHAPTER 13

"COME UP, COME up, gentlemen. Don't you want to judge the results?"

Chet Green and I stepped forward, eager to see what the man at the table before us had come up with. The speaker—black, very thin, hair tightly curled but disappearing, a professor of modern art attached to the Whitney Museum—waved us up, turning around the files he had on the desk before him, making them easier for us to inspect.

His long fingers, swinging almost awkwardly from the ends of his oversized hands, gestured in the air over the files. Smugly chuckling with himself, not vain, merely pleased with his ability to fill our wants, he said,

"I want to thank you gentlemen again for bringing this to my attention. Wonderful puzzle, wonderful." He gave us the time necessary to determine whether or not he had made the grade, then asked,

"So, Mr. Green . . . how did I do?"

A smile the size of a slice of cantaloupe from a generous restaurant broke Chet's face open, seemingly touching each ear and threatening to meet at the back of his head. He resisted the urge to dance up and down out of joy, but he did grab the man's hand and pumped it up and down, telling him,

"Spectacular, simply rip-'em-up-and-down spectacular, Professor. A+ a mundo."

The professor was Professor D. Anthony St. Rose. He hadn't bothered to tell us what the "D" stood for, and none of us had bothered to ask. Somehow it hadn't seemed important. What we had done was gone to see him with the Outliner file we'd gotten from Trenkel, and then asked him to arrange the murders in sequence based on any "artistic" growth he might see within the Outliner's work.

The gangly man had beamed when we presented the challenge, taking no more than fifteen minutes to not only correctly identify the order in which the city's latest serial murderer had completed his crimes, but also to eliminate the murder of Mrs. Sinnott as one done by the same person. This, of course, was the news we had been looking for. Green asked him,

"So, Professor St. Rose, what can you tell us about this guy? I mean, only in your opinion as an artist, what's the message this, ah, 'artist,' is trying to convey? I mean, what do you see there?"

"My boy," answered the professor, "I see enough to write a juicy best-seller just from what you are showing me. I assume, however, that your purpose here has more to do with selling editions of the *New York Post* than it does with my publishing career, so let's get down to answering your question. First off, I assume that folder of facts of yours put forth the theory that the Outliner might be a homosexual, yes?"

The professor didn't know we were using a New York City Police Department file; his assumption was that what he was commenting on were Green's gathered notes. Neither of us had seen the need to tell him any different. Chet, happy to see the professor's unprompted guesses coinciding with the police's, agreed with another smile. St. Rose smiled back, and then continued.

"Yes, I rather thought so."

"Does that mean you agree with them or disagree, Professor?" asked Green.

"Oh, I agree. I agree. Look, let's review these photos one by one, in order of the killings. Remember now, we are dealing with an artist here. To him, these are

not so much 'murders' as they are 'statements.' Now,
every murderer and artist have one thing in common . . .
they are both doing what they do for a reason. What we
must ask ourselves here is, what is this artist's reason for
making this or that statement?" Sitting back in his chair,
webbing his fingers behind his head, St. Rose told us,

"This man is, through his art, trying to tell the world
that he is a homosexual. He wants to be a homosexual,
but something is holding him back. Early church training, stern father who couldn't forgive such contact, who
knows? It isn't my job to say 'why' he is gay, just to
prove he is. So, on to the murders."

Throwing out the first photo of the plain, white-chalk-
surrounded knifing that had taken place in Harlem, the
doctor started,

"Obviously the first. Crude, fast, simple—but let's
examine the subtext of what is happening here. The
notes here say the crime took place only a few blocks
into Harlem. When a white man kills a black man without robbery for a motivation, what can the reason be?
My first guess, excuse a black man making such an
observation, would be bigotry. In artistic terms, I think
it obvious he's trying to make a statement to the world
that he is bold and daring.

" 'Look,' he says, 'I go into the ghetto and slaughter
blacks. I'm a real man. Real men hate niggers . . . and
so do I.' Well, to a scared personality, digging for the
truth within himself, yes, killing a man would make him
seem like a 'real' man, and killing a 'nigger' would make
him seem like more of a 'real' man. But what he's really
out to do is kill a 'homo.' Real men hate 'homos' even
more than they hate 'niggers,' don't they?"

Noticing, at the least, my unease with his explanation,
Professor St. Rose added,

"Oh, Mr. Hagee, please don't think I'm making some
moral judgment here. Modern art is filled with the most
hateful, bigoted, sexist damnings since the beginning of
artistic expression. For centuries, people have painted,

sculpted, et cetera, whatever they've wanted to. That's art, gentlemen, people expressing their inner feelings. Art interpretation comes in when the artist doesn't actually understand his own feelings. And," he told us, his voice filling with the power of his authority on the subject,

"If you think people paint pictures, or make movies, write books, whatever, with a complete understanding of the message they're actually trying to get across, then you don't understand art, gentlemen. Most artists don't have the faintest idea what it is they're really trying to say. That's what makes them artists—that internal struggle to get to the burning truth within them."

I interrupted then, trying to get us back on the track. "Well, Professor," I started, "then how does the rest of this all tie in?"

"Yes, back to the subject at hand. Numbers two and three were rapid pieces, weren't they? One right after another, yes?" Green nodded again. St. Rose kept going.

"Certainly they were. Look at the markings, the second in Flatbush, the third in Brooklyn Heights. Now he is killing white men. As I said, this man has nothing against blacks, merely against himself. First he rages against a black. Then a homeless man in a poor part of the city, then a wealthy man in a quite upscale part of the city. His statement is painfully obvious. 'Look, Dad, I'm no artist. I'm a killer. Blacks, the homeless, the rich. All the useless—I'm the plague that sweeps them away. I'm a righteous angel—the left hand of God.' And so on. He marks them around in white to draw attention to his murderous handiwork—sterile, policelike attention, no less—and then rests, satisfied everyone understands that he is not an artist, in other words not a homosexual.

"But then, then came the change. Can I guess there was quite a space of time between the third and fourth killings?"

When Green nodded again, St. Rose said,

"To be expected. Look at the difference. After dwelling on what he had done for a while, the stirrings within him drove him out again. With the fourth he switched to color, using blue. Blue is a very serene color. He also moved indoors. He left the man he killed, another white man, getting closer to what he himself is, in the aisle of a supermarket—on the one hand, very bold, very daring, but also very revealing. Blue is the color for men, in that Hallmark sensibility we are all surrounded with. So he draws attention to himself again . . . I have killed, and then to his problem . . . a desire for submissive white men at his feet, but he takes a step forward. He makes it more public, which is what he himself wishes, for his homosexuality to be more public, and he shows this by moving into color. To admit to being an artist is, for him, an admission of being gay. I'm quite sure that if he had had the time, the rendering here would have been more detailed, but I imagine killing someone in a supermarket aisle and then coloring around them in blue chalk *and* then getting away with it as well is difficult enough for anyone.

"Anyway, the observation deck of the Staten Island ferry, his next attack, more than makes up for it. This murder came quickly after the fourth, didn't it?"

Again Green agreed that the professor was correct, and again St. Rose continued his explanation.

"I'll try to keep this brief. Look at what he's done . . . roses growing out at all the appendages . . . very straight, long-stemmed, very phallic, life out of death, and also, let us not ignore . . . it is the most artistic murder yet. He is getting close and closer to saying what he has to."

"But, Professor," I asked, "the next victim was a woman. Doesn't that hurt things here a little?"

"Perhaps, but let's see. I'm sure none of the bodies has been sexually molested yet, have they?"

When I shook my head, he said,

"No, I wouldn't think so. And the woman wasn't molested, either, I'm sure. To tell the truth, I think she was a mistake. Look at her . . . this is no fashion model. This is a plain, very masculine woman, dressed in men's clothing. My guess would be that she was a lesbian, herself. A woman who walked, moved, thought like a man. I doubt the killer even realized until he read the papers the next day that he had killed a woman. He used the same slash across the throat to do his killing, then never touched the body again. Mixing her blood into the design of his outlining just shows his striving, reaching out all the more."

And once again the professor had nailed down everything the police had found. His guesses were a hundred percent consistent with their own strongest theory. What we had been hoping for by visiting Professor St. Rose was to get our own expert so we could publish what we wanted to without getting Trenkel in dutch for showing us the file in the first place. The plan had worked in a big way. The World Trade Center men's room masterpiece was the big finish, according to both the police's expert and ours. Taking two suicidal AIDS sufferers, the Outliner had made his final statement, "killing" what he considered to be the things wrong inside of him—white male homosexual things—turning them into his finest work yet, one that celebrated gay love, using spiritual colors and symbols to show he not only accepted what he was, but that he thought it noble and godlike.

And that, insisted Professor St. Rose, made it impossible for Mrs. Sinnott to have been his next victim. As he told it,

"Look at the progression . . . white chalk—identify the problem. Then blue to get closer. Roses, growing from the blood, strong penises reaching for the sky, then a rainbow. Heaven's gift, just like the roses, but higher, more blessed, and then, finally, Christ himself. God gives his son to redeem all sins. These are not followed by a crime like this."

The professor's hand stabbed down at the photo of Mrs. Sinnott as she had been found.

"Someone here has been very clever. They've tried quite hard to make this look like some sort of regression, but it doesn't wash. No, look at this—these strokes of black over pink, the use of these male symbols dominating the female ones. Our man has never shown that he thinks men superior to women—that's not what his message is all about. No." St. Rose dismissed the last murder entirely, not willing to entertain the slightest doubt that it had not been committed by the man known as the Outliner. "Not one chance in . . . ten thousand."

"Then, Professor," I asked, holding up the picture of Vivian Sinnott's corpse, "who killed this woman?"

"Gracious, I wouldn't know, Mr. . . . Hagee, isn't it?" After I nodded, he concluded,

"No, I wouldn't be able to tell you that. The only thing I can say, and I say this with absolute assurance, is that it is simply impossible for the man who committed these other killings to have committed this last one. In fact, I would go so far as to say that the only person this man is going to kill after this," he said, pointing to the photos of the first eight murders, "will be himself."

CHAPTER 14

CHET GREEN AND I sat at the horseshoe bar of a cocktail lounge above the South Street Café, a diner built into the corner of the building housing the *Post*. Beers and full ashtrays in front of us, we sat in silence, neither of us having anything left to add to our conversation. We'd gone there to see what we could make out of what we had gathered from the excitable yet proper Professor D. Anthony St. Rose. So far, it hadn't been much.

When the Outliner had called the night before, we'd debated as to what we could do for a while. The file Trenkel had given us made noises in the same direction. The problem was, of course, that we couldn't act on information we got from the file. The *Post* wanted its story; I wanted Vivian Sinnott's killer caught. If we simply used the police file to justify our actions, the repercussions would have rolled over all four of us. Trenkel was taking as big a chance giving us a copy of the file as we were using it.

So finally we had hustled what favors we could to gain an audience with the famed professor. Three different sources, including Hubert, had named him as the man to see for what we wanted. Obviously, none of them had been wrong. Now, we had to decide what to do next.

The night before had been an exciting one. The Outliner rang off fast, only staying on the line long enough to protest his innocence and prove he was who he claimed to be. Giving us some facts from the police file no one else could know, he cursed those trying to lay such an

insignificant work of art at his feet. He also left Green
with a rosy smile, saying that he had called him because
he felt Chet was the only reporter who had given him
a fair shake. I'd thought his coverage of the Outliner's
work had been the most sensational in the city, but who
am I to try to classify the tastes of those who read the
New York Post?

After that, we'd called Trenkel to report the Outliner's
call, giving him everything the serial killer had told us.
Trenkel let us know he approved of our handling of
the situation and that we still had his blessing. Once
he'd been placated, we gathered our sources, discovered
St. Rose was our best next step, secured an appoint-
ment with him for the next day, and then called it
a night.

After that, Sally told Rich to get back on the case
of Black Dreamer, which he agreed to, but only with
some reluctance. Like any newsman, the closeness of the
Outliner story had given him a strong case of "hands-on"
fever. I told him I would see what I could do about
getting him a clear passage to the top of Mother's Blood
Flowing. He seemed happy enough.

After that, I asked Sally if I might tag along with
Green when he went to see St. Rose. She agreed, warning me not to get her reporter into jeopardy by going off
half-cocked with whatever information I received.

"Sal," I told her, "how can you accuse me of such
a tendency? Why, anyone can tell you I'm the most
levelheaded man in New York City."

"Unn-huh," she sneered, her eyes twinkling. "And I'm
going to headline at Caesar's Palace in two weeks."

"Who's opening for you?" I asked in my most innocent voice. I ducked the book she threw at me, laughing
but protesting,

"What'd I do?"

"You're a son of a bitch, Jack Hagee," she told me,
laughing as well. Feeling that then was as good a time
as any, I asked her,

"Well, maybe so, but how about answering the question?" When she just looked at me, a little lost, I repeated the question for her.

"What did I do?"

Then she understood. It took her a moment to switch gears. She did it, though, without too much trouble. Her mouth drew into a tight line for a second, then her lips pulled themselves apart and she told me the story.

"You didn't do anything."

"Sweetheart," I told her, "I may not have done anything serious, but I did something. What happened that night? Letting me in on it might keep it from happening again."

"Okay, you're determined to embarrass the hell out of me, so here goes. When I met my ex-husband, it was at a party. He was just what I needed that night—he swept me off my feet. The moment just seemed right and . . . before I knew it, we slept together and became an item and were married in four months. And then I found out what a creep he was and in less than four months we went back to being unmarried."

She stared at me the whole time we talked, watching for my reactions. Not seeing any she didn't like by that point, she told me more.

"I know this isn't a very good excuse, Jack, but I just saw it all happening to me again. Jim was good-looking, too. He was a lot like you—same goofy charm, tough-guy act, and of course the big shoulders and all the rest. That night we met, I hadn't been with a man for a while. I went to Rich's party looking for someone—I knew I was going to take somebody away with me . . . I just didn't know it was going to be somebody like you— somebody who would be so much like all the good things I loved about Jim."

She stopped staring then, her head still aimed in the same position, but her eyes looking through me, back to some point in the faraway past. She kept talking, though, telling me in a softer voice,

"When we were finished, I looked down at you. You were sweating. Your hair—just around your ears—was slicked down just the way Jim's would get. You smiled at me—it was a happy smile, like you were trying to let me know you were glad to be there with *me,* and not just anybody. But it also had this streak of . . . being self-pleased. Okay, I guess every woman is going to see that on every man's face whether it's there or not, but suddenly all I could see was Jim's face—that hateful way he'd look at me."

And then, suddenly, she stopped talking, a split second away from breaking into tears. I'd had some idea she'd been married before, but I never knew anything about the guy. I still didn't really, except that we both sweat around the ears. I also knew I had two things I could do then: swell up with righteous indignation and complain about how badly I'd been treated by her or just be glad to finally be past the barrier that had been standing between us and not start raising another to take its place.

Choosing the latter, I asked her if she'd like to go out and get a drink. I could see in her eyes she's been half expecting me to act like every other guy she'd ever known—or at least like her memory of Jim. The other half of her, the half that had crossed its fingers and let her tell me her story, smiled, accepting the offer without delay. While she got herself packed up and ready to go, I fingered my dragons again, wondering if my break-through with Sally was more of their handiwork. Seeing my smile, she asked me what I was thinking. I told her. She smiled herself, asking me,

"So, you're saying that it really wasn't any sensitivity on your part that has you acting like a caring human being here—it's just the good-luck charm—right?"

"Oh, sure," I agreed, smiling back at her. "Everyone knows what a lout I am."

"Yeah," she answered, stuffing the last of the papers she needed for the night into her walking bag, "a magic necklace being responsible for you suddenly acquiring charm certainly makes sense to me."

I kept my mouth shut and just smiled helplessly. In truth, since I'd set up the line she'd used on me for her, there wasn't anything more I could add, anyway. Besides, the way my luck with women runs, I had a feeling it probably *had* been the dragons. Not caring to test the theory, I admitted defeat and headed the two of us out the door and around the corner to the same bar Chet and I would end up in later.

We talked for several hours, warm, friendly stuff, the things we'd missed the first time when nerves and the wine had jumped us forward too many notches. We said our "good-byes" there as well, not wanting to ruin the shaky relationship we had just started to rebuild. We'd both felt good about the way things were working, and I for one wasn't going to do anything to louse that up.

That had been at about two in the morning. Now it was thirteen hours later, and Green and I had done about as much as we could with the little we had. Finally, I told him,

"Look, I don't see where we can do any more with this as a team, do you?"

"No," he agreed with a sigh. "Sad, but true."

"So what'd you want to do next?"

"Guess I'll just file the story as is for the moment. Name the big expert, list his findings, give the Outliner's call as motivation, quote him on the fact that he didn't do Sinnott, tell the world some crazy-fuck fag thinks I'm the fairest-haired reporter in the city, and then call the bank and tell them to expect my Pulitzer check."

Lighting a new cigarette, he asked me,

"How 'bout you?"

"Got an idea or two."

"But you're not talking."

"I think it's best. I mean, let's keep at this on our own. We'll pass on anything we find out to the other, but this way I won't bring down any wrath on the *Post* by doing something without Fourth Estate immunity."

"You thinking of doing something, shall we print it in eighty-six-point type, say . . . rash?"

"Who, me?" I asked, letting the innocence flow from every pore. "Chet, you wound me. Haven't you heard? I'm the most levelheaded man in New York."

"Seems I have heard that somewhere," he admitted with a chuckle. "Somewhere recently, in fact." Taking a long pull of the beer in front of him, he asked,

"You know, Brenner'd go the limit for you if you dutched yourself up here."

"Yeah," I admitted. "I know. All the more reason to try and play it clear."

Studying me with the practiced eye of a reporter who had microscoped the city for the past fourteen years, Green flicked away the end ash from his cigarette and then asked,

"So, tell me, Jack. Did you two ever do the big Wally?"

" 'Do the big Wally?' " I quoted. "Where do you guys come up with these names?"

"Ix-nay with the runaround. You two do the bang-bang or what?"

Crushing out my own smoke, I told him,

"Sorry, Chet. Some things just aren't for publication."

"Oh, strike-out city, eh? Too bad."

"Whatever you want to believe, pal."

"I see. The boy did score. Home run on the big board."

Smiling, shaking my head the way I always do in such situations, I told Green as I slid off my stool,

"Sorry, no good. Make all the guesses you want about whomever you want. Some things really are personal, you know."

Tossing me a salute, he yelled,

"You'd make a lousy reporter, you know that?"

I snapped him one back as I kept heading for the exit, shouting,

"Figures. I make a lousy private eye."

CHAPTER 15

AFTER THAT, WE indulged in a few more minutes of idle chatter—the speculations and reminiscences of men more concerned with wasting time than using it—then Green went back to his office and I went back to mine. He had his story to write up for the morning edition. I had a business to run. After all, I told myself, even if I did plan to ignore it for a while so I could buzz around the city, chasing one of the two killers the police had a small army after, I still had to make some pretense at being a businessman.

Not having had enough to drink to affect my driving—in my judgment, anyway, if not the state's—I got into my Skylark and moved it out into the hell of midday traffic. Fighting everyone around me and the snow beneath, I managed to somehow get across and up town, pulling up on the opposite side of the street from my office next to a set of police department parking barricades.

Jumping out of the car while the motor was still running, I bucked them up onto the sidewalk and then pulled the Skylark a bit smoother into the spot they'd been occupying. A large woman in her mid-sixties came out of the newsstand next to the parking spot to help me stash the barricades out of sight. I gave her a peck on the cheek while we worked.

"How's it goin', Freddie?"

"Like shit in a blender, big boy," answered the smiling newsstand woman, snorting silver breath as she hefted the last of the blue sawhorse pieces out of sight. "Things are smooth, but they still stink."

"Sums up this city, all right."

"Don't it, though? So, how's everything in fuckin' tough-guy land, Jack?"

"Never better," I told her with mock good humor.

"Aw, jeez," she answered, her tone dripping sympathy. "That's too bad."

"Yeah, I know."

We both laughed, Freddie returning to the inside of her stand, me coming up to the front. I skipped my usual newspapers, not having the time for that day's disaster quota, requesting only a grapefruit juice from the cooler. Grabbing up a Chunky and one of those small bags of Planters cashews, I dug around in my pocket for some money while Freddie pulled out her stash bottle. Black-labeled Jack Daniel's was the taste of the day.

"J.D.? Warm, wet, and wonderful."

"I better pass. I'm floating now."

"You're gonna pass up J.D.?" asked Freddie, her voice not knowing whether to reflect shock or sorrow. "Oh, now I know this city is goin' to hell in a handcart. There go all my schoolgirl dreams, shot to fuckin' shit . . ."

"All right," I said, taking the bottle from her. "I sure don't want to be responsible for shooting all of *your* schoolgirl dreams to shit."

Knocking back a finger or two, I wiped my mouth on my cuff, admitting I was glad for the slug. It went down as smooth as Daniel's always does, warming all the right spots, numbing the rest. I squared my bill and then said my good-byes, letting Freddie know I'd only be at the office for a few minutes and then right back.

I crossed the street and went into my building. Once inside, finding no winos to chase out of the stairwell, I gathered my mail and then headed for the second floor and my office. Once I was past those doors as well, I thumbed quickly through the day's deliveries, none of it bringing any news, entertainment, or money, then flipped on my messages. There were only two, one from Spooner & Morrow, wanting to renew their security agreement, the other from Elba.

Calling Tom Oakel, an operative I subcontract most of my corporate security work through, I let him know S & M were signing up again, then I hung up and redialed to call Elba. Her message had told me that Richie would be home that night and that he was willing to talk to me.

I figured to let her know I'd be there, but there was no answer on her line. After letting it ring for a while, I hung up and turned my attention to my juice and carbohydrates. I broke the Chunky into four pieces, then divided the cashews into four more or less equal piles. Then, mashing the nuts into the candy, I knocked off the whole affair, washing it all down with the still reasonably cold grapefruit juice.

After that, I tried Elba's number again, once more listening to the other end ring without answer. Realizing there wasn't much I could do about it from my office, I closed everything down, reset my message machine, and then headed back for the street.

Crossing over to Freddie's, I pulled the police barricades back out from behind her stand, talking with her while I got them ready.

"So what's the squeeze these days, big boy?"

"Nothing much, sweetheart," I told her. "Like an idiot I'm looking into the Outliner case with Chet Green . . ."

"That ratbag? I hate his stuff."

"Well, be that as it may," I told her as we got the barricades out, ready to throw back into the street, "if I hadn't helped him, I wouldn't have been able to pull together what I needed for what I'm really after."

"You after the Outliner, Jack?"

"Naw," I told her, trying to be reassuring. "I'm pretty sure I'm not."

"Then who you after?"

"Somebody worse," I told her. After that, I climbed back into the Skylark and headed out to Queens. I didn't know if somebody worse was home or not, but I was willing to take the chance.

CHAPTER 16

THE SINNOTT HOME was in Queens Village, the money-eyed area of the borough where people owned swimming pools the way the rest of the town owned bathtubs. I guessed that it was possible a guy bringing down D.A.'s office pay could afford to live there, if he had a lot of dead rich relatives who'd liked him a lot. The thought that Rich was searching for someone dirty in City Hall who might be tied in with the most lucrative drug trade currently going was not lost on me.

Finding the mansion in question, I pulled into the driveway, cursing myself for not putting two and two together when I'd taken down Mrs. Sinnott's address some weeks back. It wasn't the largest or most expensive place in the area—not even in the top fifty percent—but it was still the home of someone who, if not high on the hog, was at least up out of the mud, holding on to its flanks.

Even in the dead of winter the grounds were interesting to look at, enough pines and firs and ivy to keep it attractive. As I climbed to the top of the stairs, I wondered which one of them did the gardening—whose personality it was I was seeing surrounding me. If it was her, I thought, it's too bad he didn't stay home and take more of an interest. And if it was his handiwork, I figured it was still too bad he hadn't stayed home and taken more of an interest. Then again, the thought occurred to me, it was probably some gardener's personality I was trying to analyze.

At that point, someone who was not Andrew Sinnott, and probably not his gardener either, opened the front door and stepped out onto the porch, closing the door behind him. Placing himself solidly between me and the house, he announced,

"Mr. Sinnott is not seeing any reporters."

"I'm not a reporter."

"Mr. Sinnott is not seeing anybody."

Sighing to myself, tired of having to run the same old cliché past the same old type of goon once again, I answered,

"He'll see me."

"Mr. Sinnott is not . . ."

I waved my hand in his face, dismissing his litany, telling him,

"Look. Go back inside. Tell Mr. Sinnott if he wants to get his hands on all the copies of his wife's videotape, he'd better get his sorry ass out here right away."

The goon from Central Casting eyed me for a moment, then went back into the house, the click of his relocking the door making me smile. I hadn't been thinking of myself as that tough-looking a guy recently. It's the little touches that make you feel better about yourself. The goon returned after only a minute, holding the door open this time, letting me know Mr. Sinnott would see me.

"Now," I asked him innocently. "Don't you feel like a moron for locking the door?"

"Nope."

"Too bad . . . you sure looked like one."

Not a devastating gag, to be sure, but then guys with size twenty-two necks rarely respond to those Oscar Wilde–type bon mots. I held off on throwing any more, however. He'd deserved one just for working for a guy like Sinnott, and like any halfway intelligent guy, he'd take it in that spirit. Any more would be asking for trouble, though, and although most people don't believe me when I say it, I really don't go out of my way to look for trouble. Why would I—somehow, it always finds me.

Coming into the Sinnott living room, I could see that it had found me again, right on cue. Sinnott was in a chair by the fireplace bathed in the light from two kerosene lamps situated on the mantelpiece. He had a drink in hand, the color and amount of ice suggesting alcohol—lots of alcohol. He looked tired and gaunt and miserable. The wrinkles in his clothing suggested it had been slept in. The wrinkles in his face suggested that the sleep had not been restful.

Despite the presence of a healthy cord of deeply seasoned wood the fireplace stood empty. Its well-scrubbed black iron stood useless, sending waves of cold through the room merely by its not being utilized. Sinnott kept his bleary, red-tinted eyes on me as I walked in, as I stood with my hands in my pockets, as I pulled them out and crossed them over my chest. I tapped my feet, looked at the ceiling, made a few noises with my lips, all these motions trying to get some reaction out of the man of the house. Finally I asked,

"How 'bout I do a little dance?"

"What?" answered Sinnott with a slight trace of a slur, his eyes finally blinking.

"You know, a little two-step—spread some sand around, do a soft shoe—something entertaining. Just looking to catch your attention."

He took a long pull from his glass, downing five or six fingers in a series of smooth gulps. Putting it aside, he wiped his mouth with a wrinkled sleeve, then said,

"Mike tells me you're not a reporter?"

"That's right."

"But I know you—saw you the other night at the press conference. You . . ." His mind kept searching its file drawers, trying to remember. I was impressed with his powers of recall if with little else about him. "You were with . . . Green. That fuck Green from that fucking *Post*."

His eyes narrowed, somehow still blinking, making his sallow, tired face even less attractive. He made to

take a drink, his arm moving toward his mouth auto-
matically, even though the rest of his body language
said he didn't want it. The glass stopped just short of
his face, his hand waving it around in a small circle—
a move so practiced the liquor inside didn't seem to
stir, let alone slosh. Finally, he broke the silence, asking me,

"If you're not a reporter, then what the hell are you?"

"My name," I told him, passing one of my cards to
his man, Mike, "is Jack Hagee. I'm a private investigator."

His hand stopped twirling his drink. It wasn't an
abrupt movement—even the ice inside the glass didn't
move. But I could see the wheels turning. Drunk as he
was, as upset and depressed as his situation was making
him, I could see he was putting the two and two he had
together. Something inside of him made him put the
drink down. He stretched to do so, putting it as far out of
reach as possible, his subconscious making sure that if he
went for it again he'd have to go through at least as much
trouble. Mike stayed off to the side throughout, ready to
move if he had to, but obviously used to letting the boss
handle things on his own—even when he was sloshed.
Looking at Andy Sinnott with a little more respect, at
least for his combat skills, I wasn't surprised when he
told me,

"You're the fucking peeper she went to. You're the
one that made that fucking movie."

"I arranged for it to be made, which is essentially the
same thing, yes."

Laughing, his eyes unnarrowing but losing none of
their shrewdness, he asked,

"So what do you want, you fuck? Money? You here
to blackmail me? Come on, give it—what're you looking
for? Let's get it over with."

"I'm looking for answers, Mr. Sinnott."

"Aren't we all, hotshot. What're your questions?"

"I want to know if you murdered your wife."

"What?" His eyes bulged believably. Since his shock could have been over my audacity and not the answer, I asked him the question again.

"No," he told me.

"Did you arrange for her murder?"

"No!"

"Did you condone someone else's plan for her murder?"

"No, goddammit!" He swelled up out of his chair, making his feet with a stumbling effort, one hand's fingers against a chair arm providing balance.

"You miserable prick," he shouted, adrenaline burning away the trace of a slur with which he'd started our talk. "Just who in the fuck do you think you are?"

"Some time back your wife hired me to get her the proof she needed that you are a contemptible, cheating bastard. Now mind you, she didn't hire me to prove it to her—she was already sure you were a shitpot. She just needed proof she could take into court so she could be rid of you once and for all. I gave her that proof and bang—what happens? Suddenly she's dead at the hands of the city's latest serial killer. Except, guess what, he didn't do it."

I gave Sinnott credit—as much as his eyes told me he wanted me dead, he didn't take a swing at me, didn't sic his guard dog on me, didn't even interrupt. Like any good politician, he let me talk, sucking in every bit of information I was willing to give him.

I gave him everything I had.

"Now you might be asking yourself, 'How does this guy get the right to say he *knows* that the Outliner didn't kill my wife?' I'll be happy to tell you."

Coming closer to his face, narrowing the boundary he'd set for us, I raised my voice as well, telling him,

"First, the police don't believe it. Second, my own experts don't believe it. And third, guess what, the Outliner doesn't believe it, either."

His eyes grew again. He blinked despite a conscious effort not to. Poking him in the chest with an index finger, I kept going, blowing steam the entire time.

"You wanted to know what the question was I wanted answered—I'll tell you. I want to know who killed your wife. Period. And believe me, I'm going to find out. If it wasn't you, if you didn't have anything to do with it, you won't have to worry about the tapes. I'll personally turn everything I have over to you and let you and your children get on with your lives. But," I warned him, bringing my poking finger up into his face,

"If I do find out you had something to do with it, trust me—I'll be doing a lot more than releasing tapes."

He stared at me for a moment, finally collapsing back into his chair. His arm snaked across to where he'd left his drink, dragging it back to its master while I headed for the door. Mike was there ahead of me, ready to open it. I took the opportunity to study his face again, reflecting the split-second glance against what had just been said. He remained impassive, which told me two things. First, I was sure he had had nothing to do with Mrs. Sinnott's death, that he even held no opinion as to whether or not Andy did. And second, that he was not emotionally involved here, that he was just a man doing a job—a fact that in the long run made him more dangerous than most of the punks I run into. I was just about to pass through the doorway when Sinnott called out.

"Mr. Hagee . . . ?"

I turned, looking in his direction, continuing to adjust my scarf. I could see he hadn't done more than sip his drink. Holding it before him, again moving it in its previous circular holding pattern, he said,

"I didn't kill my wife. To put it so someone like you can understand it—if I was going to kill my wife, or anyone for that matter, I wouldn't have done such a fucking stupid job of it. If you don't think I realized long before you got here how bad all of this makes me look, then you're not giving me very much credit."

He took a sip of his drink while what little warmth there was in his home continued to race out the open door. Coming back to me, he continued,

"I don't say this to get you to stop looking at me as a suspect. Frankly, I really don't care what you do. But besides the obvious fact that someone who, at least once upon a time, meant a great deal to me has been murdered—the sooner you or somebody else discovers who really did kill Vivian, the sooner you and everyone else nosing around will stop thinking of me as a murderer."

Taking another breath, trying to find the right voice to ask his question, one not so much designed to trick me, but get across exactly what he was trying to convey, he asked,

"I'd like that. This all"—his hands motioned to some other larger picture to which I wasn't privy—"it's just too much for me. I'm tired of it, and I just want to get past it all."

Then, after another breath, he finally asked,

"What I'm trying to ask you is . . . would you consider taking a retainer from me in this matter . . . to help you conduct your investigation?"

Maybe it was a bribe—maybe it wasn't. Right then, not caring one way or the other, I told him,

"No, sir. I don't think so. I don't want your money. All in all, from where I stand I think I may have gotten too much of it already."

CHAPTER 17

I SAW NO reason to go back to the office after pulling away from Sinnott's. It was late in the afternoon—I was tired of doing my job for the day. I was also cold and hungry and too exhausted to bear the thought of fighting my way through the traffic around me all the way back to my office. Whatever I might find there, and I knew it wouldn't be much—if anything at all—wasn't worth the aggravation.

Having drunk too much for the amount of food I'd taken in was wearing on me to the point where my apartment seemed like the best place to be. Working my way down to the Brooklyn-Queens Expressway, I hooked the Skylark out and into the erratic traffic flow, grateful to be a clear shot away from home.

I followed the other cars headed in that direction, sticking to the right-hand lane, allowing the current of the automobiles flowing all around me to move me along without having to consciously think about what I was doing. All veteran drivers have the ability; most use it without knowing it.

I hung there in the slow lane, drifting along, listening to a New Age music cassette. It was a straight music/no vocals tape Hubert had made for me of a guy named Andreas Vollenweider—just stuff no one could quite figure out so they labeled it New Age for lack of something better. Most of the time I like music a little livelier, but not on the highway. Any good insurance investigator can

give you the statistics on how many car radios are tuned
to hard rock stations at the moment of deadly impact.
For those who can't guess, the answer is "quite a lot."
Myself, I like to keep calm on the highway. As a grizzled
old state trooper, the first guy who ever gave me any
practical advice on driving, told me back when I was
fifteen,

"There are eighty-five million murderous assholes
loose on the roads of America and . . . they all want
to . . . kill you. Every last one of them . . . all they
want to do is . . . kill you. And any time you take a hand
off the wheel, start keeping time to the radio, talk to
your girlfriend—whatever—you give every single one
of them another opportunity to erase you from the face
of the earth—to render you down to nothing more than
a grease spot and an obituary notice."

The only fault I've found over the years with what
he had to say was that I think the odds have gotten
worse. All of which had me staying in the right-hand
lane. I can travel fast when I want to—weave in and
out of traffic like a lunatic with the best of them—
when I have a good reason. Traveling home for food
and warmth over slush-scummed roads with alcohol still
dogging my breath was nowhere near a good reason.

To pass the time, I juggled what I knew in my head.
Vivian Sinnott's death was a phony. I was convinced—
had been since the Outliner had told all of us at the
Post—someone had framed the stupid bastard. The question was . . . "Who?" Who else besides Andrew Sinnott
would have wanted to do it? And, more to the point, who
besides him that might have wanted to even *could* have
done it? Working in the D.A.'s office, he could have
accessed the police files and come up with the murder
as it was committed.

But the problem I had with that was that I didn't think
he did it. I hadn't given up on my other convictions, that
he was a cold, miserable calculator, measuring everyone out against the rule mark of how useful they were

to him—a self-centered, self-indulgent egomaniac without the slightest concern for anyone around him. But—something a lot of people don't seem to have learned—just because someone is a rotten human being doesn't necessarily make them guilty of every crime imaginable. As much as I would have liked to trash Sinnott for the murder of his wife, the little voice inside was telling me that he wasn't the killer. In truth, I was halfway convinced that he didn't set it up and that he didn't even approve someone else setting it up.

As I turned off at the Ocean Parkway exit, grateful for the uneventful ride and for being only a couple of miles from home, I tried to figure where that left me. What I came up with was that that left me blind in the dark. I knew I was nailed to the wall, looking at the beginning of a monstrously complicated murder investigation I had nowhere near the resources to undertake.

If Andy Sinnott had nothing to do with the murder, then I had to admit it could be the work of anyone—a worker under Sinnott trying to make their life easier, a lover of Sinnott's looking to clear the way for him or herself, an ex-lover of Sinnott's looking to make it appear as if he had done it to get back at him, the partner of one of Sinnott's lovers looking to make it look as if he had done it to . . .

It all started getting a little too involved, with no string worth following any more than any of the others. To get a clue I would have to stage massive interviews . . . people throughout the city government would have to be questioned for scandalous dirt, something the city wasn't about to allow me to do. And, I asked myself as I turned onto Sixty-fifth Street, why would I want to? What was I thinking, getting this involved with a dead client just because I saw something in her husband that I didn't like?

Wheeling my way around several large, blackened chunks of ice, most likely broken off from some delivery truck, I tried to remind that barking in the back of my brain that wanted me to become the Lone Ranger that avenging the helpless wasn't my job. As cruel and cold and, well, Andrew Sinnott–like as it sounded, my job was doing those things people paid me to do if I decided they were legal enough. And, I also reminded myself, since I had no one acting as my client in this matter, how long did I think it would take the cops to shut me down—most likely hard and fast—for overstepping my authority? I answered myself out loud,

"About one New York minute, pal."

And that, I thought, was that. I made my turn onto Avenue O, sat at the West Sixth Street traffic light like I did every day, made my turn onto West Seventh, and began hunting for a parking spot—all without any more mental battles. Common sense was finally winning, reminding me that I had done my best—if Andy himself hadn't murdered Vivian, then how far did my obligations extend?

Finding a spot only a half block from my apartment building, I parked and then started the trek back to my building through the icy shock of wind tearing through the street, continuing my mental juggling over the Sinnotts, but also beginning to wonder what I would have for dinner, and when I would walk Balto. Wait for the wind to die down or take him right away in the hopes the cold would force him to hurry himself along for once? A stupid notion, I pointed out to myself—Balto, being a German shepherd/husky mix, wasn't about to get cold before I did.

Thus, by the time I reached the elevator, I had my whole evening planned. Reheat the macaroni and cheese in the fridge, fry up a couple of the pork chops I hadn't gotten to yet, let the mutt chew up the bones and lick clean the plate, and then take him for his walk late . . . that way I could get back in time for the big Jucha/Mayo bout. True, I told myself, I'd have to listen to it on the radio, but I still wanted to know how it came out. It felt good to have everything planned so orderly. Unfortunately, the plan fizzled as soon as I got to my apartment.

Taped to the front door was a note from Elba. It told me that Rickie was home and would I please—*please*— come down as soon as I got home? Sighing, I went inside only long enough to shrug my way out of my scarf and hat and coat, knock Balto around for a few seconds— which meant getting knocked around by him in return— and then scratch him in between the ears, promising to get back to fix us both some grub as soon as possible.

Walking down to the floor below, I wondered at how I get myself into these messes. Why couldn't Elba's father do the right thing—just once? Why was I going down to lecture this kid about selling drugs? Beyond that, what did I think I was going to say to him that was going to change his mind when his own father was encouraging him to do it?

Each step grew heavier as I walked, the echo of my shoes against the marble of the old building's stairwell, harsh, lonely sounds punctuating my negative feelings about my good-guy tendencies.

"Sometimes," I said just under my breath, "I think you're watching too many cop shows."

I had to wonder—trying to solve crimes I wasn't being paid to solve, that, indeed, I had no reason to solve, lecturing seven-year-olds about selling drugs—when had I become everyone's guardian angel for Christ's sake? Then, as I hit the lower landing and started closing on the Santorio apartment, I reminded myself that going in with that kind of an attitude wasn't going to help anybody.

If I had any intention of helping Rickie at all, for any reason other than it was convenient to go down and mouth some platitudes so his sister would be happy, I figured I had better start to get some ideas in order. So far I'd said "sure, sure" and played the big man for a little girl, but I hadn't actually come up with anything that was going to do the job she asked me to do.

That, of course, started the back of my mind screaming at me again. It cursed me for wasting time chasing
around Andrew Sinnott when I could have been looking
for a real client or at least getting ready to help the friend
that had come to me for real help. Elba was looking for
me to save her brother from the evil infesting her family,
not for me to come in and do a bad imitation of McGruff
the Crime Dog.

Knocking on their door, I pulled myself up out of the
slouch my bad mood was putting me into, determined to
see my way through whatever happened as best I could.
I owed it to Elba and her whole family. If, as she had
told me earlier, Rickie's contacts were storing volatile
chemicals in their apartment, then I owed it to everyone
living in the building, including Balto and myself. Thus
armed, I figured I was ready for whatever was waiting
for me inside.

As the door opened, and I caught a look at the Colt
10mm aimed at my chest, I realized I'd conned myself
again.

CHAPTER 18

"YOU LOOK SURPRISED, Me'stor Hagee."

I was looking at a Hispanic youth—twenty, twenty-two tops. No relative of the Santorios I'd ever met—five-ten, one forty-five tops, black hair, razor cut, light brown eyes, slightly hooked nose, fair enough skin. The accent he was playing for laughs. The 10mm was serious. It wasn't the only serious gun in sight, either.

"Beebee," ordered another punk, one slightly better dressed but cut from the same mold. "Tell our guest to come in and join us."

The warning alarms went off in my head—loud and shrill. Although I couldn't put my finger on anything tangible, I knew the minute the door shut behind me I was a dead man. Noise from farther back in the apartment let me know at least some members of Elba's family were still alive. Probably all of them, I figured. I was the one they wanted, for whatever reason. I was the only one in trouble. If they were going to injure any of the Santorios at all, it wouldn't be until after I was dead. Which, my brain screamed, meant that for everybody's sake I'd better not end up dead.

"You heard the man," said the one at the door, waving toward the back of the apartment with his weapon. "Come in and join us . . . guest."

Smearing the number five goofy grin over my face that they taught us back in my Military Intelligence days, the one that said, "Sure, I'm harmless" the loudest, I gave a shrug and took one step forward, shifting my foot at the last second to come down on the toes of the punk in the doorway. I crunched the step down hard—grinding my heel—grabbing for his 10mm at the same time. Then, while my left hand closed around the weapon, I shot my right under it, burying its bent fingers in Beebee's throat. The scream he had been in the middle of cut off sharply, replaced by a harsh, sputtering cough that made it sound as if I'd done some real damage.

I didn't have time to look. The instant my fingers had touched the Colt I'd backpedaled out of the doorway, dragging the weapon behind me as Beebee started his blood-coated gagging. I turned and raced back up the stairs, knowing as I did so I had no hopes of getting into my apartment before they were on me. I could hear Spanish bursting in the hall below as I hit my own floor. Continuing up the stairs, I continued on up to the roof. As usual, the exit to the outside was unlocked. I went through, my eyes scanning the lumpy expanse of tar paper stretching away before me for anything I could use to jam the door closed. Nothing came to view.

The icy wind howling over the rooftops slashed at me, instantly penetrating through the pores of my clothes. I moved away from the door, looking for either an avenue of escape or a defensible position from which to make my stand. The fire escapes were out . . . there was no way I could get down one fast enough before they found me. Ricochets have a way of chewing up a guy's luck.

I'd only been on the roof for a few seconds, but already I was chilled straight through. I bit down against it, putting my mind on something other than the cold, hearing my old Special Forces D.I. Major Rice's friendly voice barking in the back of my mind:

"Forget the cold! Don't try to ignore it—forget it! You can't shoot straight when you're shaking and blowing on your hands. Put the cold somewhere else—remember it in the summer—but forget it now!"

We stood in the Virginia snow in our bare feet, wet ice sleeting down against our skin, soaking our underwear, squeezing off round after round, praying for the bull's-eye that would let us get back inside. It took a while, but finally our hate for Rice—hate for his mustache, hate for his accent—hate for everything about him filled us with a red warmth that steadied our hands and hung his face at the center of the target, drawing our bullets like magnets. I was the first one to score and the first one inside. Later, when we were all inside, the Iron Man told me,

"Got your fires up fast, didn't you?"

"Yes, sir," I answered through gritted teeth, my look letting him know it was my feelings toward him that did all the stoking.

"Good," he told me, his look letting me know that he already understood. "Don't lose that. That kind of hate will keep you alive."

Trying to keep his advice in mind, I kept moving, pushing the cold away from me, checking the 10mm ammo supply—full clip, convenient—as I did. After that, I cursed to myself the fact that despite the dozens of twists and bumps and ledges breaking the flatness of the roof, there simply were no good points from where I could make a stand. I had no idea if the guys chasing me were near the door yet—the howling wind cutting through the icy night was covering any noise they might be making.

I figured they were smart enough to only send one guy out the door at a time. I'd never get a cluster, and even if I did, I had no idea how many of them there were.

"Damn!"

I shouted the curse out loud, spitting it into the wind with disgust. My quick review had shown me that I only had two choices—get up on top of the small roomlike affair that served as the exit for the stairwell or go over the side of the building down the fume tube running up the north wall from the chimney of the private house next door. The stairwell roof was chancy. If I didn't get everybody right away I would be trapped—stuck in a spot from which they'd be able to pick me off without any trouble.

On the other hand, if they caught up to me going down the fume tube before I got to the bottom—*if* the ancient, rusting funnel didn't just tear right out of the side of the building—I would be just as dead. I was about to make my choice when the gang gave me a new fact to consider.

The small skylight on the top of the stairwell room blew apart as gunfire from within turned it into noise, flames, and flying glass. My decision basically made for me, I shoved the 10mm into my pants and then dashed for the side of the building. Reaching the edge, I paused for just a second, wrapping my fingers around the ivory dragons I was still wearing. Then, spending only one of my precious seconds asking Git'jing's gods of the home and hearth for a blessing or two, I hurled myself over the edge, making a second prayer on the way over that the rotting tube would hold together.

Hanging on to the lip of the building, I grabbed on to the funnel, discovering that the rust had done its work thoroughly. Although the looping braces that held the tube in place were still solid, the tubing itself was shot. Sections of it fell into red crumbs, blowing away with the sleet wherever I touched it. Trusting to luck, I let go of the roof edge, letting the first anchor brace take my weight. It held.

Above me I heard angry voices cursing in Spanish. Over the wind I picked out at least three different voices answering a central leader. A minimum of four, I reminded myself as my weight tested the third brace. It held. I continued to work my way down the side of the building, my progress feeling painfully slow.

My brain read off figures to me, trying to convince me I would be all right. My building is only six stories—it pointed out—the house next door is two stories. Its slanted attic room made that more like two and three-quarters. I could jump for it after just two sto-

ries if I really had to—just eighteen, twenty feet—
that's not much—that's not far—I could do it . . . it
was possible . . .

Above me, the voices that had been growing faint
started getting closer. I knew they would waste time
checking the fire escapes first. I also knew I had the
darkness and the wind and even the cold on my side.
I reminded myself, however, that they had a minimum
of four weapons to my one, and extra ammunition, and
a grudge.

The two sides of my brain keeping their separate tally
sheets, I stretched my foot down to the eighth brace—
it held. I rested my full weight on it and started for the
next, tubing crumpling and falling away in all directions
with every contact. My eyes and mouth filled with flakes
of rusted metal. Ignoring it all, I sent my foot out again,
struggling toward the tenth brace. I found it. It held.

I was halfway down the building, almost down to the
next roof when disaster hit. The brace at the end of the
funnel wasn't up to it. The first to receive the escaping
heat over the decades, it was far more brittle than the
rest of the tube. As I tried to put my weight on it, the
last twenty feet just ripped out of the wall, braces and
all, crashing onto the roof below.

Above me, the gunmen gathered toward the noise. I
could hear them coming, but could not make out what
they had to say. Hanging in the shadow of what was left
of the funnel, I looked up, trying to see if I could spot
anyone. I couldn't—the swirling, windblown snow cut
me off completely. Then suddenly I looked up through
the funnel itself and saw a head just coming into sight.
acting without thought I jerked the Colt from my belt
and fired upward. At least one of the shells caught the
gunman in the face, the abrupt cutoff of his screams
letting me know I'd just lowered the odds by twenty-five
percent.

Shots rang out through the night from the rooftop
above, some striking the roof below me, some the yard.

Letting go of my handhold on the brace, I kicked off from the wall, landing on the near side of the roof below. I hit on my side—badly, painfully—then rolled down to slam into the wall of my own building. Shots continued to ring out from above, but now they were getting closer, my amigos now all having some idea of where I was.

I sucked in a deep breath despite my aching ribs and then let loose a burst—not so much hoping to hit anyone as much as trying to make them step back. They did—fast. Taking the moment the spent ammunition gained me, I ran across the slant of the neighboring roof, using my building's wall as a brace, then I disappeared under the branches of the tree growing out of my neighbor's front yard.

Once I'd reached that cover, I lowered myself as quickly as I could through the branches from the ledging of their roof to the top of their front porch and then finally dropped onto their front walkway. Getting into the gutter, I ran down West Seventh Street to my car, purposely firing a few shots at the roof to draw their attention.

The gunmen returned my fire, but only briefly. They stopped long before I reached my car, giving me some hope that the bit of a plan I'd concocted while making my way to the street might actually work. For once the taken-for-granted paranoia of all New Yorkers was working in my favor. Because I'd naturally locked my apartment behind me even just to go one floor below, I had my keys with me. Unlocking the Skylark, I climbed in and slammed the door, shutting the chilling wind out behind me.

Grateful for the respite, but knowing I had no time to waste, I kicked the hulk's V8 to life again, cursing the men trying to kill me, this time for making me give up my parking place. Pulling out into the street, I checked my mirrors, looking to see if anyone was pouring out of my building. No one was in sight by the time I made the corner.

Making an illegal left, I jerked the Skylark out onto Bay Parkway, making the next left at West Eighth Street, luckily just catching the end of the green light. I couldn't afford any wasted seconds. Blasting down Eighth, I curled the left at Avenue O, and then started cruising slowly down West Seventh, hunting my pals.

I inched along slowly, scanning both the sidewalks and the cars parked next to them. There was nothing suspicious about this—no one in New York thinks twice about cars prowling their neighborhoods. Everyone knows it's signifying either someone looking for parking or thieves—two things of which the city has plenty. I passed my apartment building with still no sign of my attackers. Then, two thirds of the way down the block, I finally spotted my pals.

They had their coats on now, which meant they'd returned to the Santorio apartment before coming out. There were five of them all together—one being helped by the others, another being dragged. They were moving as fast as they could, heading straight for some objective, most likely the vehicle in which they'd come. Sliding back into the same parking place I'd just left, I grabbed up my captured Colt, exited, and then jumped out onto the sidewalk in front of them.

"Hey, boys, long time no see."

As two gun hands started to come up, I warned them, "Not bright."

It didn't matter. These were cowboys, faster, tougher, meaner than anyone in the world. I put shots in the first's head, the second's chest. This knocked them off their feet, sending their dead companion down as well. The one who was still whole, helping their wounded along, screamed at me,

"Don't kill us! Please! Oh, sweet Virgin, oh, God, oh, pleasepleasepleaseplease—pleaseeeeeeeee!"

"I don't want to kill anybody, junior. We can all get out of this real easy."

"Please! Please. Please. Please."

I tried to comfort him again, letting him know I didn't want to kill anyone, that I just wanted some answers. Unfortunately, what he and I wanted were two different things. Before I could get close enough to disarm him, both he and his wounded friend tried to get their guns out. It was pitifully slow and awkward. I had no trouble gunning both of them down, cursing them for their stupidity.

Wiping the 10mm clean of any fingerprints I had gotten on it—including the clip—I lay the weapon among the bodies and then started back for my building. I hadn't wanted to kill them—at least not all of them. That just kept me in the dark as to where they had come from and why. Without them, all I had was an attack on my life with little idea as to what made me so important. And five killers, even five relatively fumbling, bad ones, are a lot of killers for someone to send after one lone guy.

Realizing, though, that something more was up than I had previously thought, I let myself back into my apartment building, getting through the front door and into the elevator even as I heard the first sirens coming from off in the distance. I was freezing, shaking and rubbing myself, hoping no one was looking through their peepholes to see me coatless in the lobby. I knew if I could make it back to my apartment without being seen that I could beat the rap for the five bodies the cops would soon find. With luck, I knew it was possible they might not even identify our building as the initial source of the trouble.

Thinking about things as I rode upward, I smiled to myself. I'd been chased by a pack of punks trying to kill me, and then maneuvered into risking my life in a crazy stunt that in itself almost finished me off for them. Then I was forced to kill all of them, leaving me with no idea why any of it had happened in the first place. But, I told myself, at least I didn't lose my parking place. A minor accomplishment, sure, but in New York City, certainly a valid one.

CHAPTER 19

I SAT IN my apartment, nursing a black coffee, Elba and three of her four siblings with me. The two youngest ones were asleep in my bedroom, the third watching over them. Elba and I sat in the living/dining room/kitchen part of my home, waiting for an aunt of hers she had called. They had all been in my apartment when I got back to it, having gone there the minute the gunmen had chased me out of theirs. As we waited, Elba and I pieced together what had happened.

Elba had never actually *seen* Rickie that day—he had only called home earlier. When Elba had talked to him, begged him to talk with me that night, he'd said "sure." Then he'd told his boss he was getting some heat and the boss had sent over the welcoming committee I'd found at the Santorios' apartment. That much of the story Elba had gotten from the gunmen. They had told her and the other kids not to worry, that they weren't there to hurt anyone, just to get rid of an annoyance for Rickie.

Elba was fairly sure they really did not mean anyone in the family any harm. Apparently Rickie was a top-notch Dreamer salesman, one who could handle his territory and those under him with amazing adroitness, which made him one for which the boss was willing to do special favors. Like new sneakers, designer sunglasses, or chauffeured limo rides to grade school. Killing me was just one of those favors. Elba had no doubts about that, either.

"I'm so sorry, Jack," she told me, trying not to cry again. She brought over the pot from the stove to top off my cup. As she poured, I told her,

"Nothin' to worry about, sweetheart."

"But, but, I almost got you killed. I am so stupid. I never thought . . ."

"No," I interrupted. "No, you didn't. None of this makes any normal sense. I can guarantee you that if it was your father who was putting pressure on Rickie, this isn't the tack they would have taken."

"But, why . . . ?"

"Because there's something going on that we don't know about. Rickie's boss didn't react this way because he was told some guy from upstairs wanted to talk to Rickie . . . it was because he was told a private detective wanted to talk to Rickie. That still doesn't mean we made a mistake."

I looked into her little-girl eyes, so tired of being mother for her sisters and brothers, so tired of trying to be the glue her family so desperately needed. Working at keeping my voice soft, I told her,

"You see, normally such news wouldn't mean anything to these people. They know what they're doing, and they know everyone else knows about it, too. No one hires private detectives to investigate drug dealers— why would they? All that someone could find out is what they already know—that they're drug dealers."

"So why did they try to kill you, Jack?"

"Because we scared someone. We didn't mean to, but we did. When you asked me to talk to Rickie, and he told them he was going to be hassled by a private detective, they looked at him for what he is . . . a seven-year-old boy. No matter how street smart he may have gotten, they saw him as a leak. They didn't see it as me trying to help *him,* they saw it as me coming after *them.*"

"Who, Jack? Who are you talking about?"

"I don't know, sweetheart. That's what I'm going to have to find out."

I started to throw a few more words of comfort on the fire when I was interrupted by a heavy banging on the door. The sound of it was crisp and authoritative— not something I expected from her aunt. I tiptoed across the room, holding my finger to my lips to warn Elba to silence, Balto following at my heels. I checked my door's security eye, seeing two policemen in uniform standing out in the hall. I recognized the taller of the two—not one of my favorite people. He was a cop I was fairly sure was—if not out-and-out crooked—at the very least well bent . . . one who worked out of a precinct known for its shady goings on, run by Captain Mike Fisher, a man also known to be more than just a little loose with the rules. Opening the door, I said,

"Why, Officer Clements, as I live and breathe. It's about time somebody got here."

I knew the only way to play the following was to act as if I knew nothing at all. Putting on my "worried citizen, Jack Hagee" expression, I asked,

"What the hell was going on outside? I must have counted sixty shots. and a lot of that was automatic weapons fire. A *lot* of it. What the hell . . . ?"

Clements took it from there, his manner and his eyes letting me know he wasn't buying it. Sticking his hand up in the air, he warned me,

"Clam up, Hagee."

Balto stood up and made a show of backing off a pace into a crouch. Not making a sound, but baring his fangs slightly, he made both the cops uncomfortable enough for them to start fumbling at their holstered weapons.

"You keep that fuckin' mutt under control."

"He's under control."

"I don't like him," said the other, shorter one, his name tag reading "Sohl."

"That's okay . . . he doesn't like you, either. Now, let's get past the noise and down to business. I'm all clammed up, Clements. Whaddaya want to know?"

"Who's the kid?" he asked, pointing to Elba.

"She cleans my place. When she heard the shooting, she got scared. Her father wasn't home so she came here."

"From where?"

"What's that got to do with anything?"

"Answer the question."

"You answer mine," I told him. Clements looked me over, hand still on his gun. His eyes flashed to his partner, checking for something I couldn't discern. I pulled myself up a bit straighter, putting my line of vision above Clements's, forcing him to crane his head to look me in the eye. Sensing that things might be coming to a head, Balto left my side, starting to make a circle of the two cops. He brushed the back of their legs with his tail, daring them to start things. As Sohl started to prepare a kick, I warned him,

"For your own good, pal, I wouldn't do that."

"You threatening me?"

He threw the question/answer at me, his voice filled with relief. That gave me his number. He was one of those cops who relies on the fact that police scrutiny means trouble for anyone—the innocent along with the guilty—to get him the respect his eyes told you he didn't deserve. He liked me better as a target . . . dogs don't understand empty threats. They like everybody but troublemakers. No easier a target than Balto, however, I stared him down, my sneer telling him his badge alone wasn't enough to make me dance. I answered his question at the same time.

"Not me, pal," I told him, keeping my stare up until I forced him to blink.

"Would I threaten you two punks with the fact that that dog could chew your asses up all by himself—not to mention how easy you'd be to handle if I helped him? I wouldn't do that. That wouldn't be nice."

Clements pulled his service revolver then. Balto started a low growl in response. His hand almost steady, Clements ordered,

"You better call that thing off, motherfucker, or I'll kill it right now."

"Why don't you try?" I asked him.

"What?" Clements backed up a step, staring at me as if I'd lost my mind.

"I said, 'Why don't you try?' Go on, go ahead, you punk. You think you're faster than he is? Prove it. You, too, Sohl. Get your gun out, too."

Both men stared at me; both backed up a step. They were clearly at a loss, not knowing what to now make of the situation which they'd been sure they were going to be in charge of. Continuing the pressure, I sneered,

"Sure, I'll have some fancy explaining to do . . . I might even get hurt. But you two, I promise you, you'll both be dead . . . in as painful a set of ways as that dog and his big teeth, and me, can make them."

Clements's hand started to shake more violently. Things just weren't working out as he had planned them. Sohl went to back him up, started pulling his revolver out. Balto upped his throaty growls a few decibles, freezing the second cop's draw halfway out of its holster.

"Tough guys—tough talk," I told them. "Blowhard shits like you two make me sick."

Balto started clacking his big teeth together, filling his growling with a gurgling liquid sound. That was enough for Sohl. Releasing his hold on his half-drawn pistol, he waved his hands in front of him, saying,

"I'm out of this. I'm out of this."

Clements, knowing the only time he was going to have to act was right then, started to shift his aim from the indeterminate spot between myself and Balto toward the one hundred twenty pounds of muscle and fang just praying for an excuse.

Cutting them both off, though, I stepped forward and slammed Clements backward, taking the gun from his hand as he toppled onto my couch. Balto, sensing I didn't need any further help with mine, squared off with Sohl, letting the cop know that his choice to back off had been a wise one.

Holding his gun next to my head, pointed toward the ceiling, I told Clements,

"Your chances at pulling whatever you wanted to pull have just all disappeared. Now you're going to tell me what the hell you wanted here, and you're going to tell me fast, or you're going to wish you never knocked on my door."

"I—I don't know what you mean," he lied. "We didn't come here to pull anything. There was a disturbance reported at this address. I knew you lived here—just figured you had something to do with it. I—I . . . guess I was wrong."

I wanted to push him further, like I would have any other lying bastard who'd just threatened to kill me, but I knew I couldn't. You can't rough up a cop. No cops. I was in bad enough for what had happened so far. The only things I had going for me were that Clements and Sohl were obviously dirty and that although I'd made them look really bad, there'd been no one around but Elba and Balto to see it. Handing Clements his gun back, I filled my voice with apologetic embarrassment, saying,

"Oh, well then . . . ah, I guess I was, too. I'm sorry, but with all the shooting, and then you and your partner going for your guns and all, I guess we both just overreacted."

Helping him up off the couch, I searched his eyes, looking to see what his response to mine was going to be. I was creating an out for both of us, one where we could both escape an ugly mess without too many complications. I didn't expect him to buy my story any more than I was buying his. All I wanted was for him to use it as an excuse to stop and get out before one of us got in deeper than they needed to. Luck was on my side.

"Yeah, yeah," he agreed, running his hand over his weapon before he sheepishly slid it back into his holster.

I let go a sigh of relief. Clements mumbled along for a while longer, letting me know how close I'd come to the edge—blah blah blah-fucking-blah—and I assured him I was grateful a set of good cops like he and his partner had come along. As the door shut behind them, I moved into action.

"Elba," I shouted, "get everyone ready to move out of here."

"Move?" she questioned, coming back into the room with Theresa, her youngest sister, cradled in her arms. "To where, Jack? What's going on?"

"I'm not sure what's happening, but I don't think we'd better be here when those goons get back with reinforcements."

Seeing Elba's eyes grow wider than they already had when it looked like she was going to have to watch her boss and favorite puppy fight two cops to the death, I stopped to explain. Dropping to one knee, I took her by the shoulder and said,

"I'm sorry for this all, honey. I have to admit that I don't know why those two dil—ah, bozos were here, but it's not good for one of us and I have no intention of finding out which one of us it is the hard way. Get some coats and extra clothes for the kids . . . we're getting out of here."

She handed me the half-asleep three-year-old, letting me know she would be back as soon as she could. Then, taking the oldest of the boys and Balto with her, she headed out into the hall. Holding Theresa in one hand, I got on the horn with the other, punching in the number of one of my poker partners, William Norman, known to all the regulars as the Li'l Doc. I got his machine, but luckily found him hiding behind it.

"Sorry, Jack," he told me. "Can't be too careful these days."

"Quite all right, buddy," I told him. "I'm in one of those beggars-can't-be-choosers modes right now. You'll forgive me if I jump right to the point."

"What's up, Jack?"

The Doc had put me back together a couple of months earlier after the worst beating I'd ever taken. We were both guys from small towns who might have ended up in New York for different reasons, but both held the same opinion about the dump. It's a bond shared by most city residents.

I told him what had happened in Elba's apartment, and on the roof, and then in my own apartment with Fisher's goons. Since the Doc not only disliked Fisher's precinct all on his own, but also enjoyed what he called "having some peripheral interest in my cases," he didn't hesitate when I asked if I could crash in his Manhattan digs with four Spanish children and their aunt.

"You're a peach, Bill," I told him.

"This aunt isn't going to be freaked out by having her little nieces and nephews around a practicing homosexual, is she?"

"I don't know," I answered honestly. "But she's met Hubert and she still lets Elba work for me, so she's got to be some kind of tolerant."

"Right you are," laughed the Doc. "Anything I should get before you arrive?"

"I don't know," I answered in all honesty. "Go out and get some Yoo-Hoos and potato chips."

"For the babies?" he asked.

"No," I told him, "for us. We'll take the kids to McDonald's."

"I'll warm up a deck," he told me.

"For the babies?" I joked.

"Sure," he kidded back. "Can't start 'em too young."

"Great," I said. "You're going to be a big help."

"See you when you get here."

So saying, the Doc rang off, giving me a chance to make some more calls. I tried to catch Rich at home and at the office but ended up having to leave messages in both places. Then, in the hopes she might know where he was, I tried Sally's number, catching her at the office. Unfortunately, she didn't know where Rich was, either. To explain, I gave her the forty-five-second version of what had happened since I'd talked to her last. She asked me,

"Is this as bad as it sounds?"

"It's starting to look that way."

"I take it," she said, "that you've already made note of the fact that your gang was the wrong color?"

"You mean," I answered, my arm falling asleep from the weight of the sleeping Theresa, "the fact that Black Dreamer is supposed to be a Chinese exclusive and yet I was attacked by Hispanics? Yeah, that little discrepancy wasn't wasted on me."

"Any theories?"

"Enough to make my little detective brain boil, but nothing I could give you to chew on." Then suddenly, before I could continue, Elba and her brother returned with everyone's coats, Balto calm at their side. I waved her past, using sign language to indicate she should get everyone dressed as fast as she could. I handed the now-snoring Theresa over to her brother, and then I returned to Sally, telling her,

"Look, sweetheart, I've got to get going. Try and track Rich down, tell him everything. I'll get back in touch as soon as I can." Looking at my watch, I asked her, "Where will you be in, say, two hours?"

"Glued to my seat. You, you just go. I'll be here—I won't go anywhere. And if I can find Rich, I'll get him here, too."

At that moment Elba's long overdue aunt started pounding on my front door, screaming for her babies. Elba ran to let her in, Balto bouncing around her feet the whole time. I started to pull on my own coat, still talking into the phone as I did so.

"We're all here, sweetheart. I've got to leave now before anyone tries to make another pass at us."

"You take care of yourself," she told me.

A few funny answers I could have made flashed through my head, but I avoided them, telling Sally,

"Don't worry, I'll be fine. I've been doing this kind of shit for a long time."

"Go," she told me. "Just get going. I'm going to be a nervous wreck for the next two hours no matter what comforting nonsense you try and shovel at me. Don't waste time you might not have."

My throat went dry for a moment, my vocal chords freezing even though my brain had a thousand things it wanted to say. Listening to Sally's words for a second, though, I realized she was right, and that my body knew it was time to shut up and get the hell out of the area even if my brain was working on a less immediate agenda. Knowing she understood, I fought my way past the less immediate and said,

"Two hours."

Then I hung up, recradling the phone. Buttoning my coat while taking a head count, I shoved my .38, its holster, two boxes of ammo, and a box of Balto's favorite dog yummies into an overnight bag I keep ready in my hall closet for just such moments. Pulling my hat down tight over my head, I scanned the room quickly, my eyes finally returning to where I'd started . . . the phone. I thought of Sally sitting in her office, wishing I could call her back and say something that could keep her from worrying. Knowing, however, that the only thing that would do that would be the news that I was no longer where anyone could find me, I started herding the kids out the door and down the hall.

As Balto shepherded the five of them down to the elevator, I hit the lights and pulled my keys. Locking the door behind me, I said to myself in a whisper,

"Well, this is about the worst you've gotten yourself into in a long time."

Then, as I started down the hall to the elevator, the car hit our floor, stopping with a noise that startled Theresa out of her sleep. Instantly she began bawling, a noise that set all of her relatives to clucking around her and the usually unflappable Balto to barking. As I shushed at everyone, trying to get them into the elevator, I groaned over the noise,

"A *long* time."

CHAPTER 20

THE DRIVE INTO town wasn't a nightmare, but it wasn't something I'd want to do every day. Elba, cradling little Theresa in her arms, Balto, and myself were in the front seat, Auntie and the other two kids were in the back with the extra clothes. Trying to keep our charges from dwelling on what all had happened, Auntie and I let them get more than a little out of hand. It did keep them distracted, but it was also enough to get me thinking about checking into a sanitarium. I don't know what it did for Auntie.

It took us roughly forty-five minutes to get to the Doc's apartment. As I expected, everything was ready for us when we got there. He'd gotten his sleeping bags out of building storage and borrowed a few from some of the other campers in his building. The older kids and Balto and I got the couches and the floor . . . Auntie and Theresa got the guest room. He also had a spread ready. When we arrived he was still unloading it onto the dining-room table—a half-dozen large packages of cold cuts, bagels, chips, cookies, candy bars, milk, assorted juices and sodas, boxes of cereal, peanut butter, jelly, boxes of elbow macaroni, et cetera.

"Bill," I asked, just a little amazed, "did I remind you not to go overboard?"

"Hey," he said, mock-defensively, "this isn't a lot, this isn't excessive—is it?"

Picking up a two-pound package of fruit-filled Cadbury chocolates, I told him,

"Well, even if their aunt lets them eat everything you bought, which I'm not sure about, you've got enough stuff here for a month."

"Hey," answered the Doc in his own defense, "I've seen Balto go through fifty pounds of macaroni and cheese at one sitting. All by himself."

The Doc then began clawing the air as if pulling food toward his mouth, leaking garbled noises something like those that six or seven starving wolves might make as they ripped apart a deer. He carried on for a moment until he cracked himself up, finally saying,

"That's your mutt, my pal—Balto, the four-legged garbage disposal."

I laughed in spite of myself and then helped him finish getting all of his groceries stowed away. After that, I kept the kids entertained while their aunt and the Doc got a snack together for them. We all sat around his living room feasting, all the adults maintaining the picniclike atmosphere in the hopes that none of the kids would remember why they weren't sleeping at home that night.

It didn't work, of course. The kids knew why we were all there—they weren't the kinds of circumstances people can forget that easily, no matter what their age. Some of the time they took advantage of the fact—some of the time their faces were nothing more than large sad eyes, filling with tears. Luckily for the Little Doc and me both, auntie understood how helpless bachelors really are in these moments and took care of all such situations.

My two-hour time limit ran out during the middle of the festivities. Going to the kitchen, I used the phone in there to call Sally. She had found Rich and gotten him back down to the *Post*. I spoke to both of them on a conference line, reviewing everything that had happened. We kicked around the story, Rich deciding that the question of why I was attacked by Hispanics when the city "knew" that only Orientals were involved in the Dreamer trade was worthy of a column. I told him that

I'd be looking forward to seeing the next day's paper and what it might stir up.

Then I talked with Sally for a few minutes, letting her know that I was all right and that I'd get back in touch as soon as I had anything to add. I reminded her that we didn't know for sure if the Dreamer attack and the visit from Clements and his partner were related.

"So what are you telling me?" she asked. "Total?"

"I'm saying that I'm not sure what's going on. I have a run-in with a Chinese gang. That gets you and Rich interested. A client of mine is murdered by someone trying to make it look as if the Outliner did it. That gets you two more interested. Her husband is a city official. I go to see him and come away with the feeling that he didn't do anything to his wife, but then get attacked by drug types and gone over by the police."

"Jack, do you think the cops are mixed-up in this? Not for publication . . . just between you and me."

"In all honesty, Sal, I don't have the faintest idea. Fisher is a corrupt bastard all right, but Dreamer is moving through Manhattan. How's a Brooklyn police captain get involved in that kind of crime, especially if it is being run out of City Hall, which seems possible since it looks as if they're covering up *some* kind of involvement."

"What are you going to do, then?"

"I'll see what I can find out tomorrow before Rich's column comes out. Then I'll see if that stirs anything up. There's a good chance that that alone might bring things to enough of a boil to show us the way to finding out just who's guilty of what."

When Sally made no response, I asked her why she was being so quiet. She told me.

"Just a little nervous, I guess."

"You?" I answered, more than a little stunned. "You nervous? About what?"

"Stirring things up is what Mrs. Sinnott did, isn't it, Jack? That's what got her killed, right?"

"Possible."

"Be careful, will you? Don't stir things too hard, Jack." Sally paused for just a beat—her voice strained, almost breathless. It was only a beat, though, after which she told me, "I'd hate to think we got past our differences, ah . . . too late for it to matter."

"You'll turn my head with talk like that, lady."

"I'll keep that in mind."

We talked for another moment, flirting like teenagers with nothing better to do. I let her know that I'd be all right—she threatened to kill me if I wasn't. We hung up finally when one of the kids came in to complain to me that one of their sisters or brothers or someone wasn't being fair about something. Sally laughed at my predicament and then rang off, extracting one last promise from me to call her the next day.

After that, I went back in and mediated all disputes, got people eating, helped with the cleanup, and then finally got all the beds filled and all the lights out. It was pretty far past the bedtimes of most everyone in the apartment, but under the circumstances it seemed as if I was forgiven.

As I lay in my sleeping bag, I wondered at how I'd gotten myself into the situation I was in. Knowing I wasn't going to come up with the answer there at the Doc's, however, I rolled over onto my side and tried to get to sleep. The next day was going to be a long one and I was going to need the rest. It took me a lot longer to finally drop off than I thought it would, though. No one ever told me that little kids snore.

CHAPTER 21

I MANAGED TO rouse Hubert a little after ten. It was not the best of conversations we'd ever had, but for once that wasn't his fault. I clued him in on everything that had happened since I'd seen him last. When I told him about what Rich was going to do in his column, he told me,

"No, he didn't."

"What're you talking about, Hu?"

"I'm sayin', g-grouchy, that I've already read today's *Post* and Rich doesn't have a column in it."

My first reaction was to do a little cursing and then go out and get my own copy of the *Post,* but as irritating as Hubert can be, the one thing he usually isn't is wrong. Cutting off my negatives before they got started, I asked Hu to flip through the paper again and double-check. He did. Rich's column still wasn't there. I told him thanks, then let him know I was going to ring off and do some checking. Promising to call him back as soon as I could, I got off the line fast, and then punched in Rich's desk number. He was in. He told me what had happened.

"Things are getting awful juicy awfully fast, Jack. The story was spiked."

"By who? Any ideas? Any reasons? What?"

"Calm down," Rich advised me. "You'll live longer. Let me give you what I have. It's a mix of a few facts and a lot of intuition, but it's all I've got."

"Good enough for me," I assured him. "Spill it."

"We were ash-canned by City Hall. No idea how high up, but high enough to put pressure on the publisher. He jumped up and down on Sally's ass and she had to pull the carpet on it. How they found out about it, I don't know, but anyway, their reasoning is that part of the support for your theories rests in exposing the fact that people know how the Outliner is operating. They say part of their plan is to try and trick him by appearing to not know what he is doing."

"What a load of bullshit."

"Uuuoohhhh . . ." drawled Rich sarcastically. "Why, I never thought of that. City Hall lie to the taxpayers. Gee, Jack, that's a pretty strong allegation. You wouldn't have any facts to back harsh talk like that up, would you?"

"All right—you can the comedy—I'll apologize. But shit, what're we going to do now?"

"I've been giving that some thought, actually," answered Rich. "I'd like to get a little luncheon together. I figure with guys throwing lead in your direction, you're going to be keeping a low profile, so that means Louie's is out. Got any alternatives?"

"If we're looking for a place where no one would expect me to show up, let's make it fast food. I can't tell you the last time I had a frozen patty."

"How about the Colonel?"

"Sure," I agreed, "we're not getting together for the ambience."

"And," added Rich, "they do chicken right. There's one with a second-floor dining room at Thirty-fourth and Seventh."

"Pretty close to Penn Station? What if they've got the train station covered?"

"You'll be coming from uptown. They're not going to have twenty square blocks covered."

I reined in my paranoia, agreeing with Rich. He said that he could get there first and secure both a table and lunch enough for the two of us, letting me know I could square the bill with him when I got there. I told him "fine," but to make it lunch enough for three, telling him I was going to ring Hu back and get him to meet us. He agreed, suggesting he try to get Trenkel there as well.

I thought about it for a moment and then said "sure," figuring that Ray was in the same mess we were by having pointed us in the right direction. The least we owed him was a chance to find out what had happened, especially if there was some way for his higher-ups to discover he had given us the boosted file. After that, we simply set a time and then rang off to make our calls. I punched in Hu's number, getting him back after a few rings. He was on another line, which forced me to go on hold. I got through after another minute and told him of Rich's and my conversation. When I asked him to meet us at the restaurant, he said,

"KFC . . . ? Sure, they do chicken right, you know?"

"Yeah," I told him. "So I've heard. Thanks for the information. Just be on time, okay?"

"You just get that b-bucket o'chicken," he answered. "I'll b-be there."

After finishing that call, I conferred with the Little Doc over what to do with Elba and her family. He said it was no trouble for him to disappear for a few days to his cabin in the Poconos. At first he thought he'd have to rent a car big enough to get them all up there, but I nixed the idea. He asked,

"What's the difference? What else do we doctors make the big money for?"

"I understand all that. I was just wondering if you'd mind switching cars? First off, mine's big enough to get you all there. Second, that way Balto will be more comfortable, not riding in a strange car without me, and third, my car will be out of the city and I'll be driving around in something that whoever is after me won't know about."

The Doc agreed that the idea made sense, tossing his home and car keys to me at the same time. I thanked him as strongly as I could without sounding like a jerk,

some for the loan of his apartment and his BMW while
he was away, but more for taking my largest problem
off my hands. Without the kids to worry about, I could
get back on track again. The Doc took it all in stride,
making it seem as if I were the one doing him all the
good turns.

"Relax, Jack," he told me. "This'll be great."

"Baby-sitting this pack?"

"Sure. After all, their aunt will be doing all the work.
And me, I get to play with Balto in the woods, feel like
a great guy for doing such a good deed for my pal, and
when you get back, I assume I'll receive my standard
reward of lots and lots of drinks while you tell me all
the grisly details of your adventure . . . correct?"

I nodded my head to let him know he assumed correctly.

"So, what more could I want? You go out and track
down and bust up all the bad guys, Jack. Then come
back to your loyal, number-one fan and tell me all about
it. I'll be hiding outside of the city while you shoot the
place up."

That taken care of, I said good-bye to everyone, gave
Elba some pocket cash just in case anything came up
that none of us had foreseen, and then took off for
my luncheon. By the time I managed to somehow get
downtown through the lunch-hour traffic, find an open
meter for the Doc's car, and fight my way through the
icy bog of slush surrounding the Penn Station area, I was
amazed that I wasn't late.

By the time I finally reached the second floor of the
Kentucky Fried Chicken, though, Rich, Hubert, and Ray
Trenkel were already there, crowded around a small
table. Last but not late is okay by me.

They had an ample feed spread out in front of them—
the jumbo bucket of chicken, little containers of may-
onnaise salads, mashed potatoes, gravy, biscuits, and a
side tub filled with ears of corn. A take-out bag from
the Oakwood let me know Rich, not trusting fast-food

beans, had brought coffee in for everyone—a nice gesture, considering he was having his usual seltzer. The table was a flurry of hands, each of the trio wanting something that was in front of someone else. As they grabbed at the food, fumbling for napkins and plastic silverware, I announced my presence.

"Well, well," I said "if it isn't another meeting of the Gentlemen's Club."

"Yeah," answered Ray, throwing a piece of chicken at me. "That's us."

Managing to catch the thigh out of the air just before it hit me in the head, I saluted Ray with an obscene gesture and then started gnawing at the chicken as I weaved my way to our table through the other patrons. Taking my seat, I fished a coffee out of the bag and started assembling my own lunch, joining in with the general nonsense at the table. As always, when a group of men with something serious to do gets together, there is always a certain amount of silliness that has to be endured before things get under way. I don't know why that is; I don't know if women suffer from the same problem. I just know that for guys it seems like something of a duty.

That day's manly duties involved offending quite a number of the Colonel's other patrons with some of the more childish shenanigans I've seen come out of our group in quite some time. We coughed up Outliner jokes, puke humor, child rape and necrophilia banter, and all the usuals, as well as tossing some more food at each other, laughing like general horses' asses for about twenty minutes. By that time, Hubert was starting with oldies.

"Hey, Rich . . . you hear the *latest* Helen Keller joke?"

"No, I don't think so."

"N-neither did she."

As Hu started up his dying duck laugh at the sight of Rich's pained expression, I cut in.

"Okay, boys, enough's enough. Let's try and do at least a little business, shall we?"

We got down to work, comparing notes, building theories, trying to hash out a formula for what was going on that we could understand. We knew that the rest of the city was trying to do the same thing, but we also knew we had an advantage. When most people work on a problem, they only have others like themselves—people in the same office, people with the same outlook, people using the same information as a starting point—to whom they can go for advice. They might call in a specialist now and then, but for the most part, people tend to work things out within their own circles.

Our group definitely crossed a lot of boundaries. Ray obviously brought all the information available to the police department, both the official and the unofficial. Rich had one of the best sets of ground runners the city had to offer. If anyone in the media had a fact we could use, he could find it. Hu, of course, had his usual cross-reference of sources that has never failed to amaze everyone else at the table. Maybe it was his bizarre position in the New York art scene. Whatever it was, however, people from all walks of the city were willing to give him information, which he sold or gave away or kept to himself, all according to his own whims.

Myself, all I have is my own viewpoint. My main strength has always been in being able to notice and then make the connections that the people around me miss. It keeps me from having to say much when people are throwing their facts around, but once they want some answers, they all start looking toward my corner. Sometimes, when nothing comes immediately, things can get awful quiet and awful uncomfortable. Like, say, in February, on the second floor of a crowded midtown Manhattan Kentucky Fried Chicken.

We had put together a scenario between us that made things look pretty grim. The first thing we establish-ed was that the Italian mobs had nothing to do with Dreamer. Apparently, they had been edged out on this one because they no longer had anyone very powerful

on their payroll in the city government. After the new
mayor had come in, all the old deals between City Hall
and the outside world had been cut loose. The Italians,
having backed the wrong candidate, were now having
more trouble than they had had in a long time as far
as street-level ventures were concerned. I was surprised
by this information, but I seemed to be the only one at
the table who was.

Another thing also apparent to us—me included this
time—was that something was wrong with the city's
accusations about Dreamer. I had been in Chinatown for
a long stretch recently and I could vouch for the fact that
Dreamer was no big hit on the local streets there. On my
breaks from the store, or even when I would watch the
dealers out through the front window, I saw a lot of the
usual—grass, pills, crack, coke—but little Dreamer.

Both my run-in with Rickie's pals and rumors all of
the others had heard made it look as if it was the Latin
American pipeline and not the Asian connection that was
flooding the city. It was true that a lot of oriental kids
had been hired as sales personnel in the high-visibility,
a.k.a. high-risk, marketplaces. But it was also true that
no one above street level who'd been busted over a
Dreamer connection of any type was oriental. And, sus-
piciously, when taken in our current context, none of
the non-Orientals had remained in custody more than a
few hours.

The trouble we had in making any definite statements
was that with a new administration in place, none of us
could be sure how high the corruption was flowing or
in which directions. Not yet, anyway. Ray summed it
up best.

"Okay, let's clear the horseshit. I think it's obvious *some*one downtown is clearing the way for the
greaseballs. There's stuff coming down from up top
that's pushing us after both sides of Canal Street. But
if what we've pieced together about both the Italians
and the Chinese being on the outside looking in here

is on the level, then the wetbacks have definitely got somebody in their pocket."

He maintained his whisper as we all had, not wanting to alert the rest of the patrons as to what we were up to. Taking a breath, he asked me in the same low tones,

"So, what do *you* think, Jackie-boy? You got any ideas who's at the top of the gimmie-gimmie pole these days?"

"No," I answered. "But I bet I know who does."

We stared at each other for a second, both knowing what was in each other's minds, wondering if we were both stupid enough to do what we were thinking. Ray set his mouth in a straight line, which let me know he was. My guess is he saw something in my face that told him the same thing about me. Taking one last napkin, all of the wet-and-wipes long gone, Ray degreased his fingers while I knocked back the last of my coffee.

"You two up to something?" asked Rich.

"It's possible," I admitted.

"It's a long drive out to Queens this time of day," he said.

"Yeah," added Hu. "I s-sure hope Andy invites the two of you in for some hot c-cocoa."

I guess you can't fool anybody these days.

CHAPTER 22

RAY AND I took the Doc's car to Queens. Guys with money only respect money. A BMW pulling up in the driveway was going to impress him more than anything else either one of us could commandeer. Also, since his people had seen my car already, this gave us a slight bit of surprise. That, added to the fact that they wouldn't expect Ray to be a cop, gave us a number of small rugs to pull out from under anyone in our way.

Ray and I discussed the fact that we had no plan on the drive out. We'd known that when we left, of course, but—having no other best next move open to us—we were stuck with what we had. We wondered at what we would say to Andrew Sinnott. What kind of pressures do you bring to play on a man in his situation?

If he was innocent, if he'd had no part in his wife's death at all, then what kind of heels were we for accusing him of it? And in today's world, with its litigational answer to everything, could we end up in court being sued for emotional damages? Ray's being with the police was no protection against that.

Then, on the other hand, if Andy Sinnott, the party boy table-hopper from the tape I'd viewed with his wife, was responsible for her murder, where did that leave us? What kind of pressures did we think we were going to be able to bring to bear on the kind of monster who kills the mother of its own children—and then can blithely lie about it with a straight face?

As much as I don't like to become smug about my own abilities—because of the personal danger involved in doing so if nothing else—I have to admit that I've always been a fairly good judge of character. After my previous talk with Sinnott, and the time I'd spent thinking about him since then, I had to admit that I didn't think he did it. Willing to trust my instincts, neither did Ray. All in all, it was not an interview to which either one of us was looking forward.

We pulled up to Sinnott's under a gray sky. It was still an hour or more until sunset, but the clouds were doing night's job well enough. It was going to snow again— soon—snow or rain or something. As Ray and I went to the front door, I noticed that no one was opening it and stepping out to head off intruders this time. Not really anything to be suspicious about—just different. Maybe, I thought, Mike had the day off, or maybe they just weren't chasing people away that afternoon. Whatever.

We rang the bell, listening to the chimes bouncing off the walls inside. We continued to stand in the cold, waiting. Ray said,

"Gee, nobody's coming."

"I noticed."

"What'll we do, pick the lock?"

"How about we try the bell again?"

"That's the thing wrong with you private guys," said Ray as he set off the chimes again. "You got no sense of how to do things. Don't you ever want them to make a movie out of your life and get the babes in the audience all hot with your exciting exploits?"

"Yeah, Ray," I answered, the cold seeping in at me through the layers of my clothing. "Yeah, that's just what I want. Women who can't tell fact from fantasy—who don't even know what they want. Oh, yeah—they're the ones for me, all right."

We stood around for another minute, rang the bell again, cursed our luck at having come when everyone was out, rang it again, then started cursing each other. Finally, Ray said,

"Okay, fine, fuck it—let's just get the hell out of here."

I almost agreed, but then pointed toward the end of the driveway, saying,

"Ray, this place has a gated drive, right? So . . ."

"So," he finished for me, "if everyone's gone, why ain't the gate closed? Good question, Jackie-boy. Okay, let's snoop around a little."

We tried the front doorknob, but unlike the gate, that proved to be locked. Not wanting to move immediately to breaking-and-entering, we decided to check the first-floor windows to see if they offered us any kind of view. One did. As we took a peek through what appeared to be Andrew Sinnott's den, we found the man himself, or at least what was left of him.

Sinnott had danced on his last tabletop. His wrists and ankles were lashed to the posts of his bed, his body covered in blood from top to bottom. The end of something, possibly a glass soda bottle, was visible protruding from his rectum.

"Shit!" roared Ray, cursing the sight inside and us for finding it the way we did. "Goddammit—look! The window's up a crack. Probably the point of entry and exit. We're right in the middle of the goddamn crime scene!"

Not wanting to disturb any possible evidence more than we already might have, we circled back to the front of the house, debating what to do next. Slapping myself to beat away the cold, I said,

"Look, if there were any prints on the doorknob, we messed them up when we tried it earlier. What say, in the name of the law and all, we just force the door, go in, call some more cops, and turn this over to the proper authorities?"

"Do we have any right to be here?"

"Sure," I answered. "Sinnott offered to hire me. We came out here to put a few questions to him to see if what he wanted was going to interfere with police business. If you said what he wanted was kosher, then I was going to take the case. Hell, it's eighty-five percent the truth anyway."

Ray thought about it for a minute, mulling the idea over in his mind. Ray Trenkel is a straight shooter, for a cop, one of the best there is. But he's also an ambitious guy, one who doesn't particularly want to end his days behind a captain's desk when there are fancier desks with larger paychecks in their drawers possible further up the line. I've seen him mentally debate situations for their career-wrecking/enhancing potentials before. I kept my mouth shut the handful of seconds it took him to make up his mind and waited for his answer, continuing to do my little slap dance to keep warm.

Whether it seemed like the right thing to do or Ray had decided he was just as cold as I was, he finally said,

"Fuck it, let's do it."

We both started for the door at the same moment, bumping shoulders halfway there like a scene out of a Three Stooges short. I backed off, pointing my palms toward the door, giving Ray all the room he needed. If the cop wanted to bust up the property of private citizens, who was I to argue? Ray bent down and inspected the lock, grunting with satisfaction after only a moment. Reaching inside his coat, he pulled out his wallet, taking a burglar's jimmy from behind his credit cards. As he bent again to work on the door, I told him,

"My, my, now there's something I never thought I'd see a cop with."

"What?" asked Ray, slightly surprised, holding up the B&E tool. "One of these?"

"No," I told him. "A credit card."

"Haw haw," he answered moodily, growling out his words. "I have to laugh."

"Ahhh, don't be so sensitive."

"I ain't sensitive," he spat back, still working on the door. "It's just that I wish . . ."

What Ray wanted to wish for I never found out. The door's lock popped at that moment, a satisfying *click* letting us know we were in. As Ray swung the door open, I admitted,

"I've never been able to get the hang of that."

"What? Crack a door?"

"Yeah. I've done it a few times, but it just takes me forever."

"Join the force," said Ray, restoring the tickler to its place in his wallet. "Learn a skill."

"No thanks," I told him. "I picked up enough of those in the service."

We walked into the living room, careful of where we put our feet, mindful not to brush any walls, or furniture, doors or railings, or anything. Standing in the center of the main room I'd been in the day before, I looked for anything I might recognize as out of place. Ray crossed the room carefully, heading for the phone. Picking up the receiver, he started to punch in his office's number when a voice came from behind us.

"Put the phone down and turn around slowly."

Looking toward the bedroom, I saw Mike, Sinnott's brick wall of a bodyguard, coming at us carefully, each step a measured pace. At the sight of the gun in his hand, I offered,

"Calm down, jumbo, we're the good guys."

"That's a new name for what you are, motherfucker."

The new voice had come from behind the ex-bodyguard. Its owner popped into view from around the same corner Mike had—along with his partner—and their guns. When I saw who they were, the first thing that ran through my head was that it didn't make any sense for Brooklyn cops to have responded to a murder in Queens. The second thing that ran through my head was that if I thought Clements and Sohl were there responding to a murder, instead of being responsible for it, that maybe the service hadn't taught me enough skills after all.

CHAPTER 23

"FUCK 'EM!" I yelled, throwing myself backward with everything I had. Ray managed to duck behind Sinnott's desk while my action luckily got me completely back out of the line of fire. Mike hesitated for a second, startled by my dodge, not sure who to shoot at first, or even if he should shoot at all.

"Christ! You shit-for-brains, you you you . . ."

Clements's voice raged at the ex-bodyguard from around the corner. The sound of fists punching flesh came from the hall. Who was hitting who and why was unclear, but neither Ray nor I felt like risking a peek to find out the answers. I had pushed myself back toward the front door, getting my .38 into my hand as quickly as I could. From my vantage point I could see Ray had done the same. He was crouched behind the desk with his .9mm in one hand and the two-shot special he carries on his leg in the other.

I could have made a dash for it, leaving Ray to cover me, I even gave the idea a moment's thought; Ray was a cop; a guy like me they might kill and get away with it—easy. But a police captain was another matter. Right—sure. I dismissed the notion—fast. The facts were adding up quickly to show that neither one of us had a chance for a fair deal out of the mess into which we'd stumbled.

As their voices came at us from around the corner, I could tell there was only the trio we'd initially seen. That still meant someone felt it important enough to send three guys to deal with Sinnott. It also meant things were dirty enough that Sinnott's own bodyguard had been in on it. Clements's voice rang out.

"Give it up, Hagee. Make it easy on both of you. There's no way you can get out of here. No way you can beat this rap . . ."

"Whatever you say, Officer. Tried to arrest any unlicensed dogs lately?"

"Fuck you, you prick! You shit cum fuck suck bastard! You're dead! You're both dead!"

While my pal ranted, I combed the room with my eyes, looking for some way to prove him wrong. He was right about the fact that there was no way we could shoot our way free. There was, however, the possibility of a diversion. As long as Clements continued to scream, I knew the three of them weren't making any plans. Looking over at Ray, I caught his attention and then, waving my lighter in the air, I pointed him toward something I remembered from the day before—the kerosene lamps sitting atop the mantel of the unused fireplace. Spotting them, he nodded and crawled flat-bellied back to the wall.

Luckily the desk was able to block him from the others enough that they couldn't tell what he was up to. Making it to the fireplace, he grabbed down both the metal-based lamps, shook them, then gave me a thumbs-up sign to let me know we'd hit the jackpot. I got out a Camel and popped it into my mouth figuring, What the hell, it might be my last chance to have one. Lighting it, I left my lighter's lid open, praising myself for having the good sense to never switching over to throwaway lighters. Then, with my fingers mentally crossed, I gave my dragons another lucky rub and started talking.

"Now wait a minute, Clements," I offered, hoping to ease them into a false sense of security. "What kind of a deal are you offering here?"

I said anything that came to mind, not caring about the words, only hoping to stall the gang in the hall long enough for Ray and I to silently coordinate our plan. While I blathered, Ray unscrewed and set aside the tops to each lamp. Then he ripped open a dozen or more holes in each for good measure using his pocketknife. The noise did not go unnoticed.

"What the hell are you two up to?" demanded Mike, showing more brains than I'd originally given him credit for.

"What?" I answered. "What're you talking about? Look, do you want us to surrender to you or not?"

There was a moment of chatter we couldn't hear, and then Clements yelled at one of the others with him,

"Fuck you! Fuck them, you idiot! They're up to something. *Rush 'em!*"

Ray threw the first spraying lamp through the air just as Sohl came through the hall entrance. It went over his head trailing kerosene, splashing Sohl as it did, noise telling us it bounced off a wall before hitting the floor. I flipped the open lighter For the largest puddle I could see just as Ray threw the second lamp.

As the lighter hit the floor, Ray came to his feet and shot around the desk as the hallway, livingroom floor, and Sohl all exploded into black smoke and flames. Panic voices flooded the hall.

Sohl's mouth flew open in a shriek of clawing screams. His hair, face, and half his upper body afire, he ran blindly back toward the hallway, slipping in the burning fuel on the wooden floor. By this time Ray and I were out the door, taking wide, jumping steps down the walkway to the drive. We were halfway there when the first shots rang out behind us. Not daring to lose our head start we both fired wildly behind us, not caring who or what we might hit. More shots followed us, equally wild. We made it to the car, ducking down behind the bit of wall between us and the smoking house. Sohl's screams seemed louder outside.

"Get the fucking doors unlocked!" ordered Ray. "I'll cover you."

"Okay," I agreed, the keys already in my hand. "I'll get it running and then flip open the back door."

Ray leaned out into the open and squeezed off half a clip, forcing the opposition back momentarily. I fumbled at the lock for a second, cursing the fact that even in a neighborhood as rich as Sinnott's I'd still locked the doors as a matter of course. A bullet shattered the driver's window as I opened the door. Ray let loose with the other half of his clip. Gunning the ignition on the first try, I blessed the Doc for his good taste in automobiles and then made to open the back door. My fingers fumbled at the cold metal. I instantly fought down the urge to start punching the door, cursing my panic. Getting the button up, I flipped the door open and then screamed,

"Come on, goddammit!"

Sticking my .38 out of the shattered driver's window, I fired at the house, emptying my cylinder. The move didn't tag anyone as far as I could tell, but it did give Ray time to clamber inside. He hit the backseat before my last bullet cleared the barrel. Then, the second I saw Ray's head in the mirror, I floored the pedal, backing us into the street as fast as I could, narrowly avoiding a UPS truck.

Clements and Mike charged out of the house, thick smoke belching through the doorway behind them. Dozens of shots rang out behind us, several more hitting the Doc's car. Luckily, none of them hit us. I purposely drove away from the house toward the north, waiting until we were out of sight to cut back toward the south.

"Where are you heading?" asked Ray.

"Down toward the Beltway."

"Fuck that," growled Ray angrily, not used to being on the receiving end of police violence. "Get me back to town—I'll deal with those motherfuckers."

"Shut up and think," I snarled, trying to keep the anger raging within myself capped. "What do you think just happened back there, for Christ's sake? Those were cops. Brooklyn uniforms dorking around in Queens. The plainclothes guy was Sinnott's bodyguard. We figured someone high up was controlling this thing—now we know for sure."

I tried to relax, fighting the tension that was turning my fingers to iron rods wrapped around the steering wheel. Driving the icy streets of Queens was no time to be distracted. We were in deep trouble now. It was obvious we had shown up just as Clements and the others were putting the finishing touches on a nasty execution—perhaps another killing to be laid at the Outliner's door. Ray and I debated how much sense the idea made.

"You could be right," admitted Ray. "Hell, I'm sure of it. Sinnott's bodyguard was probably given to him by someone from downtown. That would make things a snap."

"Absolutely," I agreed. "Our downtown figure says that Sinnott has to go for some reason. Maybe he really didn't want his wife killed, and when someone else did it he didn't fall in line the way they thought he would. So, they call Mike, he subdues his boss, lets in the cops, they work him over, maybe for information we don't know about, or just to get him out of the way."

"Yeah," growled Ray. "And it doesn't even matter if they go in in their uniforms. Why would it? It's a setup from the word go. 'The bodyguard found the body . . . police investigation calls it clean . . . why, it must be that horrible Outliner again. He is a homo after all, see—he really wanted Sinnott, so he killed the wife first and then when he was spurned he killed the husband.' Excuse me if I throw up in your backseat."

"Go ahead," I told him. "It's not my car."

I understood Ray's anger. It certainly wasn't fear, nor was it simply curses thrown at our bad luck. To Ray, bad cops were something to take personally. He didn't like them and didn't tolerate them whenever he found them. I'd been a cop for a few years myself, back in Pittsburgh. I'd seen so many bad ones there I didn't care much one way or the other. Cops were just more people to me, most of them too stupid to really think about what they were doing one way or the other. Ray didn't feel that way. To him, one rotten apple spoiled the whole barrel.

Trying to ignore them for the moment, or at least rechannel the energy the thought of them was wasting, Ray suddenly chuckled out loud, saying,

"Jackie-boy, you know, this was just our fuckin' luck, wasn't it? We show up like two prime idiots, waltz up and ring the fuckin' doorbell and let the bastards know we're out front, just give them all the time in the world to set us up. Shit, we're lucky we got out of there alive."

"Yeah, I know," I answered. "I was basically just thinking that myself."

"You know what really bites, though?"

Not knowing, I asked. He told me.

"If we're right, about them planning this as another Outliner scam—I was thinkin' about all the people he really did kill. If they say that now he's killing the relatives of his victims, think of the panic that's going to run through the other surviving family members. All those folks thinking that he's going to come after them now, just so these fucks can get away with whatever they're up to."

"Not to mention," I added, "the fact that this will refocus the media's attention off our pals and onto the Outliner. But, then again, I don't think we have to worry about them doing that."

Now it was Ray's turn to not know something. He asked, "Why not?"

I told him.

"Simple—most likely we're the ones that're going to get the blame now."

Ray's face froze for a second, and then his head began moving up and down slightly, his look one of frustrated realization. Seeing that look in the mirror, I suddenly knew that as much as I'd thought I was making a bitter joke, I was actually probably right.

Outside, a type of half rain, half sleet started to fall. Swell, I thought. Just swell.

CHAPTER 24

MY VIEW WAS of twenty-three different television screens. They were all of different sizes, some black-and-whites thrown in among the color. All the sets were running at the same time, each showing a different station. I brought the sound up on the screen showing a Pat Metheny video and then closed my eyes, scrunching myself farther back into the cushions of the green-and-pink fringed sofa on which I was stretched out. I had no choice in my position. The control board for the sets was positioned in front of that couch, and that couch had a dresser on top of it. You either crawled inside of the setup and then stretched out, or you stood. I'd had a tiring day. I stretched out.

Ray was somewhere else in the warehouse, making phone calls. The place was a used furniture shop located along the main drag in Coney Island. It's run by a self-styled anarchist named Rubin Wave who lived there with a large number of cats. The cats, as usual when someone they didn't know was on the premises, were off hiding somewhere in the maze of furniture and old guitars and toasters and other miscellaneous, thirdhand junk.

I have to admit that I've never been quite clear on exactly what it is Rubin's anarchistic drive is aimed against. It's not the Democrats or the Republicans, law-and-order, the social welfare system, Jews, *The New York Times,* blacks, or women in particular, but I've heard him go off on every one of the above, and a lot more, in his time—making all of them sound as if they could be the ones in charge of the coming apocalypse. All I know for sure is there is one hell of a conspiracy going on out there, and Rubin is keeping tabs on it for us.

"It's those fuckers in City Hall, Hagg," he said, suddenly appearing at the corner of the sofa. "City Hall fuckers, City Hall."

He placed a handmade table next to my head, the top of which was made out of holders for various-sized bowls, bottles, and glasses. Each spot was filled with a different beverage or snack except for the ones on each corner shaped to hold the ashtrays. Digging one hand into the cat's paw-shaped Cheetos while pulling a beer from another, I asked,

"What exactly are we laying at their feet this time?"

"Channel seven," he answered.

I shrugged and hit the control button for the local ABC affiliate. Once I saw the subject matter, I agreed with Rubin. It was almost definitely the work of those fuckers in City Hall. The moderator told us:

"This, of course, is not the first time the private investigator has found ways to insert his name into the nightly news, but it is certainly the most shocking. Many may remember the spectacular resolution he brought to the murder of Ralph Morgan early last year, the 'Millionare Mugging,' as it was known in headlines across the country. Viewers may also remember hearing his name in connection with the assassination attempt of black mayorial candidate Andrew Taylor Lowe during last year's primary race. The murder of Assistant District Attorney Andrew Sinnott, however, is not an event . . ."

I killed the sound, not needing to hear anymore. Rubin had filled me in on the gist of what they had been saying across the band since literally fifteen minutes after we had backed out of Sinnott's driveway. As it was being told, the police had caught me red-handed trying to make Andy's death look like another Outliner killing, just—went the theory—as I had his wife's. I then made a death-defying escape with an unknown partner. Well, I thought, they've got about twelve percent of their facts right. Not bad for a television news broadcast. Watching the soft-faced puppet smilingly mouth the fabric of lies being manufactured about me, I asked Rubin,

"And it's all been about this bad?"

"Oh, yeah. Oh, yeah. Big, bad Hagg the slicey-blood monster man. You sure turned an evil corner since the last time you was here."

"Yeah, didn't you hear," I joked back. "The mayor's ordered everyone who lives in Bensonhurst to be thirty five percent nastier until President's Day."

Rubin laughed. I waggled my eyebrows to show him how serious I was. I was ready to dismiss the broadcast simply because I knew it was wrong, but then a nagging thought forced me to ask,

"Hey—you study the tube like it's the Bible, Rubin. What do you think? Are they doing a good enough job to turn anyone's head who knows me?"

"Be serious, Hagg. Nobody believes anything they hear on the shitbox if it contradicts their own reality. Unless, you know, they're just some brain-damaged case—which, I must admit the truth, New York has plenty of. But anyway, I mean, yer friends and all—why would they believe anything they heard on the TV?"

He paused and then added,

"*I* let you in, didn't I?"

"Yeah, you did," I admitted. "Thanks, Rube."

"Fuck it, don't worry about it. Worry about the Confederation. Whoever's fittin' your frame and gettin' ready to hang you on the wall. Scum-zum, Hagg—fuckin' scum-zum. Bastards, bastards."

Rubin took a long pull from his beer and then asked,

"Who did do it, though? Who killed Sinnott true, Hagg? Who bumped him and his wife . . . real time?"

Before I could answer, Ray came back into the room. He did not look happy. Taking one of the beers from the handmade snack table, he knocked back nearly half of it in one draw. Then, wiping his mouth, he told us,

"You can update my 'unknown partner' status."

"What's up, Ray?"

"I made some calls to see what I could find out. I was hoping none of those pricks recognized me. I'd of been a lot more use to us on the outside."

"Somebody did?"

"And a half." Ray spit the words angrily. "They had a message waiting for me at my office. I called them back through that relay number your friend here gave me. Smart move—they didn't want to talk about surrendering, But they did have a deal all worked out."

"Let me guess," interrupted Rubin. "You provide Jack's carcass . . . they supply the 'unknown partner's' body."

"Something like that," admitted Ray. "Hell, I was even supposed to get to take credit for the collar. Would have been a nice career move."

Ray drained his beer, then reinserted the empty into the spot from which he had taken it. Grabbing a pair of beef jerky strips from another slot, he said,

"And even though I have faith in Mr. Wave's relay system, I think we'd better move to a Manhattan location. I doubt they could have pulled a trace, but we're awfully far out of town sittin' here. Take us an hour—minimum—to get to anywhere from here if we needed to."

"He's right, Jack," agreed Rubin, getting up out of his chair. "Don't worry about it. I'll do the pound and grind to Doc's wheels. You guys take the panel truck in the back—the red one. That one can't be traced back here."

Disappearing around a corner created from stacked chairs, he came back in a minute with a set of keys that he threw to me, saying,

"Do it, go on—I'll be okay. I'll get to the car right after *MacNeil/Lehrer,* the third part of that inner-city special, and *Fantasy Island.*"

Bringing up the volume on the three sets in question, Rubin settled into my seat on the couch while Ray and I tried to thank him, receiving only a loud, obnoxious "ssshhhuusshhh" for our troubles. Dragging our coats on, we walked toward the exit at the back of the shop.

"You got any safe houses in Manhattan no one, and I mean *no one*, knows about?" asked Ray. "The more I think about it, the more I'm realizing I don't have a single place some other cop doesn't know."

"Yeah," I told him, opening the door. "I got one."

"Where is it?"

"Let me put it to you this way," I said as I worked the keys Rubin had given me, trying to find the one for the door. "How would you like a good home-cooked meal? Just like Mao used to make?"

CHAPTER 25

"NO, NO," PROTESTED Papa Lo, waving me into his place at the dinner table. "You sit here. Sit here."

The Los welcomed us as warmly as any fugitives have ever been welcomed anywhere. As they put it, anyone they knew who was being hunted by the government had to be all right. All I can say is, having friends who used to live under communism does have its advantages.

The family had seen me on the television and had already lit two bundles of incense in front of the Buddha they kept in a back corner for just such emergencies. Having me show up on the doorstep a couple of hours later took on almost a religious significance. I've had people happy to see me in my time, but this was something else.

We got there just at the start of dinner, "always best time to arrive," as Mr. Lo put it. Ray was accepted without question. If he was my friend he had to be innocent, too. Of course, they had seen him on the news as well. They were mightily curious as to "what could cause someone as powerful as a captain of the police to be hunted unjustly."

After a few phone calls we were happy to sit down to dinner and give them the whole story. In fact, hearing all the facts out loud again even gave me a new slant on some of it. When you're stumped over a puzzle, there's nothing like talking it out with someone else to give you a new perspective. Before I could put any of that new perspective to work, however, Lo's son Kong spoke up.

It was obvious that he did not like having Ray and I there. We were a threat to the family—outsiders—to him, an unwanted threat to the peace and security they had all tried so hard to build and maintain. I wasn't worried about him turning us in—he was too well disciplined, too respectful of his father's wishes to do anything like that.

He was not above harassing us, however. Starting in with the same kinds of questions he plagued me with during my earlier stay with the family, he asked Ray and I,

"I've been in this country for seven years now and my dad keeps telling me that we're so much better off under capitalism than we were in China. I'd like to know what you think about that."

Being even more of an outsider than I was in the Lo home, Ray let me field the question. Like any adult, my first try at an answer was the easy way out.

"Well, Kong, I think your dad is right."

"Why?" he shot back, not letting go. "Just because you're an American and it's the American way, or just 'because' period? Have you ever lived under communism? Have you ever even seen it?"

He was ready to blow more air but I stopped him, saying,

"No—and not just because I'm an American. I'd dump our rotten system in a minute if there was anything better out there to take its place. Oh, and yeah, kid," I told him,

"I've seen communism."

My mind flashed back to my service days, memories of ducking commies around the world for Military Intelligence—mass graves of schoolteachers, killed not for what they were teaching but because they could teach at all; entire countries, once green and prosperous, now in ruins, their fields all dust, because the Soviets had planned their planting; industrial centers that had been the pride of Europe, now merely jokes for businessmen from democracies . . .

I remembered, all right.

I looked into this teenager's eyes and I remembered a convent in Latin America. The nuns there were raped repeatedly, just so they'd sign statements to attest that the Catholic Church was aiding the rebels the communists wanted stopped. When they wouldn't do it their fingers were broken one by one, then their ribs. Finally, when it got too boring for the glorious heroes of the workers' revolution, they simply had the poor women murdered. Then some semiliterate party official signed the papers himself.

The statements were accepted, of course, by the world press—*embraced* by the American media—as gospel, even after it was pointed out that only two of the eleven Christian college graduates executed for their crimes against the state had been able to spell their names correctly.

That and the fact that all of them had chosen for some strange reason to sign their names in the same handwriting never seemed to bother the reporters and editors and anchormen and women giving us the facts—the same crew of rabid dogs who hounded Reagan the entire time he battled the communist monster, the sniveling hypocrites who covered the fall of the Soviet empire as if it was their liberal agenda that had brought it down instead of supporting it as it had for decades.

Shaking off the memories, though, trying to push the trash, if not out then at least to the back of my mind, I told Kong,

"I've seen it in every corner of the globe and the further it falls, the better off we all are. I'll admit that the people running things at the top of both systems are complete and utter scum. No question. The only essential difference is that here we're allowed to say so. I know that doesn't seem like a lot, but believe me, someday you'll understand that your right here to call the big boys on any point makes all the difference in the world."

"And you think you could just catch the president doing something illegal and blow the whistle and somebody will do something about it?"

"Maybe, maybe not," I admitted. "We've got secret police and mobsters and hired assassins, just like everywhere else. The difference, I guess, is here they're more like exceptions than the rules."

But then, before more could be said, the downstairs bell for the street rang. Mr. Lo called me over to a mirror setup he had rigged to view the street from the upstairs during our earlier troubles. Taking a look, I verified that our visitors were both people I had telephoned before dinner and gave him an "okay" sign. That sent Git'jing running downstairs to open the door. A minute later she returned with Rich and Hubert in tow. The two were ushered to seats at the table, an action neither protested.

"You guys haven't had dinner?" I asked innocently as they both accepted chopsticks from Mrs. Lo.

"Sure we have," answered Hu. "So what?"

"Wouldn't want to seem inhospitable," said Rich in dry agreement.

I laughed. Ray snorted. We both fell back to our meals, however, kicking around the happenings of the day and stuffing ourselves with Mrs. Lo's usual impressive spread. This went on for about twenty minutes until the doorbell rang again. Again I checked the mirror and again I gave the high sign. A minute later, Git'jing returned from the store, ushering a trio of oriental youths up from the street.

"So, Big Hagee, glad to see you're still alive," said the one in the lead. Allowing one of his seconds to take his jacket as he crossed the living room, he said,

"I've seen the news—very nasty stuff. Lies, I assume?"

I gave him a look to let him know he assumed correctly.

"That's what I thought. Not that I don't think you're capable of killing parasites in, shall we say, a 'colorful' manner. It is just my assumption that you would never be as clumsy about it as they're trying to make you out."

The young man took in the others at the table, smoothing back the sides of his brush cut.

"Interesting group we have here," he said, showing off his knowledge of the others gathered.

"We've got the most fearless store owner in the neighborhood, the very fair and highly respected Mr. Violano of the *Post*, and, good evening to you, too, Captain Trenkel. I assume you are as innocent as Big Jack."

Ray snorted, demanding,

"Who is this punk?"

"Why, Cappie," answered Hubert. "You don't know Jackson In, the lord high, grand poobah of Mother's Blood Flowing?"

"My fame precedes me," said Smiler graciously. "Well, Big Hagee, let us get down to business, shall we?"

CHAPTER 26

THE FIVE OF us talked for some time, sequestered off by ourselves in the living room, the television turned to the local news in the background. The Los were taking a big enough chance just harboring fugitives from justice and letting them meet with known criminals. Knowing what we were talking about would have made things even worse.

Things started coming together quickly after Smiler showed up, bringing us the last of the puzzle pieces we needed. We began working on a plan of operation before midnight that, truth to tell, was fine by me. Being wanted by the law—not being able to walk the streets because I didn't know which cops were dirty enough to shoot me on sight and ask questions later—was not sitting well with me. I'm not well known for my ability to wait out such circumstances. I *can* do it—I'm not stupid enough to just bull my way into a situation from which there's no way out—I'm just not famous for being able to do it very easily.

The big news Smiler had for us was confirmation that Black Dreamer was not a Chinese connection product. His people had looked into the drug months ago when it had first "surfaced" that the stuff was flooding the city via Chinatown. They had discovered it to be a type of cooked rock, made from heroin the way crack is made from cocaine. After the cooking process, however, Dreamer was then coated with PCP laced with some designer taste put together to boost the high by sharpening the PCP's edge. That made it one nasty drug. Smiler also admitted he'd only looked into it to see who was making money that he wasn't. When he discovered it was no one within his grasp, he'd lost interest, knowing that until he crushed the Time Lords that he wouldn't be able to do anything about it, anyway.

So, besides lying to the public about who was selling the stuff, City Hall was even lying about what it was. Ray was sure whoever was highest up in the cover-up had a typical set of stories ready to cover their lies: "We had to mislead the papers to cover the fact we knew what we were dealing with." No one bothered to debate his guess—we'd all seen it too often before to doubt his logic for a second. It's unbelievable how much shit you can shovel on the media in New York if you've got their blessing to do it . . . and the new mayor and his team had the media's blessing.

The local papers and television stations had all screamed at the voters to do the right thing and throw out the incumbent. As usual, without bothering to think for themselves, the people had rallied and done the press's bidding. And now that the city had played out-with-the-old and in-with-the-new, the people were stuck with a set of bloodsuckers even more vicious than the last, ones condoning, and most likely profiting, from the sale of the most dangerous street drug in years and Ray and I were stuck with murder raps. Of course, I couldn't really complain too loudly. I hadn't bothered to vote myself.

Hubert summed things up best.

"Can—can somebody t-tell me how shit like this goes on? They're lyin' about where it comes from, lyin' about who's sellin' it, even lyin' about what the fuck it is, for Christ's sake . . . How do they think they're goin' to get away with it? And for that m-matter—somebody tell me—how *do* they think they're goin' to get away with it? With a million cops and reporters and all sniffin' around this stuff every day—how is it that *nobody* fuckin' catches on?!"

"Good questions," admitted Rich. "I think you have to remember, Hu, that the people you're talking about don't think the way you do. Look at Andrew Sinnott. How did he think he was going to get away with doing the things he was doing? You wonder why it never dawned on him that events were going to catch up with him because that's the way your mind works—if *you* were doing the things he did, *you* would expect to get caught sooner or later. But Sinnott? I'd venture the guess that he never once thought about the possibility that he might go down for his crimes."

"True enough," interrupted Ray. "You remember a couple of years back—that guy who killed two women and put them in the trunk of his car? Now there's a guy who never thought his crimes were going to catch up with him."

Ray accepted a new cup of tea from the fresh pot Mr. Lo had just brought in. The older man stood back to listen as Ray continued his story.

"The jerk rented a parking space in a public garage and then just parked and left it there with two rotting corpses in it. He knew he was under investigation from the police. He knew we were checking out his properties, looking for some angle to get him on. What—did it never dawn on the asshole that a car registered in his name would be considered his property? Fuck, I mean, he even paid for the spot with a check."

"Hey, man," added Smiler calmly, an amused look on his face, "haven't you heard? It's just part of the criminal mind-set."

"You'd know all about that, wouldn't you?" asked Ray.

"Who, me?" asked Smiler innocently. "I'm just a simple American citizen, looking to make an honest buck."

Ray snorted in contempt. The smooth look on Smiler's face cracked slightly, a hardness flashing across his eyes for just a moment. Not wanting to see our fragile treaty wrecked, I jumped in, trying to salvage Smiler's honor before he was forced to do it himself.

"Gentlemen, let's just sum this up and get back to business, okay? Yeah, sure, there's such a thing as a criminal mind. No problem. I think the thing you're all leaving out is that breaking the law doesn't necessarily make one a criminal any more than upholding the law makes one a good guy."

I took a sip of my own tea, allowing anyone who wanted to get a word in their chance. Everyone kept quiet, waiting for whatever I was going to say. Taking the floor again, I said,

"The law by itself is nothing. When Washington and Jefferson and that bunch put together the Constitution, they wrote up a truly great piece of paper. The American Constitution has served as the model for, I don't know, hundreds of other countries' constitutions since then. So how come the world isn't filled with places like the United States? You want to know why? I'll tell you why. Because words on a piece of paper don't mean shit unless someone's ready to back them up— with their blood if they have to."

"Why for you argue?"

Everyone's heads turned to Mr. Lo. Setting down his teapot, the older man said,

"What? Someone have problem to understand some people no good? What so hard? Everyone born same. Some grow up, think only of them—what they can eat, what they can take—their pleasures, their comforts. Others, they think of everyone around them, how they connect to each other, how what they do come back to them through those connections. Judge, cop, president, gangster, teacher, no matter—all same. Laws never make no difference. Criminal write law all time. What good law? Only can trust people. You . . ." Mr. Lo stabbed a finger in Ray's direction.

"You criminal. You break law—kill man. Television say so. What to do? Should I get cop, turn you in?

Communist say I should. Say forget truth, forget justice. Is good idea? What you think, huh?"

Ray's eyebrows pushed down, leaving him with a bitter glare. Everyone in the room understood his problem. Ray Trenkel was not the kind of man who liked to be told that the loan-sharking, prostitution, and drug overlord sitting next to him just might share the same moral high ground he reserved for himself. Being a man who did lay claim to such acreage, however, he answered,

"What I really think is that we should get back to business. Maybe the rest of you are happy shoving this philosophical crap back and forth at each other, but me, I'd rather get myself clear of this mess and get things back to normal."

"Status quo, eh, qua'lo?" said Smiler. "Okay, Chief. Whatever you say. Here's a bit of juice for you. And you remember this . . ."

The boy gangster leaned in close to Ray, speaking quietly, staring him in the eye,

"I'm only here because of Big Hagee. I would piss on this whole city and laugh as it slipped into the ocean. I could care less if every one of you fools, white and black and brown, killed yourselves and your women and your children. You probably will anyway. But I like your friend's style. So, because of him, in this thing I will help you."

"I'm touched," spat Ray. "Let's hear what you've got."

"There is a truce among all the families. Not just all the Italians . . . all of us. All of us outside the Latinos have formed a coalition. The elders of each house have come together in the hopes its combined strength will frighten the city officials into cutting open the box around the drug pie."

Smiler took the teapot, graciously refilling the cups of those who needed more. He covered everyone, including Mr. Lo and his own men, walking around the room pouring as he continued to talk.

"You are correct. Black Dreamer is definitely a Hispanic product, one under the complete protection of the city. These pigs think they can safely ignore both their Mediterranean and Asian competitors. This, as you might understand, has caused quite a number of these 'business rivals' to consider drastic measures."

Then, before Smiler could continue, Hubert called our attention to the nightly news as it turned back to Ray and myself. As the strident figure of the new district attorney, Judith Siegel, the most honest woman in New York City politics, came into focus, Hu boosted the sound.

" . . . men will be caught. They will be punished. No one is above the law in New York City—not its own police captains, and certainly not rogue cowboys like Jack Hagee."

I stared at the set as the camera shifted back to the anchorman, listening to the politically correct meat puppet in the well-pressed suit as he informed the public that the manhunt for Ray and myself was rapidly boxing us in, and that the police were expecting results from their informants very soon. He let the world know that we were extremely dangerous fugitives, and that no one should try to apprehend us themselves.

Doing everything possible within his journalistic province to help protect the poor, frightened public, he flashed the toll-free number people were to use if they saw us, showed the public our pictures one more time, and reminded everyone about the fifty-thousand-dollar-apiece reward that had been offered by some caring private citizen for any information leading to our captures. His smile reassured the world as to what scum we were. I told Hu to turn off the set before I did it permanently.

"You know, of course," said Smiler, "that it was the Helmendez Reality Company that made the generous donation to the city of your reward money."

"Let's say I'm not surprised," I answered. Madder than ever, knowing that someone as careful as Smiler seemed to be wouldn't have taken the floor without a reason, I turned things back over to him, saying,

"Something tells me you have something up your sleeve."

"It is so refreshing to deal with you, Big Hagee. I like men I cannot stay three steps ahead of. Oh, yes—I have a few thoughts to share with you all."

Taking a seat on the couch, Smiler said,

"In anticipation that you gentlemen might be receptive to an audacious plan, I just happened to have one in mind."

Smiler talked. We listened. Audacious wasn't the word for it.

CHAPTER 27

EVERYONE ADMITTED THAT it was a truly amazing plan. If the glass teat's blow-dried marionettes thought I'd "found ways to insert my name into the nightly news" in the past—they hadn't seen anything yet. I was surprised at the nerve of it all, and truth to tell, by the time we were done refining what Smiler had come to us with, half of it was my idea.

With everyone in the media sucking up the party line, the main thing Ray and I had to do was to focus attention onto something besides ourselves—something like City Hall's involvement in drug trafficking and murder, for instance. Smiler'd found a real interesting way to do it.

It hadn't taken us twenty-four hours to get everything planned, mapped out, and prepared. A lot of that was due to things Smiler had set into operation before he had even arrived at the Los'.

Showing the guts of a John Wayne era cowboy star, he had called a meet with the head of the Galibento family—the mob branch apparently feeling the biggest pinch from Dreamer—and then gone in alone and unarmed. He had told them that now was no time for false pride and that those who stood alone were going to go down alone. He had then told them that if information he had was correct, those in City Hall who had allied themselves with the power behind businesses like Helmendez Reality were about to take a long fall. He said that if they wanted in on the kill, that he would arrange it.

They had—and he did. With a phone call, he brought Vincent Galibento himself to the Los' home. The resplendent Señor Galibento, or Vinnie the Scissor as they had called him until around 1957—after which such familiarity became unwise—came into the Los' as if there were nothing more natural in the world for him than to be visiting a second-story walk-up in Chinatown at two in the morning.

Once he was there, our planning came down to nothing more than establishing who would supply what— why they would do it and when. Interestingly enough, territory was not an issue of the meeting. Both Smiler and the Scissor were content to simply regain their old business grounds. Smiler, of course, merely wanted to consolidate his recent gains in the big-time mobster biz. The Scissor, he was simply too old to take the lack of respect shown to him by City Hall's latest dealings lying down.

"Fuck them," he said, holding one of the Los' delicate teacups in his left hand and several of their homemade, moon-shaped New Year's cookies in his right. Delicately apologizing for his language to Mrs. Lo who had come into the room to make sure we had enough tea, he waited politely for her to leave again, and then told the assembly,

"Too many years, this all gets to be too fucking political. I've been telling the young ones—the ones coming up behind me, these morons who are supposed to take everything over, right—for the last forty years I tell them . . . 'You can't trust the fucking politicians.' But do they listen—would I be here if they listened? Fungoula . . ."

The Scissor made a familiar motion with his hands, executing it with surprising ease considering the cup and cookies. Then, his face hardened over as he said,

"Enough talk of what should've been—let's sign some death warrants."

Our Italian connection was more than happy to supply

all the muscle needed, nice big boys who fit into the
New York City police uniforms Smiler obtained for
them under Ray's direction. Hubert had managed to
tickle his connections enough to discover the address-
es for three different Dreamer factories. Two of them
were small, nearly insignificant chemical shops. The
third, however, was a major storage and distribution
center.

Our plan was simple. First we would hit the two small
shops and wipe them from the face of the earth. If we
could dig up an informant—great. If not, on to the third.
At the very least, we were hoping the sight of a supposedly paid-off police force moving in on their properties
would be enough to shake up the cozy setup between
the Dreamer lords and their bed partners in City Hall.

There was only one way to find out, though, and we
were on our way there. I sat in the back of the unmarked,
armored van Smiler had provided, fingering the shotgun
in my hands, turning it over and over. It had been a long
time since I'd worn a police uniform. Sitting there in
a stolen one was not making me comfortable. Looking
around the back of the van at the mobsters in their police
uniforms, I seemed more uncomfortable than they did.
Figures, I told myself.

I glanced at my watch. It was only minutes before ten
o'clock—the time our coordinated attack was supposed
to begin. I tensed again, biting at my lower lip. It felt
like the gnawing edge that would hit before a mission
during my service days, but it was more than combat
stomach. I'd never really worried about dying before,
never cared if there was anything on the other side of
the line or not.

My philosophy has always been . . . if there's a heav-
en and I get in—great. If the way I've lived my life
doesn't please some white-beard who thinks I don't fit
the angelic corporate mold—then I'll take what I get.
And if the last breath *is* all there is—if you die and then
all the pain is over with once and for all, but that is it, no

afterlife, no reincarnation, no nothing but the cold grave and the ravenous maws that invade it—then that's fine, too. I've never expected anything out of life except that which I can wrap my hands around. No, it wasn't the thought of dying that was bothering me, it was dying under the present circumstances.

My life has never meant much to anyone. I've never mattered in the grand scheme of things, or even much in any of the smaller schemes that exist around us all. In fact, I've purposely kept myself as removed from them as I could, pulling back every time I've found myself crossing over into somebody else's circle.

But, the little voice inside kept telling me, if I died then, in a stolen police uniform shooting up a Dreamer den, there was no way the truth was ever going to come out. My dead body was all my enemies were going to need. Rich wouldn't be able to uncover the truth—whatever that was. And even if he did, no one would care.

In fact, it was that apathy, the average New Yorker's world-famous disregard for everything around them, that had protected whoever my enemies were for so long in the first place. In a city where everyone is a transient, no one cares who destroys what, who steals what, who murders who, who rapes who, et cetera. Why should they? After all, they're only there to make a buck, just like everyone else. If I didn't stir things up, if Ray and I died, we'd just be another headline, replacing the names of the dead from the day before. The brands they marked us with would stick forever, or at least until this set of monsters was unseated and replaced by another.

Then, *if* our current foes were toppled, *maybe* the truth would out and people who had never heard of Jack Hagee and Ray Trenkel, who were only in New York to make their own pile of bucks and get out, maybe on some ride home from their wretched jobs, or over their morning coffee, for a few minutes they would be made aware that, hey, we were innocent after all.

Swell, I told myself. Afterlife or not, it just fucking wasn't enough. One way or another, even if I had to go down to do it, the guilty were paying for this one. I hadn't been asked to play this round. Other people had suckered me onto the court. Well, even if I lost the game, someone else was getting stuck picking up the markers.

I looked at my watch again. We had two minutes until we were supposed to hit the front door of our target—two minutes from the time Ray and his team would hit the front door of their target. By now Rich and Hu were off checking my apartment and my office, to see what the real cops had or had not done. By the time Ray and I were finished, and the four of us compared notes, we would know if we were going to have a chance or not.

Another glance at my wrist showed me we had ninety seconds left. The group of us, the six mafiosos hunkered on the van wall benches and myself, all checked our weapons a last time and smiled at each other. Some of the grins widened, one guy spit on the floor. Another followed him.

Thirty seconds were left. The doorman's hand moved to the release handle. Up front the driver was gliding us in toward the curb. Fifteen seconds—we could hear the brakes catching, feel the van slowing. Seven seconds—the click of the emergency lights coming on echoed throughout the cabin. Four seconds—the spokesman for the Italians pointed toward the door, saying,

"It's your show, Mr. Detective."

"Then let's fuck 'em up."

The doors flung open and we poured out of the van. Not worried about following the same safety book as real police, two of my men took the door—one slapping a massive bubble wad of C-4 plastic explosives on its center, the other giving him a two-second count to get clear before he punched his detonator. The door flew inward. We followed.

The resistance inside was minimal. The doormen were the last in, following myself and the others. We didn't leave them anything much to do. There were only five workers inside—one chemist, two mules, two guards. The guards went down under a hail of shotgun blasts, some from me, some from others. One of the mules pulled a .45—both he and his partner went down under another hail of tearing shot. The chemist dropped to the floor, the air around him filled with his voided bowels. Two of the Italians grabbed him up and dragged him to our van.

The rest of my small force worked at destroying everything inside the lab while I went outside to contain the general population. Regular citizens were staring out their windows up and down the street. The brave were pouring into the open, heading toward the factory. I scanned those approaching, watching for anyone who might be a hidden member of the Dreamer team looking for payback. None of the faces I saw read that way. Many of them were shouting slogans or singing with joy. Others were crying.

"Thank you, O dear holy Mother above, thank you," said one woman, touching at my sleeve as if I were the pope.

"We've tried for so long to get you to do something about these bastards," said another, talking to the stolen uniform I was wearing, not really to me.

"Kill them all!" shouted another. "Kill them! Kill them all—kill them all!"

I spoke to the crowd, ordering them back, telling them the area was far too dangerous for them to get any closer. As my team came out, assuring me that there was nothing salable left inside the factory, I picked out two of the more venerable of the citizens in the crowd and then told them,

"They'll be some more police here soon to clean up this mess. We have twenty more of these dens to hit today. I'd like you two to keep everyone back for their own safety until the others arrive."

The two older men, both Hispanic from the look of them, filled with pride. Their faces reflected their joy in being able to so visibly align themselves with the forces that had removed the drug factory—the one everyone had known of but hadn't been able to do anything about.

Getting back into the van, I gave our driver a smile to let him know we were all still alive and the high sign to get him moving again. Then I just settled back for the ride to our rendezvous point with Ray's team.

So far, I thought, so good. I'd managed to do something to keep the locals from pouring into the factory, as well as planting the notion within the crowd that we were going to be raising a lot more hell in the drug community A.S.A.P.

The captured chemist was on the floor, gagged as well as cuffed at the wrists and ankles. We were at the meet point in less than five minutes—the next site less than ten more away. Ray's team was waiting for us. Pulling up to the other van, I stuck my head out and asked,

"Any luck?"

"Naw," answered Ray. "Got in and out clean, but this bunch of trigger-happy lunatics didn't leave much. How about your bunch?"

"Clean. We got the chemist. You want to risk the time to question him or go for it?"

Ray weighed our options rapidly. If the chemist could give us a lead to follow, there was no need to hit the large factory for which we had the address. But if he didn't have anything, at the very least the wasted time would assuredly give the team there time to prepare for our assault. If we hit them fast, there was a much better chance we would all live through the attack. At that point, after what we'd both been through, I could see in Ray's face that he really didn't care how many drug dealers he killed that day.

Smiling at him, I asked,

"Well, why didn't you say so?"

He allowed one side of his mouth to curl upward slightly as we both climbed back into our vans. I let everyone know we were going for the next site as I made my way inside. Our driver had the van floored before we could get the doors shut.

CHAPTER 28

WE ARRIVED AT the main Dreamer den in eight minutes and twenty-three seconds. I timed the trip. So did everyone else in our van who was wearing a watch. The two who weren't just kept asking what time it was. People were happy to answer—how long our trip was taking was a matter of some importance to all of us. We knew our timing had to be just right.

We had to get there reasonably quickly—but not too quickly. Likewise, we could not take too much time, either. Too fast and we would get there before they had time to start dismantling their operation—if they thought we were headed for them at all. Too slow, of course, and everyone would be gone by the time we got there.

We had to hit them once they had the news that the cops were breaking their deal—throw them into a panic. They would have plenty of triggermen at a factory this size. We had to arrive just as their panic was setting in— not when they were expecting nothing and thus relaxed enough to do their jobs efficiently, or after their panic had passed and they were ready for a fight.

Having no way of knowing what time it was inside the Dreamer den when we arrived, we didn't bother with any fancy tactics. Ray's van took the drive-through doorway of the east side of the block, ours hit the two walk-in doors to the south. We took the same approach, hitting both doors with the same type of plastic explosive charges as before. Ray's group took the direct approach, driving their van straight through the corrugated metal entrance.

We poured through the doors as we had previously, pumping shot in all directions. Men flew backward and splattered against walls like water ballons exploding against the sidewalk. The battle was a lot less one-sided this time, however. More heavily armed, staffed by many more guards, and forewarned, the opposition began whittling our numbers down immediately.

Two of the Italians to my left went down almost instantly as we came through the doors. One was hit by vicious, rapid machine-gun fire, the burst coming unexpectedly from above. While others fired back at the hidden sniper, the first hit was cut in half by the spray of high-caliber lead, his legs falling forward, his torso backward—his mouth screaming for the entire time it took his lungs to empty. The other was hit in the head by enemy shotgun fire. His face disappeared in a red splash, flying along on the blur of metal pellets that ripped it away, smashing the bone underneath, smearing his brain into drops of gray rain that spread out in a sickening, moist circle on the wall behind him.

I pumped shells in the direction of the sniper until I had exhausted my first clip. Coming up empty, I dove behind a forklift where I could reverse my taped-together clip arrangement. I slid it out and back in quickly, watching as several rats raced by me in panic. Two of them spun around in tight circles, chasing themselves and each other, while the other bit each of them savagely. The third kept biting at the others for a handful of seconds, until finally they turned on it, all three of them swarming over each other, tearing bloody hunks away from wherever they could, one of them even biting himself.

I watched, fascinated for a moment, then turned back to the battle raging around me. Listening to large hunks of lead bouncing off the other side of the forklift, searching for a way to me through the steel and iron, I realized the "moment of proper attack," as Rice used to call it, was at hand—that single instant at the beginning of any skirmish when your enemy is at his most off balance.

Deafening noise came from every corner of the warehouse—weapons fire of all types, men shouting orders, begging for mercy, screeching prayers, puking at the sight of their friends' wounds, screaming mindlessly from the pain of their own. Then the ability to hear disappeared completely. I'd gone into the factory wearing standard-issue earplugs, knowing from long experience what a confusing, as well as painfully deafening, experience indoor gunfire can be. Even through the plugs, however, I'd still gone deaf from the incredible decibel ceiling being raised inside the metal warehouse.

Bullets ricocheted off every surface, heavy shot rebounded from the steel walls, gouged the cement flooring, all of it echoing over and over to create a brutal silence that made every moving mouth an empty gesture. It was the moment I was waiting for. Too many people accept movies as reality, not understanding that there isn't a single thing filmmakers won't lie about. What goes on in a gunfight is one of them. The cinema has given people an idea that you can shoot off guns inside and still hear, still talk to the guy next to you, still see through the clear air. In a word, this is bullshit.

Everyone in the warehouse was effectively deaf at that point, unable to communicate with each other, unable to see more than a few feet in front of them. The air was clogged with smoke and dust and flying Dreamer. Clouds of the drug, stirred by all the shooting, were filling the place. As I had expected, as is usual in such places, only the chemists had face masks. I had told the Italians what was sure to happen when we attacked. Now that it had, the earplugs and nose filters I'd recommended were making more sense to them.

Knowing I'd have no better chance, I stood up from behind the forklift and started firing blind into the smoke and dust above eye level. Moving forward into the confusion, I motioned for the rest of our two teams to follow me, and then left them behind, not caring if they were with me or not. I'd reached that moment in the battle when looking to see if someone is on your left or right is futile and dangerous.

In any such fight, although you certainly hope there are a few people on your side, to count on them for anything is practically suicidal. Your senses have to take over for your brain—conscious thought pushed aside in favor of instinct. Every direction, every avenue of attack, is up to you to cover. It's like any other part of any other day, basically—just more intense.

Reveling in the intensity, I stopped worrying about dying and charged into the enemy, working at making them worry instead. My mad dash took me from the southeastern corner of the warehouse in a straight line for the northwestern one. I pumped shotgun shells in all forward directions as I ran, screaming at the top of my lungs to pump my own blood as I plowed onward. I dodged my way through the drug-laden tables and crates leaving dying men on both sides of my attack line.

Halfway to the back my second clip emptied. I chucked the double away and slapped in another while still on the run. Two figures loomed up in front of me at that moment. Instinct brought my shotgun to level—common sense assured me they couldn't be members of my own team—fear of their abilities pulled the trigger, the one shell blowing one of the figures away into the distance, spinning the other around and off to the side. The body slammed into several packing crates, toppling them. It had been a woman. Part of my brain wondered if she had deserved to die, the rest ignored her, knowing she was of the enemy, knowing than nothing mattered except staying alive and killing everything around me.

I scrambled into the protective nook they had vacated, slipping in a smear of blood greasing the floor. I went down badly, my upper arm crashing against something rounded but hard. Not able to handle the shotgun with one arm numbed, I grabbed the .38 out of the side holster of the uniform I was wearing and cocked it, waiting for a moment to catch my breath.

Machine-gun fire slammed along the wall of crates I had my back against, sending another cloud of Dreamer into the air. I pushed myself down lower, worming my way away from the bullets I could see but could not hear.

As another figure came into view I sighted for a second, determining whether or not it was wearing a police uniform. When the haze cleared enough to show me that it was another of the enemy, I let fly with two shots, spinning the body around twice. When I saw that these were not enough to put the man down, I fired again and again, and then again, finally knocking the machine gun-toting figure over.

Two more men came up behind me, my own team this time. The first pointed ahead, making a shrugging motion with his shoulders indicating his concern over whether we should keep moving forward or not. I started to answer him when suddenly the other pointed forward. Looking in the direction he indicated, we saw flame spreading wildly throughout the warehouse, burning away the drug dust in the air, replacing it with various grades of smoke.

Before we could move, an unhearable explosion rocked the floor, knocking one of the Italians off his feet. A monstrous pillar of fire blasted upward from the back regions of the warehouse, splashing against the ceiling and raining back down on all inside. The look of it told me it was a chemical fire, one that would burn even if flooded over.

My companions, having made the same connection, made to head back for the way we had come in. I joined them. We dashed for the ruined entrances, no longer worried about being shot. Everyone within the warehouse who could still move was on the run, abandoning their fellows and their guns, racing for the doors.

Burning money floated on the superheated air, a fiery confetti raining down equally on all the frenzied escapees. Flame spread to every corner, springing up in a dozen more places every second, blocking exits, catching on the clothing of many of those who tried to simply run through it.

We stumbled into the street, choking, coughing, some of us so dazed they stumbled out into the freezing slush and simply stayed where they fell. I looked back at the black smoke belching out of the building, my eyes blurring with tears as I continued to hack. A roaring thrust of flame threw itself out of the door through which we'd just exited, one so superheated it melted the ice on the sidewalk beneath. It was fairly easy to see there were going to be a lot more dead than we had planned on if the warehouse didn't have a back way out that we hadn't been able to discover.

Ray came over toward me, dragging a Hispanic man who continued to retch in the snow throughout the entire trip. He was wearing an expensive suit—the jewelry on his hands was worth more money than I'd ever seen in one place.

"What do you think?" coughed Ray, screaming to be heard over the ringing in his ears.

I nodded my head, still coughing myself, barely able to hear him. Wiping at the soot stinging my eyes, I slid the .38 in my hand back into its holster and then took the shotgun from Ray's hand, using it to cover him while we made our way to the van in which my team had come. By that time, the streets were filling with citizens, slapping their arms against the cold, jabbering and screaming at each other, wondering at what was happening—illogically attracted to the gunfire, flames, and explosions the way the bored are everywhere.

In no position to be slowed down at that point, Ray and I, along with about two-thirds of the men we had started with, piled into the remaining van, cramming in those few prisoners we had been able to grab. Then, hitting the illegal siren taped to the dashboard, the driver forced the gathering crowd out of our way. We abandoned the area to the fire trucks we could not hear but assumed would be there soon.

We had what we wanted.

CHAPTER 29

I'D NEVER PARTIED with mafiosos before—it was refreshing to find out they didn't do it much different than anyone else. While our van was still in sight of the burning warehouse, one of them had already pulled a bottle of Martell out of his bag and begun passing it around. It was empty before we saw the first of the fire trucks. I took a healthy pull, just to clear the smoke and gritty scum clogging my throat, if for no other reason.

The man next to me took one twice as healthy, then grabbed the head of one of our prisoners and poured one of equal strength down his throat. The handcuffed man sputtered and coughed, spewing a mouthful of smoke-grayed phlegm down his chest, but did not protest. Another bottle followed that one, another appearing before the first could be drained. I caught Ray's eye as one of the bottles reached me, the other reaching him at the same moment. Ignoring the whooping and shouts all around us, we tilted our bottles toward each other in salute. and then we both threw our heads back and drank, long and hard before passing the bottles on to those waiting for them.

An hour later we were hidden in a Chinatown basement, reviewing our options. The van, police uniforms, and all the other equipment we had used was gone, sunk in one of the rivers flowing around Manhattan. No one bothered to tell me which one and I didn't ask.

The surviving Italians had all departed as well. There had been a lot of shaking of hands and hugging, most of them letting Ray and I know that we were *"Tu bene, mia frattello."* Always a goal of mine to be considered a brother to the Mafia. But I took it in the spirit it was given, remembering that I'd been the one asking these guys for help and that I'd called people a lot worse than them "friend" in my time.

After the separation, we took our prisoners—four in total, the chemist from the smaller factory, and two mules and the Suit from the larger—back to Chinatown to see what we could learn. The mules weren't talking, but it didn't matter. The questioning of only a few minutes let us know that they didn't know anything. The chemist was perfectly willing to talk, but he didn't know a thing we could use.

The three responses were to be expected. Mules are a dime a dozen. A mule who displeases his masters in any way at all, let alone dropping a dime on them, is easily killed and replaced. Good chemists, however, are hard to find. Subsequently, they are told next to nothing almost all of the time because it's realized that they will talk because they know they are valuable. The Suit was another matter, however.

He was the kind that can go either way: maybe have something, maybe not—maybe talk, maybe not. With Smiler's men standing around him in a semicircle, Ray took it upon himself to outline the man's options for him, throwing in a few lies to help the mix.

"Let's get cozy here, buddy. I want to explain something to you, and I want you to get it straight right from the beginning." He flipped his badge in the already frightened man's face, telling him,

"The deal days are over. You people can't pay us enough for protection anymore. Now, you remember that because I'm going to ask you questions and you're going to talk. You know why? Because if you don't, I'm going to make your life a fucking nightmare that never ends. If you don't give me what I want—exactly the way I want it—you're going to live in a hole the rest of your life. You're going to be my dog. Do you understand?"

When the Suit chose not to respond, Ray cuffed him across the face, a single-fisted backhand that knocked the man over backward. Signaling to three of the Chinese strong arms behind him, Ray directed the trio forward, ordering them to strip the Suit. Happy to comply, none of the three was gentle in their work. Then, once the trio had backed off from the naked man on the floor, Ray came forward with a length of chain attached to a choke collar, which he slipped around the man's neck.

"Now, Spot, let me give you a little bit of an idea what I'm talking about here."

He kicked the man in the side, his winter boot raising a bruise larger than the one on my arm.

"Heel, you mutt."

Dragging Spot across the room, he pulled him over the cold, wet cement of the basement floor. Jerking him hard, he kicked him again, bouncing him off of the wall.

"Heel, you motherfuckin' bastard."

Then Ray jerked the chain, cutting off Spot's air. While the man clawed at the constricted collar, Ray took the opportunity to deliver another sure kick—this one to the side of the head.

"You think I don't have time to get you properly trained, mutt? You think your ass isn't going to win blue ribbons for obedience when I'm finished with you? Think again, Spotty-boy. Think again."

Seeing that Ray's tactics were going to take a little while, but having faith that they would work in the end, I excused myself and headed upstairs to where I could find a phone. A woman assigned to help us led me up the various stairways and through the halls to Smiler's office. I looked around as I came in. Smiler had had his personal area done up in a style that might best be described as suitable for the CEO of Fu Manchu, Inc.

It was a clever blending of the standard furnishings of a typical Manhattan executive's office with a number of stereotypical props straight out of a 1940s pulp magazine story, right down to a brilliantly colored macaw in a delicate bamboo cage and a loose marmoset that scampered from corner to corner as long as I was standing. As soon as I sat, the monkey perched itself atop the high-backed chair of its master and stayed there. As I looked around, Smiler asked,

"Do you like it?"

"Well," I admitted, "if nothing else it proves you have a sense of humor."

The young gangster laughed, nodding his head to let me know I'd given him the reaction he was looking for. Then he fed a small piece of banana to the chittering marmoset while asking me,

"So, are we a success already?"

"Not quite. But," I assured the young gangster, "you can see in this guy's eyes he knows something we can use. And I think you can see that he's going to tell it sooner or later, too."

"Excellent. This is good for us both, then . . . yes?" When I only nodded in return, my mind drifting off toward some nagging problem I couldn't yet quite focus on, Smiler continued, saying,

"You are a very interesting man, Big Jack. Can I get you anything? Whiskey, a cigar, Coke-a-Cola?"

I told him that some cigarettes and some aspirin would be best at the moment. The smoke I'd inhaled during the escape from the warehouse fire was still making my head pound. Of course, why I wanted a cigarette then I'm not sure, but it was provided by one of Smiler's lackeys before I could even question my motives.

My requests were brought on a small silver tray along with a glass of water. I washed down the pair of Advils, then lit up one of the Marlboros on the tray. Not one of my usual Camels, but not bad. While I exhaled my first drag back out into the office, Smiler told the woman who had led me to his office to massage my temples.

"Lie Shiu is very skilled in these matters. She will break up the pain in your head even faster than the drugs. Please allow her to try."

I acquiesced, leaning back in my chair far enough to allow the woman to more easily reach my forehead. Trying to be a gentleman, I even crushed my cigarette out after only one more drag. Her fingers were soft but strong. It seemed only a matter of seconds before the tensions and pains that had been eating at me began to disappear. As Lie Shiu continued to work, Smiler said,

"If it seems I'm taking advantage by asking you what I now will, please tell me so. I will find another time. But, Big Jack, there is something I do wish to ask you, and since the timing now does seem so very advantageous to me, I thought I would at least put the question in the air and see what your reaction was—if that was all right with you."

"Go for it," I told him.

Even though my eyes were closed I could feel him smile. Immediately, he said,

"Very well, I would like to establish what grounds would be acceptable to you on which the two of us could continue to work together in the future."

I opened my eyes at that one. Back when I'd been with Military Intelligence, the government taught us all how to control our faces—how to move our eyes when surprised, how to keep the blood from flooding our cheeks, when to smile, when to laugh, et cetera. I'd been caught off guard on a conscious level, but I could feel the correct look of quiet interest settling on my face—a much better response to show externally than the mildly nervous shock I was actually feeling.

Figuring I knew where Smiler was headed, I asked,

"Can I be honest without jeopardizing our present relationship?"

"Men like you are rare in this world. I would always seek your friendship, Big Jack, even if we became enemies. Tell me what you wish."

Sitting up, I pushed Lie Shiu's hands aside gently. I wanted to be able to see Smiler's eyes—show him mine—while I gave him my answer.

"I won't work for *anyone* except on my terms. I tried the government, I tried the police . . . I guess maybe I just don't play well with others."

I picked up the glass of water that had been brought with the Advils, using the device of taking a drink to break the moment, giving me the chance to repeat myself when I put the glass back down so that there would be no mistaking what it was I had told him.

"Whenever I work for someone else," I told him again, thanking my service days for the few useful things they'd taught me, "it's got to be by my rules. If you have work to offer me, I'll judge it by the same criteria I do any other job. In other words," I told him, settling back into my chair,

"I respect you—you're welcome in my home. We're getting to that point where it's hard to tell who owes who a favor. I'd trust you to take care of my dog. But like you or like anyone, there are some things . . . I just won't do—period."

"Good," answered Smiler. "I'd hate to think I'd mis-judged you, Big Jack." Sitting back in his own chair, he pulled his marmoset down into his lap. Scratching the monkey behind the ears, he asked,

"But I have been running this meeting where I wanted it to go and have not asked why you came up. You did come to see me, yes?"

"Actually I just wanted to use the phone."

Smiler pointed to one positioned on his desk for the use of those sitting on the other side. "Unless," he said, "it is a private call?"

I smiled innocently, as if I thought there were actually a private line somewhere within the young gangster's complex. He smiled back, playing the same game. Telling him the one right there would be fine, I grabbed up the receiver and punched in Hubert's number. I got his machine, but he picked up as soon as he heard my voice.

"Hey, hey, Hagee. What's up, Dick Tracy?"

"That's what I want from you. Did you get to do a pass-by on my apartment and office?"

"Yeah, sure did. And like the little Nazi used ta say, 'Veeeerrrrrrrry interesting.' "

"Spill it."

"Both yer castle and yer workshop got a royal trashin'. But take a wild guess at what they took?"

"I'm in no mood for guessin' games, Hu. Will you just get on with . . ."

I was forced to ask Hubert to hold for a moment, however, as a commotion from the hall stole the attention of everyone in the room. A number of Smiler's people entered the room, some preceding and some following Ray and his new pet. Ray dragged the naked drug dealer along, purposely walking faster than the man on his leash could keep up.

Finally getting him into the office, though, he stopped the Hispanic at the side of Smiler's desk. Giving the chain a short jerk, he said,

"Our host's shoes are dirty. Be a good dog and lick them clean."

The man on the floor, his puffy eyes tearing again, bent his head low without hesitation and began running his tongue over Smiler's shoes. As everyone in the room watched, suddenly the young gangster's marmoset leapt down from his perch to Smiler's desk. Leaping from there to the kneeling man's back, Mighty Joe Young stuck its nose in between the man's cheeks and then leapt back to the desk, chittering in wild disgust. Everyone in the room laughed or chuckled or at least smiled. The man on the floor kept crying and licking Smiler's shoes. I got back to Hubert, telling him quietly,

"I'm going to have to get going—looks like there's going to be a breakthrough here. So tell me quick, what the hell did they boost from me?"

"Okay. It was the cops, right? You know? More of Fisher's men, right? Anyway—both places, right?—they put the grab on all your videotapes."

Taken slightly aback, I asked Hu to hold on again and then asked Ray if his pet had talked yet. His answer was to give a demonstration. Ordering Spot to sit up and speak, he finally got us the last piece of the puzzle.

"I swear to you," blubbered the drug dealer, "I swear—it's the D.A.'s office. They're in charge of everything. Sure, the mayor is their friend. Sure, everybody's got their hand in it, sure—what else—you expect it. But, I swear—to the Holy Mother, I swear it—we deal directly with them. They do everything. I can give it all to you—I will, I will. I swear, I swear—everything I know. Where the drugs come in, who gives the payments, who gets the payments . . . yes, I can tell you who ordered that stupid woman killed, yes, yes, I will . . . everything—*everything*."

And then, after that, the man fell to crying hysterically, thrashing on the floor, wailing as if the last of his sanity had snapped. People laughed even harder than the last time. Even the monkey and the bird joined in. Then suddenly I remembered I still had Hubert on the line. Getting back on with him, I said,

"Listen, Hu, you still have a copy of the Sinnott tape, right?"

"Sure—that thing's f-funnier than shit."

"Swell. Get over here as soon as you can with it, will you?"

I gave him Smiler's address and then rang off. Sitting back in my chair, I shut my eyes—weary and tired—too exhausted to be a part of the festivities unfolding in the room. As soon as my eyes closed, Lie Shiu moved forward as if it had been a signal and started massaging my temples again. I let her, using the blessed, healing motions to help block out the noise of the revelers and their whining object of torment.

Going back in my mind, I called up the image of the tape Carmine had shot, watching the late Andrew Sinnott go through his paces. I knew that that tape was the one the cops had been looking for. Now, the question was—why? What was there about it that made it important—important enough to get an assistant D.A.'s wife murdered, and the assistant D.A. himself. Important enough to get me framed for murder along with a police captain, and yet so unobvious both Hubert and I had watched the tape—him more than once—and noticed nothing.

Letting Lie Shiu distance me from my surroundings, I lived in the darkness behind my eyes, concentrating on the videotape. Remembering it as sharply as I could, I replayed it in my head—scene for scene—following it from the beginning. I watched Andy enter, order, and sit down. I watched him throw his money on the floor, make a big deal out of finding it, call the waitress over. I watched her reaction—arms going up, mock surprise on her face . . .

And that was when I told myself that it couldn't be that easy. Replaying the woman's face in my brain, I froze the image of her in my mind and then went back to the last time I'd watched television, replaying that image on another screen in my head. I compared the two scenes, looking closely at the women in both of them, moving them around in my head, trying to see if I could lay the one over the other. After a few minutes I found they fit with no trouble at all.

After that I canceled the images, finally just sitting back and relaxing, allowing myself to slide totally under Lie Shiu's gentle ministrations.

Yes—I told myself as I surrendered to the gentle hands on my forehead, a little sad at the truth, but relieved nonetheless—yes, it could be that easy.

It's always that easy.

CHAPTER 30

RICH AND HUBERT arrived at Smiler's in the early afternoon. Ray and I had called them to meet us because it was finally time to straighten out the mess I'd started by taking Vivian Sinnott as a client. Of course, in theory, taking Lo's case was what had actually caused the mess, unless one wanted to get really technical and point out that it wasn't the people trying to avoid the thieves and killers who had started anything.

Whatever the case, however, before trusting my freedom—let alone everyone else's involved—to my memory, I checked out the tape Hubert brought with him carefully, making sure what I'd put together was correct. Everyone else checked it out with me. Now that we knew where to look, what we saw seemed like more than enough. After that, having come to an agreement over the value of what we had, we outlined our next steps and then put them into immediate operation.

In truth, it might have made more sense to wait until the next day when we were rested, but I just couldn't. Neither could Ray. We'd spent too long being the only ones called murderers. We were tired of waiting for the chance to do a little name-calling of our own.

The first thing we did was to dispatch Rich to City Hall. His job was to convince the mayor that we had enough to bring down most of his corrupt little government and that if he didn't play ball with us, we'd work at bringing him down along with it. Our promise was that we wouldn't do anything to implicate him if he gave us a clear path to those we wanted. Rich was the only man for the job, probably the only man in all of Manhattan whose reputation could allow him to walk in and make such assurances, let alone threats, and be taken seriously on both counts.

After that, while Rich was on his way to Gracie Mansion, Ray started the gathering of a number of real cops, men and women that he knew he could trust. They were told to gather at Gracie with as much legal hardware as they could muster. At the same time, Hu was on the phone, alerting the Chet Greens of New York to what was upcoming. Getting through to the top muckrakers at each of the city's papers, radio stations, and television news divisions, he gave them just enough to make sure that when everyone else showed up at the mayor's home that there would be someone there to record the event.

The obvious reason for that was that none of us had any doubt that if Ray and I were to waltz in to the mayor's by ourselves we would end up as so much hamburger being passed out to the homeless in some Bowery shelter. We also knew that trying to go straight to the media would only start a press war with City Hall issuing its statements and us issuing ours. That would go on until the downtown boys could get someone close enough to us to take us out, and then, without us to focus on anymore, the media would assume City Hall was right after all. And that would be that.

No, if we were going to survive, we had to have the mayor in our pocket—ready to cut off those who had slipped up to save his own oily backside. All of this left me with nothing much to do save wait around while everyone else took care of the last loose ends.

I thought about calling Sally, but decided against it. We were too close now for me to blow it by making some lovesick high school boob slip. Maybe it was paranoid of me to think that the opposition might have bugged phones at the *Post* in their attempt to find me, but like the man said, "Even paranoids have enemies." With that in mind, I settled for sitting back and waiting.

I spent a little time feeding banana slices to Smiler's marmoset. I spent some more playing cards with three members of his muscle squad, one of whom had tried to brain me with a baseball bat in the middle of Mott Street a few days earlier. I didn't let it get to me. We'd been unknowns to each other then—it had just been business.

He apologized for it quite properly enough when we finally recognized each other after a few hands, a sincere act that bought him considerable face with the two older hands at the table. I told him there were no hard feelings, which was true. What did I care? It had to be remembered, I was trying to kill him, too.

After a while, though, it was finally time to go. One of the old hands had done slightly better than the rest of us, but no one had lost very much. We'd all been too tense about what was going to happen next to get overly concerned about our cards. The way it sat, if the mayor played things straight and went for covering his losses, then everything was in the bag. If not, then a lot of people were going to get hurt and the whole house of cards was coming down anyway. Rich assured us the mayor had promised to play ball, but what in hell was a politician's promise worth?

Smiler met us on the street, standing in the newly falling snow to hold open the door of the car he had donated to the war effort. I had to admit, for a gangster, it was a nice touch. He extended his hand, palm open. I gave him mine. As we shook, he offered,

"Good luck, Big Hagee. We just put a fresh platter of oranges out and lit another bundle of incense for you."

"Thanks," I told him, grateful for the human contact. Some people may not like it, may feel cheated that I didn't have some flip line ready to throw in his face after all he had done for us, but I really couldn't care less. You don't question "who?" pulls you out of the fire, you only ask "why?" Then, if you go along with his motives, no more questions are allowed.

A gangster had owed me a favor that when I'd needed it, I collected; now we were even. Anyone who has trouble with that, well, all I can say is, they've never really been in any real trouble. As we stood for those last seconds on the sidewalk, working at ignoring the piercing cold of late afternoon, Smiler said, more to Ray than to me,

"You know, I do have my own reasons for helping you two. Sure, I want to break the Hispanic lock on the Dreamer trade, but not for profit. I'm just tired of my people having to take the rap for the stuff. Clean?"

"Clean," said Ray, only a trace of grudge left in his voice.

"Are you sure, Captain?" asked Smiler, only half kidding at him. In a condescending voice, he added, "You know, I'm still a bad guy. My people sell drugs, run whores, they break the legs of borrowers who don't meet their payments . . ."

"Yeah," agreed Ray. "But, fuck, so does the mayor and we're ready to make a deal with him, too."

Smiler laughed then—clear, high, young laughter that turned the heads of every passerby in the streets, no matter how hard they were consciously trying not to notice their young lord. Ray and I smiled, too. Hell, why not? It was funny.

Then, after that, not really caring what came next, we got into the backseat of the waiting four-door and let it take us off in the general direction of the mayor's mansion. The snow fell all around us, prompting Ray to dig a flask out of his inner jacket pocket so we could toast the weather.

After we'd both had a good slug, we passed the flask up to the driver. He took a slug of his own and then passed it back. After another round, he passed it back again and then for some reason or another started to sing "Jingle Bells."

By the time he reached the chorus Ray and I had each lubricated our throats once more and joined in ourselves.

CHAPTER 31

WE ARRIVED AT Gracie Mansion just as the festivities began to get out of hand. Neither of us was anywhere near as drunk as we would have liked. After a few minutes of searching faces, Ray spotted one of his men, my pal Detective Mooney, standing with a quartet of Ray's handpicked police. The five opened to let us get into their center and then closed ranks, trying to hide us with their bodies. On one level I wished we could have found someone else who Ray trusted. On another, though, I knew that when people were playing fast and dirty, even I would trust Mooney before most other cops.

While we got out into the freezing cold, one of them whispered to another and then took off while Mooney reported,

"It's a mess, Captain."

"Give it."

"There's Brooklyn all over the street; Fisher's got all his dirt squad goons mixed in here. I think the mayor might be hoping for the 'accidental death' route here."

The man who left returned with two others. Each of them was holding a street-patrol winter jacket and hat. Ray started to shrug off his coat, telling me,

"Put one on. I told the boys to have a set ready for us. Least it gives us a chance to get inside without getting gunned down out here like the mad dogs we are."

"Works for me," I told him, throwing my own coat off back over my shoulders. Once we had our rookie disguises on, Mooney continued,

"We've got a squad car waiting up about ten blocks. When we give them the signal, they're going to make a running entrance. All of our guys know it's a dodge. They're going to rush the street, let everyone know that you're coming in. Once all that's goin' on, we figure we can get you inside in one piece." He indicated me with a wave of his thumb.

"Maybe even dog shit here, too."

"I don't expect to live through this, Mooney," I told him. "After all, if a decent, upstanding organization like the New York City Police Department can be corrupted, what chance is there for scum like me?"

I could tell Mooney had a good comeback, but Ray cut it off, growling,

"You two shut the fuck up—now. We have absolutely no time for this shit. Am I understood?"

"Yes, sir," Mooney told him.

"Hey, I'm everyone's pal," I said innocently. "I couldn't say an unkind word if my life depended on it."

"I'm so glad to hear it," answered Ray. His voice had grown terse. I didn't blame him. It was his show now. Proving it, he started giving orders.

"Okay, Jackson, give us ten minutes to get as close as we can and then give your signal. Mooney, you and Hawkes are with us. Hoffman, take the point, if we see you coming back toward us we'll take it that there's trouble we're not ready for and back off until you report."

Hoffman snapped a salute and started making his way through the crowd. Turning to the tallest cop in the crowd, Ray said,

"Thornton, you watch Hoffman from about ten, fifteen yards—if he hits trouble use your judgment, help him or get back to warn us. Whichever gets the job done."

Another salute and another uniform disappeared into the crowd. While Thornton moved off, Ray kept a tight eye on his watch, gauging how long it was going to take his point men to get far enough in front to make them effective, all the while watching the ten minutes until our diversion continued to run out. With eight and a half minutes left, he said,

"Let's go."

We moved through the crowd slowly, trying to look like the others in the area. The front of Gracie Mansion was littered with both print and electronic reporters, as well as dozens of police and hundreds of just plain citizens. We inched along, avoiding everyone we could, working our way toward the front doors, trying not to draw any attention to ourselves.

The top of Thornton's hat never left Ray's sight. First we saw Hoffman move inside, and then finally Thornton. The coast was either clear or it wasn't. Coupling to that the fact that time was running out, we started up the front stairs. I ducked my head down to light a Camel as we went past a group of cops who seemed a bit too interested in who we were. I sensed one debating with himself as to whether or not it was worth his time to investigate. He had a shotgun, as did three others in his group. Then, just as he was making up his mind, a rookie with a large box of foam-cupped coffees came up to the group. The welcome sight of the steaming cups broke the man's concentration, letting us slip by.

Ray checked his watch again. As we came through the doors, he could see Hoffman and Thornton waiting for us behind the first indoor checkpoint. Ray was timing our entrance to hit along with the sound of sirens. Right on cue, as the street broke into pandemonium, everyone inside crowded the doors. Ray led us past them all, fairly sure of where we would find the mayor.

Within another two minutes, though, we were hearing a flurry of shouts and curses from outside—it hadn't taken the opposition long to realize we weren't in the cars. Now everyone who had been waiting outside was storming the building. Panic filled the air, our foes, our allies, and ourselves all realizing in one single moment of clarity that the moment of truth had finally come. We reached the mayor's den before anyone else. The right honorable lord of New York City was inside, entertaining Judith Siegel with an open bottle of brandy.

The D.A. recognized us, did a double take, and then exploded to her feet, cursing,

"Fuck, they're here? You let them get in here?!"

"Now, now, Judith . . ." started the mayor. "I'm sure that nothing is going—"

"You sold me out," she screamed. "You fucking horse-sucking shitpile!"

Siegel started swinging, rapping the startled mayor two good ones to the head before Mooney could pull her away from him. Still swinging while Mooney held her off her feet, the D.A. screamed,

"You don't have anything! I'll get all of you! I'll drag down this whole administration. I'll take the—"

"You won't do anything but shut up," Ray told her.

"It is all over, Ms. D.A.," I added. "Your goons were pretty thorough, but they didn't manage to get all the copies of the tape. It was a nice try, though."

Ray looked at me, waiting to see where I would go with things next. I looked the panting dark brunette hanging in Mooney's arms up and down, hating her as much as I'd ever hated anyone in my life. Then, talking fast, I told the mayor,

"Things you may or may not know, Your Honor. Judith here had a down-and-dirty fling with Andrew Sinnott. We never made the connection because we were studying the key we had to things, Sinnott himself. Mrs. Sinnott, though, she studied what any cheated-on wife would—the other woman. She recognized her husband's boss—like any woman would. The blond wig, the change over to the whore makeup, stuff like that fools guys—but not wives. So, finally having the goods she needed, she told Andy she was going to get her divorce."

Switching my direction, I blasted at Siegel, telling her,

"When you heard about that, you knew it would only be a matter of time before you'd be identified. I'm sure you could see the headlines coming—THE D.A. OF T&A—no, nobody likes a scandal. Especially not when they're directing the city's drug traffic, and they're smart enough to know that one investigation can always lead to another."

Pausing for a breath in the best Perry Mason–like fashion I could muster, I turned up the volume in my voice and then bore down on Siegel, growling in her face,

"So, you had Mrs. Sinnott killed. Your access to the Outliner's files made setting that up easy. Then, when you found out Andy didn't like what you'd done, you had him killed, too. Hell, why not—right? He was okay for some cheap thrill partying, but that kind of action had already caused you enough trouble. After that, when Ray and I stumbled onto your hit men, you tried for us, too."

I stopped for one last breath, and then asked the still struggling D.A.,

"Tell me how close I am."

"You fuck!" she screamed. "You bastard fuck! I was supposed to let my career go down the tubes over a dare?! I go to that damn club and throw wild with an office boob one miserable time and I lose everything?! Rot in hell, you fucks! *You fucks!!*"

The mayor hung his head, calling quietly into the hall for some officers to come and take Ms. Siegel away. My instincts sent my hand toward my .38 when three officers came walking in, one of them Clements. He smiled as he walked past, giving me a conspiratorial nod as he did.

I burned at the sight of him, my hands not understanding why I simply didn't gun the bastard down and be done with it. Watching me, the mayor gave me a slight shake of the head, almost as if he knew what I was thinking. Then, before anything else could happen, the three new arrivals took the screaming woman away.

I looked over at Ray and could see he felt the same way I did, his hand as anxious to find a gun as mine was. As we shared our silent thought, he started to say something, but before he could, suddenly gunshots tore open the air in the hallway. Everyone crowded for the door, scrambling to get it open. When we did, we were told that everything was under control. The two cops I didn't recognize were both all right. They were the only ones.

Clements was sprawled on the floor, his gun out of its holster. He was shot through the heart. It was easy to see that there was no chance he would survive the wound. Judith Siegel was dead as well, sprawled on the floor in a broken heap. The most honest woman in New York City politics had gone to her reward.

EPILOGUE

YOU WOULD THINK it would be raining. Most times when everything winds down around a funeral you think of everyone standing around in the rain—black coats, black hats, black umbrellas. It wasn't raining on us that morning, though. It was too cold. We got freezing wind, instead.

As I stood listening to the sermon, looking at the other faces around me, I accepted that I wasn't going to find anything to take my mind off what had happened two days earlier. It was the lousiest deal I'd ever swallowed, and believe me, I've swallowed some beauts in my time. Every other time I've done it, I had good reasons. I had good ones this time, too, which is the only reason I'd allowed the mayor to get away with only delivering us Siegel and Clements.

He had done it, of course, because they were the only ones on which we had something and he could live without them. The way they put the story together for the media ran like this:

As the three officers the mayor had called in escorted Siegel out, she grabbed Clements's gun out of his holster and managed to kill him before the other two could shoot her in self-defense.

Ray asked the mayor point-blank if we were supposed to accept such an obvious setup as the truth. The mayor sent everyone from the room but Ray and me. In a low voice, he told us,

"You two have what you want. You're cleared. The

media will lick your asses and make you stars for handing them a big fat juicy story to fill their page ones and their eleven o'clock lead spots."

As Ray began to raise an arm in protest, the mayor shot him a hard look and warned him,

"Don't you say it, mister. Don't you say a word before you think a little bit about what I'd have to say back. You've got what you wanted, all of it. You've avenged Vivian Sinnott, even Andrew Sinnott if you wanted to. Your fucking justice has been served."

Allowing a second of silence to make his point, he continued then, saying,

"And on top of that, all the people who tried to kill you are dead. Clements's partner, the man you two doused in kerosene—you may remember that little prank—died in the hospital a few hours ago. Sinnott's bodyguard, Mike, you remember him? Surprise, surprise, he was found only minutes ago facedown in the river."

Then the mayor turned his back for a minute, ostensibly to light a cigar, more likely just to break eye contact with us. With his back still turned, he spoke in between puffs.

"So before we make any threats, before the D.A.'s office is put to the bother of deciding whether or not it wants to press charges in the before-mentioned murders, let's let sleeping dogs lie. You boys have done the city a great service in helping us rid ourselves of some nasty embarrassments." He turned again, all happy, election-winning smiles.

"So now, go on," he told us. "Go reap the rewards of being heroes. Go get laid, get drunk, tell your story to Channel Eleven, get some groupies, whatever the fuck you want out of this. Go get it. Judith Siegel made a terrible mistake, and now she's paid for it. Let's just work to get past all this and try to heal our poor city, shall we?"

The mayor extended his hand. Ray was on the edge, deciding whether or not to blow his stack. Taking the

mayor's extended hand during Ray's moment of indeci-
sion, I shook it soundly, saying,

"Thank you, sir, thank you."

"My pleasure, son," answered the smiling face.

"Oh, and, sir . . ." I added, prodding Ray toward the
door, talking over my shoulder,

"Yes . . . ?"

"Don't make any 'terrible mistakes,' yourself, okay?
Elsewise we might have to be heroes all over again."

What his smile might have turned into after that I
don't know. We left to go have all the fun the mayor
had suggested we have, hours and days of turning away
reporters, dodging embarrassing questions, trying to keep
on the tightrope set out before us. It wasn't easy.

First off, not only did we have the downfall of the D.A.
laid at our feet, but the Outliner as well. Mike's body
hadn't been the only one found. The former scourge of
the city had been found as his own last victim. His suicide
letter had been addressed to his father, letting him know
that Dad had been wrong, that he . . . "had never taken
it up the ass. Not me, Dad. I killed the ones that did. I
know you'll be proud."

Chet Green had written up his story, laying out all
of our work at St. Rose's, making it sound that by our
having doped everything out correctly, we had somehow
pushed the Outliner to take his own life. Thanks, Green.
Now, he was on his way to the Pulitzer the *Post* had
always expected Rich to win, and Rich was stuck going
along with the party line because that was all Ray and I
could give him.

It galled me to not only use Rich as my "exclusive
source," giving me a stick to beat away all the other
reporters, but also to then not give him the whole story.
He knew I wasn't giving him everything, but he also was
smart enough to know why. He didn't bother me about
any of the sensitive stuff, making me feel all the more of
a heel for selling out. I knew there wasn't anything else
we could have done, that Ray and I, and probably Rich,

would have joined Mike in the Hudson if we would have handled things any other way. The little voice inside was annoyed with me, however, not caring that I had responsibilities now outside of pleasing my own ego.

I looked down at Elba, standing next to me, wiping her freezing tears aside, absently fingering her necklace. Her brothers and sisters were there, as well as their aunt. Sally had come with us, as had the little Doc, and something close to fifty of the media's choicest scumbuckets, prying monsters with no scruples whatsoever about ramming their microphones into the faces of children trying to brave their way through the funerals of the last parent they had had and one of their brothers.

Their father's body had been found badly burned in the warehouse Ray and I had attacked. The flames hadn't killed him, however. The autopsy had revealed he had been dead for some time before the fire hit. An execution-style bullet, just behind the right ear, had made his passing a great deal less painless than being burned to death . . . the way Rickie had died.

Rickie had been caught in the same inferno, but he had been roasted alive. And, worse for everyone, the gun found in his hand was the one that had killed his father. Those prisoners taken by the police who had arrived after Ray and I had left all said Rickie had committed the execution because his father had been causing too much trouble. When the murder had been ordered, Rickie had volunteered. The boss had been very proud of his protégé. That, of course, was before Ray had taught the boss how to shine shoes.

Sally held my hand, looking into my eyes, asking me silently what exactly I was going to do. All I could do was look back at her sadly and let her know I wasn't sure. Elba and her brother and sisters had no one now. Their aunt could barely support herself, let alone four more mouths. There had been no time to think about any of it. The Doc had brought everyone back from the mountains barely in time for the funeral.

In front of us, the priest had called for people to throw their symbolic handfuls of dirt into the first of the graves. As hands lifted and dirt fell, and as the sounds of weeping grew in volume, I looked over at the second hole, wondering how the four children with me were going to get through that? And if they did, how were they going to get through the mob of filth with their videocams and their pads and pens and their digging, prying, shameless attitudes, all of their steel-hard obnoxiousness poised to make these poor kids cry for the cameras just one last time?

And if they got through that, then what about the next day and the next day, and the thousands after that, living apart from each other in foster homes, or struggling dime by dime, robbed of their mother by sickness and their father by greed, their family torn apart by the worst the city had to offer.

As I watched her, Elba fingered her necklace again, nine ivory dragons that I had given her. If they worked at all, I thought, they had saved my life over the past few days more times than I could count. With what Elba had to face, though, I wondered if even they could be of enough help to get her through it all.

She looked up to me then, her eyes asking me for some kind of assurance that somehow she would survive. Listening to the freezing wind whip through the tombstones all around me, as well as the intruding clicks and whirs of the cameras between us and the road, I gave her the best look I could, one that I hoped would give her the courage to hold herself together—at least long enough to get home.

Then, I looked out over the graves stretching to the horizon, and somehow I knew that just nine dragons would never be enough.